Candy

Candy

luke davies

BALLANTINE BOOKS • NEW YORK

A Ballantine Book
Published by The Random House Ballantine Publishing Group

Published in the United States by The Random House Ballantine Publishing Group, a division of Random House, Inc., New York, and simultaneously in Canada by Random House of Canada Limited, Toronto.
Originally published in slightly different form in Australia in 1997 by Allen & Unwin, Australia, and in Great Britain by Vintage UK.

A version of "Crabs" appeared in *Blur*, Random House, Sydney, 1996.

www.ballantinebooks.com

Library of Congress Cataloging-in-Publication Data
Davies, Luke, 1962–
Candy / Luke Davies. — 1st American ed.
p. cm.
ISBN 0-345-42387-9 (alk. paper)
I. Title.
PR9619.3.D29C36 1998
823—dc21 97-48390
CIP

Text design by Debbie Glasserman

Manufactured in the United States of America

First American Edition: August 1998

10 9 8 7

Have the gates of death been opened unto thee? or hast thou seen the doors of the shadow of death?

Hast thou perceived the breadth of the earth? declare if thou knowest it all.

Where is the way where light dwelleth? and as for darkness, where is the place thereof?

JOB 38: 17–19

CONTENTS

Part Two: The Kindgom of Momentum

Part Three: The Momentum of Change

Epilogue

Prologue

EXAMPLE OF GOOD TIMES: SUMMER AND LOVE

In the beginning: Sydney, summer

Everything's fucking beautiful! I'm so in love. I've just met Candy, it's been a month or two. We're discovering each other's bodies. Candy's just discovered smack and I've just discovered she's got a bit of money. Keen as all fuck to get dirty.

Candy's got the bluest eyes I've ever seen, a kind of mist you fall into. It's weird how you can be going along, and all you're thinking about is heroin, and then you meet someone, and other thoughts get in there. It makes it like meeting Candy was meant to happen. Things were getting hairy, as they tend to when you're using. As always, I was enjoying the dope. It can be all right being alone. But partnership is a good thing and helps focus your energies.

We did a credit card scam together, and Candy's still reeling from the adrenaline rush. She thinks we can be like Bonnie and Clyde, me handsome, her beautiful, both of us glamorous and full of sex and ready to take on the world. I suppose I mean Dunaway and Beatty. Anyway, falling in love is kind of exciting. . . .

EXAMPLE OF BAD TIMES: SUGAR AND BLOOD

Much later: Melbourne, winter

My day in the light, the day is darkening. I'm hurling all the little joys against the greater sadness. The sadness is a giant weight. It presses down. Its meaning: "What's the point?" The little joys are pebbles. The pebbles are getting smaller and smaller and the weight of the sadness is growing, the sadness is gaining density and mass, until in the end I'm throwing handfuls of dust at matter so thick there's no space between the molecules. Nowhere anywhere for anything to move. The years roll on.

I can't stop. I just can't stop. I can't stop anymore.

I'm sure it is possible, but no leap of the imagination can make it seem like it's possible.

There's a drought. Or you could say a flash flood. A flash flood of no heroin. Once every year or two, these things seem to happen. It's probably just a coming together of circumstances, like the way an eclipse occurs and it seems to be a message, that slide into darkness.

For two or three days, all the panicked phone calls, everyone ringing everyone else. Just enough dope to scrape by, deals from a friend of a friend of a friend, crap cut with so much sugar you barely feel it. Everyone saying, "I hear there's some pink rocks coming tomorrow."

Some phone calls come our way. "If you get on to anything, we're waiting here with money." I go right through my phone book. I call Dirty Julie, so treacherous and unreliable she'd never get a call under any other circumstances. Hangs out with some fucked-up guys, the rumor is they do home invasions and kidnappings. Very violent types.

But Dirty Julie says she has dope. "What do you want?" she asks. I tell her I'll call her straight back. I make a few calls. Everyone gets revved up. Secretly, I make up a packet of powdered sugar. Survival of the fittest in times of drought.

O'Brien and Victor and Maria and Schumann and Martin come around. Everyone piles into Victor's car, nobody wants to leave their money for too long. Candy waits at home. I'm the connection. Everyone is nervous, nobody is stoned. Drought brings out the worst in us and it's easy to hate your fellow human beings. We drive silently to Dirty Julie's, suspended inside the terrible tension in the car like pieces of fruit in gelatin. I direct them to park around the corner. "Wait here," I say. Five of them crammed into the car in the dark street, and the space where I had been. Everyone smoking cigarettes, the inside of the car like a dark mist in which hover fireflies.

Dirty Julie and some of the boys are waiting in the lounge room. "Hurry up, let's get this done, we have to go too."

I should listen to my instincts. I know I'm getting ripped off, that they're hanging out too, that they're waiting for my money so that they, in turn, can go get on. But there's no turning back now. It's more than eighteen hours since I've had any smack. I just hope there's a little bit in the deal, enough to hold me until things get better. I'm buying dope for seven people, including Candy and me. Surely half of seven people's dope, even if it's a rip-off, should be enough to hold me. And then tomorrow, maybe, good times will come back.

I go through the motions. I taste the dope. It's got that doughy taste of a big cut. But I'm trapped in the momentum of ignorance now. "I'm just going to take a little for myself," I say. They're all watching me, edgy. They're standing. I'm the only one sitting.

I take out half the dope, put it in a separate package, slip it down my socks. I add the same amount of my powdered sugar, give it a quick stir. This is what will happen. We will get back to the warehouse and try the dope—I will have to go through the pretense and hit up what I know to be mostly sugar—and everyone will realize they've been ripped off. They will all complain and grumble and I will apologize and say, how was I to know, what could I do? Finally they will disperse. And then I will have my private hit, and be okay. Even Candy can't know about this one. Times are tough.

But I get back to the car and they check the dope and freak. "Take it back. We don't want it." It's the official word. Everyone dipping their little finger and tasting it on their tongue. "Take it back. This is shit."

I've done a dumb thing. I am caught between a rock and a very hard place. But I have to pretend. The situation is fraught with peril. I will take the dope back, knowing that Dirty Julie and the boys will refuse, knowing that they saw me cut it.

Martin and Victor are angry. "We're coming with you," they say, following me around the corner. "No," I say, "you'd better not come. They're heavy people." It's the truth. "You're not supposed to know where they live." But I can see they don't trust me, and they keep following.

I don't have time to think. I don't know what to do. We arrive just as Dirty Julie and the boys are pulling the front door shut. "Who the fuck are these guys?" the boys ask, gesturing angrily toward my friends.

"We want our money back," Martin says behind me. "This dope's shit."

Everyone starts shouting at once then, and I'm in the

middle trying to calm them all down. If the rumors are true, I know one of these guys has killed. We mean nothing, my skinny St. Kilda friends and I.

The boys are puffing their chests and leaning into our faces and shouting and it's getting menacing and ugly under the streetlight. Martin and Victor sense the violence and back off, hands in the air, saying, "Okay, okay, forget it." Everyone moves away, grumbling, but heading in opposite directions.

My heart is beating. I'm thinking, Phew. Still got the dope down my sock. We get to the car, but Dirty Julie and the boys have changed their mind. They screech around the corner in their own car, pull up to a halt outside ours. We know this is heavy now.

One of them jumps out, pointing at me. "He cut the fucking dope anyway, he cut the fucking dope!" I'm almost in the door, last one in, but I step back out.

Arms in the air again, trying to calm him down. "Okay, okay, it's over, forget it."

He's like a locomotive coming at me. He swings so hard and fast I don't even blink. His fist is a hammer cracking all over my face. I feel my nose break and I'm in the air and as the back of my head hits the gutter, hard, I become unconscious.

Then there's a gap in what I remember.

Because it's like coming out of a deep sleep. I'm groggy, and arms are pulling me into the back of the car. I must have been out for five or ten seconds. I can hear the squeal of tires as Dirty Julie and the boys pull away, I can hear them screaming, "You fucking arseholes! You fucking arseholes! Don't youse ever come back here again, you motherfuckers!"

And I'm thinking how there's not much likelihood of that.

My nose is broken and both eyes are closed up and I'm crying because it hurts so much. The blood keeps pouring out. It's all over me, but someone's trying to hold an old rag to my face.

I'm sobbing, "I didn't cut the dope, I didn't cut the dope," because I have to make them believe me. I don't know if they do. They may well be torn between sympathy and anger.

And we get back to the warehouse and everyone has a hit and no one feels a thing. It's a ruined night.

Finally they all go, everyone resigned to their personal despair. Candy's bathing my face with warm water and a washcloth. Even though she is sick, she is loving and gentle, and I love her. She says things like, my poor baby my poor baby it'll be all right. I keep wincing. Even the warm water hurts. After a while I can't wait any longer and I tell Candy I have to go to the toilet. The toilet is outside the warehouse, on the roof courtyard. I get some water in the syringe and lock myself in the cubicle and mix up. I say, "Please, God, if it's not dope, please make it dope."

I inject it and nothing happens.

There is no warmth in my body. I drop the syringe and untie the tourniquet, usually an act that occurs in the onrush of bliss. Ten seconds, thirty seconds, a minute. I feel absolutely nothing. I drop my head in my hands, my fingers still sticky with blood.

I can no longer cry. I groan a few times. Through the slits that are my eyes, I stare at my shoes, at the gray swirls of the concrete floor, at the bright orange lid of my syringe. And I realize—it's a kind of horror—that this is my life.

And I can't stop. I just can't stop. I can't stop anymore.

PART ONE
Invincibility

"Now as soon as they had tasted the honey-sweet fruit of the lotus, they wished for nothing better than to stay where they were, living with the folk of that country and feeding on the lotus. They remembered their own homes no longer, nor did they yearn any more to return to their own land . . ."

Homer, *The Odyssey*

CROP FAILURE

There were good times and bad times, but in the beginning there were more good times. When I first met Candy: those were like the days of juice, when everything was bountiful. Only much later did it all start to seem like sugar and blood, blood and sugar, the endless dark heat.

But I guess the truth is, it didn't really take all that long for things to settle into a downward direction. It's like there's a mystical connection between heroin and bad luck, with some kind of built-in momentum factor. It's like you're cruising along in a beautiful car on a pleasant country road with the breeze in your hair and the smell of eucalyptus all around you. The horizon is always up there ahead, unfolding toward you, and at first you don't notice the gradual descent, or the way the atmosphere thickens. Bit by bit the gradient gets steeper, and before you realize you have no brakes, you're going pretty fucking fast.

So what did we do, once the descent began? We learned how to drive well, under hazardous conditions. We had each other to egg each other on. There was neither room nor need for passengers. Maybe also we were thinking that one day our car would sprout wings and fly. I saw that happen in *Chitty Chitty Bang Bang*. It's good to live in hope.

There was a time, after that Indian summer of our falling in love—after we'd gone through the money Candy's grandmother had left her, after we'd done a few scams and had a pretty good run for six months or a year—when we knew it would be good to slow down or stop and see where we were. It's funny how difficult that would turn out to be. It would be almost a decade before the car finally came to a silent stop on an empty stretch of road a long way down from where we'd started. Almost a decade before we'd hear the clicking of metal under the hood and the buzzing of cicadas in the trees all around us.

In that first year, Candy developed her first heroin habit. Like all the rest of us, no amount of words and warnings could prepare her for the horrors of drying out. So when we were forced to give it a go, she was a little shaken by the power of the thing.

This was in Melbourne for her. Candy grew up in Melbourne, and she went back there to dry out because we figured it would be too tempting to fuck up if we tried to do it together. It was her first habit, so she probably just needed a week at a friend's place with some good food and a trunk or two of pills.

I'd been gunning it now for a few years, so the plan for me was to go to detox for a while. I'd been getting this good brown Sri Lankan gear from my dealer T-Bar. There was lots of it, and everyone wanted it from me. It wasn't all that heavily refined—it wasn't the Thai white or even pink rocks. It was alkaline, and you could say rough as guts. But it was pretty pure, because three or four times a year it came into the country in condoms up T-Bar's arse. I stepped on it one-to-one with chocolate Quik, and still everybody was more than happy.

But Murphy's Law in the world of heroin said that if things could get out of control, then of course they would. T-Bar's brown was still in abundant supply, but I was starting to owe him more and more money, and he was getting pissed off with me. So I had some motivation to get things together in that department. I wasn't the world's greatest dealer. The simple equation was that the more dope I had, the more I used. I noticed that some of the people I sold to regularly were calling me less often; maybe I wasn't so reliable anymore. Detox seemed like the ideal opportunity for a breather.

The signs to stop were there. The plan was that Candy and I would link up in a week or two and be happy and healthy and maybe Candy would get pregnant. Then maybe we'd move to Melbourne, just to be on the safe side. Start a new life down there, away from the gear and all my Sydney connections.

Or maybe we could stay in Sydney and go back to hanging around with my old friends, my pot-smoking friends who held down jobs and went out on the weekends and seemed to enjoy their lives.

Mason Brown was one of these friends. Mason was six-foot-three, with a craggy face and sandy hair and a permanent grin. He loved his life like nobody I'd met before. He loved smoking buds and he only ever had the best, the lie-back-and-laugh stuff. He loved live music. He even loved—loved with a passion—his job as a field officer with the Department of Wildlife and Fisheries.

We'd grown to like each other a couple of years earlier, when we'd done a lot of business and smoked a lot of bongs. Mason had stood by me as others started to avoid me. He was never one for getting moral. He got a little sad when he saw me fucking up. He never said anything stronger than, "You really ought to stop this shit." He bailed me out of little financial holes on several occasions, and never asked for the money back.

A few days before Candy left for Melbourne, we went out to see a band. Be social, be normal, have a bit of a preview of our life to come. There were lots of people I knew there, and a few of them gave me the dirty eyeball, and some of them spent a fair amount of time staring at Candy, who always stood out like a beacon of beauty.

Mason Brown was there. I hadn't seen him in a few months and we caught up on the news. After a while he gave me one of those searching looks and said, "So—you okay?"

I shrugged my shoulders.

"Things aren't too good, Mason," I said. "I've got to stop. I really like Candy too. But she won't put up with it. It's not going to last if I keep this up. I want to travel. I want to go overseas. I want to do things. I'm going nowhere. I just need to knock it on the head. Go back to smoking. I wish I could do it like you."

"You can, mate, you can."

Mason seemed to have a blind faith in me that even I found embarrassing.

"I'll tell you what," he added. "I'll do you a deal. Grow a crop with me. We plant it, we look after it, we sell it, we go halves. We'll sell in bulk, don't fuck around with small things. You'd know a buyer. We'll make some good bucks. You and Candy can travel for a year, see a bit of the world, have some experiences. Get that monkey off your back."

It was endearing and charming, the way Mason used the corniest old expressions. He even said "junk" sometimes, as in, "Keep off that junk and you'll be right, matey." But he got me going with dreams of solid cash and a bright future. And he was the bud man, the gardener. I couldn't go wrong doing a crop with Mason. I knew also that he could grow a good crop quite successfully without me. That he was trying to be a friend.

"It's September," he said. "It's time to plant. It's already a couple of weeks late. But let's do it. I'm willing to bring you in on the plan. But here's the catch." He looked at me sternly. "Tonight's Friday. Next Friday night, or Saturday dawn, we leave. I know the spot, I've been checking some maps. So you've got seven days to dry out. If you're fucked up, we don't go ahead with it."

I was stoned to the gills on the good Sri Lankan brown, so of course I could promise him the world. I was an endless reservoir of enthusiasm. We shook hands on it and I hugged him. "Good on ya, mate," we said to each other.

I found Candy in a crowd near the bar. I pulled her aside, bursting with the news.

"Guess what, sugarplum? We're going overseas, in a few months."

I quickly filled her in. She seemed pleased enough. She knew that Mason represented a healthier life, so something involving Mason and me was better than something involving me and my own brain.

Seven days to get off smack. A new life. No problem, with this in front of me. I could do it on my head. The very thought of a successful detox made me feel warm and relaxed. I went to the toilet and found a cubicle with a lock that worked and had a nice blast to celebrate. Then I went outside to enjoy the band.

The next day I still had a gram of T-Bar's dope and some money to give him, and it's not like I was about to flush the gear down the toilet or anything. I'll make Saturday a good one to go out on, I thought. Things drifted into Sunday, and Candy and I were getting sad about leaving each other for a week, so I gave T-Bar his money and got two more grams on credit. We sold a bit and used a bit.

On Monday we had our last blasts, several times, and we caught a cab to the bus depot for one of those sad and tawdry Greyhound good-byes.

"Hang in there, Candy," I murmured as we hugged. "When we see each other next week we'll both be feeling fine. Just get through this week, that's all."

"You too," she said. "Don't fuck up."

"Don't worry," I said, "I've had my last shot too."

"I love you."

"I love you."

But the bus pulled out and we waved good-bye and suddenly I could feel the magnetic force of T-Bar's house dragging at the iron filings in my stomach.

As long as I stop by Tuesday night, then I should be half okay by Friday night, I reasoned to myself.

By Tuesday I decided I might as well just keep using, get the crop planted, then go to a proper detox (which was the original plan) next week (which wasn't). I decided I would have a big hit just before we left early Saturday morning, and leave my dope at Mason's house, and white-knuckle it for twenty-four hours as a test of strength. I'd grit my teeth and be helpful and agile for Mason, and I wouldn't have small pupils, or nod off and have him cancel the whole deal.

So it was business as usual Wednesday and Thursday and Friday. At some point I called Candy, who was sick, and told her I wouldn't be far behind. She was a little pissed off at my lack of stamina, but I assured her that I really just wanted to concentrate on the crop business for the time being, and that things would be fine, whatever the timetable.

Friday came and I organized to meet Mason at the pub where one of his favorite bands was playing. I hit up some coke before I met him so my pupils weren't too small. I told him I was feeling okay and that I'd gotten through the week. I smoked joints with him on the fire stairs and drank lots of beers as if to back up my story.

We got home to his place about one A.M. I was pretty drunk and we pulled some cones and I really could have done with a big sleep. Mason set the alarm for a quarter to five and said, "We're out the door by five-fifteen, okay?"

I figured the beginning of a business venture must be the hardest part.

Mason shook me awake when he got out of the shower at five to five.

"Coffee's on. Jump in the shower."

I took all my stuff into the bathroom and locked the door.

The Sri Lankan gear was alkaline, so I'd gotten a slice of lemon at the bar in the pub, wrapped it in a tissue, and stuffed it into my shirt pocket. It was a bit dry and stiff now but it would have to do. I put the water and the heroin and a drop of lemon in the spoon and heated the mix and whacked it up.

I could have stayed in that fucking shower for hours. I'd had a real lot of heroin, thinking of the twenty-four hours ahead. It was a massively peak experience, drifting under that jet of water. Mason banged on the door and shook me out of the silver heat and dream-steam.

"It's ten past five. What are you doing in there?"

I dried myself, dressed, and walked out into the kitchen.

"Sorry, Mason," I groaned, "I'm a bit hungover."

The kitchen's fluorescent was very bright. I shielded my eyes.

I took my coffee upstairs to the spare room and hid my syringe and spoon and dope under the bed. I felt a twinge of nervousness leaving it there, but I knew it would be good to have it to come back to. I felt certain I could make it through a day or a day and a half.

We were away at twenty-five past. It was dark and the streets were empty, so we had a good run northwest through Sydney. Mason was thoroughly prepared. His sawed-off animal of a pickup truck was loaded down with hoes and shovels and star posts and chicken wire, brown and green spray paint, fertilizers, cooking gear, and sleeping bags and a tent. His professional attitude was reassuring to one in such a dissolute state. I felt I was in the hands of a winner. I told him I needed to sleep and I closed my eyes and enjoyed the stone.

A couple of hours out of Sydney there was a bright clear morning sky. The roads were getting narrow and we moved into some pretty isolated stretches of bushland. Mason eased the pickup off the road and into a fire trail.

He pulled out one of those maps that serious bushwalkers

use, a government-printed topographic thing with the squiggly contour lines and the heights in meters. It didn't mean much to me. Creeks, roads, fire trails, contour lines: they all looked the fucking same.

Mason was in his element. He directed me with his finger. I tried to focus my eyes and look interested, nodding my head here and there at concepts I couldn't grasp.

"This is where we are now. We're going to drive the pickup as far as we can down this fire trail. Then we unload the gear. Then we drive the pickup back to here, and put it over behind those trees. We want as much distance between us and it as possible.

"So then we walk back along the trail to the gear. If we muscle it, we can carry all the gear between the two of us, so we don't have to do any backtracking.

"We'll follow this track along the creek for, let me see, it's about fourteen K's. That'll be quite a slog. It should be nice to camp here, on this sandy bit. In the morning we have to get into some pretty rough scrub. We have to get away from any walking trails, that's the only way for this to be a success.

"We'll head off through this bush here and come up on that ridge. That'll be a couple of hours. After that it's downhill for an hour or so. Now, see this spot here? See how these contour lines spread out near where these two creeks meet? That means there'll be good dirt there. Good alluvial soil. This is our spot. It's the middle of nowhere. We're looking at about ten hours heavy walking, the rest of today and a little in the morning.

"We'll hoe out a patch and clear the vegetation. Fertilize, plant, put up the fencing, camouflage, get the hell out of there. The trip out will be quicker and easier, we won't have so much weight from the star posts and seedlings. Maybe only five hours, maybe a little less. If all goes well and the rainfall's good this summer, we won't need to visit more than once or twice to check on it."

It began to seem daunting. I hadn't been expecting so much bush bashing, but I guessed it made sense to do it that way. Anyway, I felt committed and strong.

It was a big day. It was hard on the shoulders. We were fully laden, with a backpack each and several star posts on our shoulders and picks and shovels and mallets and rolls of chicken wire. We were like some tiny strange circus struggling through the heat. I could barely see for the sweat in my eyes. I could feel my face getting badly burnt. Every so often I'd have to stop for a cigarette and collapse in a heap for a while.

Until about midday I felt fine with the dope in my system, and even at five in the evening I still felt neutral and all right. I thought maybe the descent into sickness wouldn't happen, maybe there wasn't enough time, maybe I'd make it without a hitch. It had been so long since the last time I was sick, I think I'd forgotten how bad it could be.

Near dusk we set up camp and Mason lit a fire and we drank billy tea and ate a stew that tasted good. We had swigs of whiskey and a couple of joints. I felt kind of eucalyptic and all-Australian and a little euphoric in my exhaustion. I was shocked by the number of stars in the sky. I was bone-numbingly fucked and I knew I'd sleep well.

We crawled into the tent. I lay in my sleeping bag thinking, It'll be okay. Only half a day or so to get through. Just think of the dope back there under Mason's spare bed. We talked for a while about our hopes for the future and how things would be all right. Then I fell asleep hard and deep.

I woke at dawn, bolt upright in the clear consciousness of the idiocy of my predicament. Mason was shuffling about outside the tent, getting the fire going, whistling, pissing.

"Come on, mate," he chirped. "It's going to be a beautiful day."

I opened the tent flap. The ground was covered in a late frost. My bones ached. What had I done? I hadn't brought the heroin with me! Here I was in—I don't know, a place with no name, Government Map No. 9030, 1-N, grid reference 130873—and my dope was at Mason's house in Ultimo. Ultimo. Near the center of Sydney, the Heavenly City of Heroin.

Ultimo! It was all I could think of. It was a long way away. I just had to go through with this. I wanted to die. I really needed some smack in a hurry. I could hardly share these sentiments with Mason. I wanted to close my eyes and ignore the pain.

I groaned and tried to go back to sleep. But all I could think was: What the fuck were you doing, thinking it would be okay to leave the dope back there?

I had to make a show. I couldn't stay in the sleeping bag all day, though that misery would have been preferable to movement. I dragged myself out into the cold morning and rubbed my wired eyes. Mason handed me a coffee.

"I'm heating the last of that stew. You want some?"

He was disgustingly healthy, and I stood there trying to muster up some hatred for him.

"No, mate. I feel sick."

"Well, you've got to have something. We've got a big day on. Here, have an apple and a banana."

I sat on a log chewing miserably. Neither apples nor bananas were mood-altering substances. Coffee hardly counted.

"Can we have a joint before we go?"

I was thinking, Anything. Any fucking thing.

It was already rolled, of course. He flipped it out of his pocket and gave it to me with a grin.

Let me tell you, pot's a nice drug, but it's not so pleasant when it's not what you want or need. The morning remained sour and the awful feeling that I was in a nightmare trailed me like a shadow.

We packed up our gear and got going. Or really, Mason packed our gear. I helped straighten the tent before he folded and rolled it. I asked if I could have some of his whiskey, even though it was an embarrassing question at seven in the morning. It was acrid and hot down my throat, and for a moment I felt I was going to vomit.

I staggered my way, literally, through the day. The weight of the posts and shovels on my shoulders was two- or three-fold from Saturday. I kept telling Mason how sick I felt.

"Maybe I've come down with something."

"Maybe," he said.

He was always ten giant strides up ahead of me, pounding through the dense bush like David Attenborough pumped up on cocaine.

It was an ugly, ugly day.

At ten-thirty we stopped on the high ridge he'd spoken about. Mason breathed in the air like it was a form of happiness.

"Down there," he pointed, "not far now."

But it was all too apparent that Mason's concept of "not far" was very far removed from mine. I squinted my eyes into the distance, but the valley seemed to quiver in a ghostly heat haze.

An hour later we reached the approximate spot. I dropped everything off my shoulders and fell into a heap. The last time I'd felt this bad was never. Mason scouted around for five minutes, running soil through his fingers or consulting the oracles or whatever the fuck he did. I lay in the soil sniveling and sneezing, and the sun drilled through me.

"Over here, this is it," Mason shouted. "Between these two trees."

I willed myself to stand. I dragged the gear through the undergrowth.

"Mason," I puffed. "I need a fucking rest, man. I need to lie down. I'm really sick."

He looked at me and shook his head. "You do what you have to," he said. "But the quicker we do this, the quicker we're out of here. Just help me clear this patch."

He moved around and dug a line in the brush and soil with the toe of his walking boots. He formed a rough square about five meters by five meters.

"You take the hoe, get rid of all vegetation. I'll take the pick and churn the soil."

I did the best I could, under the circumstances. It was not a real lot. I couldn't stop sneezing. I was covered in a film of sweat, I was gasping for air. I thought I was going to vomit or shit. Finally Mason got pissed off, or as pissed off as he ever got.

"You've got to use a bit of muscle there, mate."

I stopped. "I can't do it, Mason. I think I'm going to collapse. I have to lie down. I'm really sorry. Just for ten minutes. Then I'll be okay."

He didn't lose his temper, but I think around this time would be the moment when I'd definitely stopped being his business partner. I curled up beside a tree, trying to wedge myself into soil and shade. I could hear Mason working furiously in the background. He cleared the plot in half an hour, did stuff with fertilizer, planted forty seedlings. Then he needed my help with the fencing.

I held the posts in place while he whacked them with a mallet. I'd come on the expedition in a long-sleeve shirt, and now I'd rolled the sleeves up in the heat of the day.

"Missed a vein, did we?" Mason asked out of the blue, between swings of the mallet.

I was taken aback. He nodded to my right arm. There was some bruising halfway along the inside of my forearm, a blue and yellow blush where I'd been searching for new vein territory.

"No, no," I stammered. "That's just . . . I mean, er, it's . . ." My voice trailed off. "I don't know what it is."

It was a poignant or pathetic moment, depending on which way you looked at it. I knew there was no crop future between me and Mason. I'd never find this place alone, and even if I could, I'd never rip Mason off. It was not my crop and I knew it. I was not a partner. I'd failed the test. Fucked up.

I was all at sea, here in the bush. Okay, then. I'd make my money the way I knew how, with my dealing, or something like that, and then I'd stop using and Candy and I would still go overseas. Fuck the crop. Besides, my dope was still back at Mason's. Things were looking up. We'd be back there before long.

Mason sprayed the chicken wire in random patterns of brown and green, explaining to me that it wouldn't pay to have a helicopter see any metallic glints in the bush. He secured a rich assortment of foliage to the enclosure, using baling wire and pliers.

Even in my sickness I could recognize that it was a work of art. It disappeared from view no matter which direction you looked at it from. You couldn't even see it from ten feet away. It was wallaby-, wombat-, and helicopter-proof. Insects and frost were the only real problems. But somehow I knew that they wouldn't be my problems. I only had one problem at that moment, as we packed up our gear and departed.

I was like a horse returning to the home paddock, going faster. I bashed through the bush with abandon. It was a long afternoon, but the pain had moved into a kind of delirium, and with the help of a special Mason after-work joint, I somehow made it alive back to the pickup.

It was five in the afternoon. I figured that, barring weekend traffic snarls, I ought to be in heaven by seven or seven-thirty. At any rate, even though it was bad to be alive and breathing and thirty-six hours without hammer, it was good to be sitting in the cabin of the pickup compared to hauling through that evil bush.

As we moved off the freeways and into the suburban streets of Sydney, the only thing I could really concentrate on was traffic lights. Orange is not a good color, and red is even worse.

I felt like I'd failed, but we didn't talk about the crop at all. Finally we pulled up outside Mason's house. It's a peak thing, a gorgeous feeling to know the dope is there. Just as amputees are said to experience a "false limb" syndrome, so the knowledge of that tiny package under Mason's spare bed imbued me with a strange happiness that I could have sworn was real.

But there was one more obstacle to conquer. Mason's flatmates were home, relaxing in front of the TV in a Sunday night bong fog. On Monday morning they would all get up and go to work as solicitors and graphic artists, whatever it was they did. My slice of lemon was gone, so I had to somehow get some vinegar from their cupboard. But the kitchen opened onto the lounge room and I was in full view of everyone.

I had to pretend to be hungry, fuck around with biscuits and cheese and shit. It was awkward sliding the vinegar along the counter an inch at a time, toward the bathroom door.

Finally I did it. Got in there and locked the door and had the big reward. My veins were like rivers bringing warm bliss on the king tide through the glacial landscapes of my taut muscles. The melting. It was good again, everything.

Not that Mason and his flatmates didn't know, I'm sure, seeing the way I drooled and scratched and nodded off when I went back into the lounge room and tried to be social.

A month later, anyway, I was talking to Mason and he said, "By the way, mate. You know the night we came back from planting the crop? You left your spoon on the bathroom shelf."

I looked him in the eye to see if he was joking. He wasn't. I could feel my ears burn red.

"It's the little details that count, you know," he went on. He had a strange way of being kind even at his most sarcastic.

Mason also told me how he'd been out to check on the seedlings, and guess what, the unthinkable had happened: attack by insects. The little crop had never stood a chance. It was ruined, gobbled up before it had time to grow even six inches. I guess it was just Mason's polite way of saying no thanks. I don't know, maybe there really was a plague of fucking locusts. I wasn't interested by then. Candy and I were talking more seriously about moving to Melbourne.

God, it was good to get back to Candy. I knew that with her I could overcome anything. She'd come back from her drying out, a newly clean Candy, keen for a one-off reward blast, and then things kind of just kept going, the way they do. Pretty soon she was back into the swing of it. It's hard, I suppose, to stop at a year or less, when you still look good, when it still feels good. We decided to put off drying out until some other time. We had each other to get into first.

PROBLEMS WITH DETACHABLE HEADS: 1

Sydney was a harborside paradise of cheap heroin and corrupt police, but nonetheless there was a time back then, before we finally succumbed to the Beast, when we would regularly try to stop. We worried about careers or things that looked like careers or the beginnings of careers: acting for Candy, God knows what for me. And did that awful cold turkey thing that seems so possible when you are merely young and stupid and life has gone a bit hairy and haywire.

It was tough going too. This one time, we were coming off the back of a neat little scam on a doctor's cashcard. Candy was still just getting into smack and it was the gravy train, lots of hitting up—I used to do it for her, slipping the steel into those marble-white arms—and lots of meandering sex that never really went anywhere. But the coming down was hard. When is it ever not?

Every day for four weeks we'd popped five hundred from an automatic teller, until one day the doctor's card got chewed. PLEASE CONTACT BANK, the screen flashed, a rather comical instruction. It was the sudden reduction in funds after a period of plenty that made us decide once again to try drying out. We spent a week taking lots of Doloxene and sleepers and smoking some pissy blond hash. We were legless and uncomfortable. Crawling out of our skin. We lay all day in front of the daytime soaps, which were always funny when stoned but hideous without smack. We sweated it out because we thought we had each other and the future.

We seemed to get through it. On about the sixth day we were beginning to perk up.

"We should do something tonight, Candy," I said. "Spruce up a little and get out of here. I don't think I could stand another night at home."

"Okay," Candy said. "How about a movie?"

That night we caught the train into town and saw something dumb at the Hoyts. It was the beginning of our new life, and this was what normal people did. It felt a little bit awkward with Candy, since our relationship was fairly new and had only ever been based on lots of sex and increasing amounts of drugs. This domestic shit was new territory, but we were sure we were willing to give it a go.

After the movie we bought an ice cream and walked along George Street. It was one of those swooning summer nights in Sydney when the air is awash with the smell of jasmine and take-away satay and salt from the harbor. In Sydney it's so easy to fall in love but so hard to go deep.

"It's nine-thirty," Candy said. "I feel really light. I feel wide-awake."

I watched her licking her ice cream and tried to imagine that it was my dick. But this was dangerous territory, since heroin and sex could so easily become confused.

"Me too," I said. "I don't really want to go home yet."

"What should we do?"

I looked in her eyes for that flicker. We were circling each other, baiting, fishing. My gut started to roll and I knew without doubt what was going to happen.

I acted casual, like I was plucking random suggestions from the warm air. This was part of the game, so no one could ever say that fucking up was a deliberate act.

"There's not much to do around here," I said. "We could go up to the Cross and check the nightlife."

"Are you sure?" She gave me a token admonishing look, but the edges of her lips were quivering.

"Hey, we're just going for a walk, we don't have to use!"

"That's the problem." She frowned. "I wouldn't mind some."

The sweet dam had burst, the Dam of Relief that would bear us tumbling up William Street and into our own veins and home.

What was it about love? Coming down off heroin, it was so hard to think of anything but pain. When we were stoned, we loved each other, we touched each other, we laughed a lot, it was us against the world. We spent every moment together, ambling through the musky days, aware only of the way our boundaries seemingly had dissolved, reveling in the sensation of submersion and inundation. But the future made me edgy. It would be good not to use drugs, I thought. I wanted us to live our lives, to laugh and touch and share things, but without hammer. I thought that surely must be a place you could get to. And yet here we were, six days down the track of another expedition into sobriety, jumping out of our fucking skin.

I could have said no. It was a moment in my life when I could have said no. But I grinned weakly and then looked away and then looked back at her, chewing my lip.

"I wouldn't mind some either."

"Do you want to?" she asked. "It's been a week. That's okay, isn't it?"

"Let's do it," I said.

And we were off.

At this time of night there was nowhere to get syringes. We racked our brains about the situation at home. With good intentions, of course you throw all that shit out. But had we put out the garbage in the last week? It was unlikely but possible. Anyway, we couldn't take that risk. And having made the decision to score, it was like instant craving. That acidic anticipation in the gut.

We certainly couldn't buy some heroin now and wait until morning to use it. That was more than inconceivable. It was silly and absurd. Snorting it or chasing the dragon was on the very outer rims of the possible. Pussy stuff.

There was only one thing to do: we had to buy the dope, *and* somehow get hold of a pick or two. Hopefully unused.

We were okay for cash, we were six days healthy, we were feeling pretty cruisy. A nervous edge about the syringe situation, but we would work that out. Even when I lived in rat holes I was generally meticulous about the vein and hygiene factor. AIDS was everywhere; I wanted it no more than the next person. Occasionally, however, fate dictated that you had to take a chance. As a junkie you had to spend a lot of time crossing your fingers and hoping for the best.

We took a table at the Cockatoo Club, which was empty at this early hour, and ordered drinks. Yusef the manager came and chatted to us for a few minutes. Just then Ronny Radar walked past the window. I was out of my seat and moving.

"Just saw Ronny. Back in a minute."

I caught up with him and we talked the talk. I gave him the money and told him where we were sitting.

"One thing, Ronny," I added. "I need a pick. Where can I get a clean one?"

Ronny looked at his watch. "Buckley's chance, mate. Buckley's. There's nothing open now."

"Haven't you got any?"

"I'll tell you what," he said. "I'll give you one that only I've used. All you have to do is give it a good clean. I'll go without until I get home later."

A regular saint was Ronny. It would have to do.

"Thanks, Ronny. You're a champion. Oh, and a spoon. Can you get me a spoon? The fucking teaspoons in the Cockatoo have got holes drilled in them."

Ronny moved in too close to my face. "Mate," he hissed. "I'm not a fucking supermarket. I'm a heroin dealer. Got it?"

"Sorry, Ronny. It's just that . . . I've been away. I'll give you five bucks if it helps."

He sighed deeply and held out his hand. I gave him five more dollars.

"Sometimes . . ." he said, shaking his head and letting the sentence trail away as he walked around the corner.

I went back into the Cockatoo and smiled at Candy. Yusef was over at the bar touching up the topless waitress. We finished our drinks and Ronny came in and sat down with us. I introduced him to Candy and all of a sudden he was a friendly kiss-arse. He handed everything to me under the table and left.

We ordered another drink and I looked down and checked the syringe. Shit! It was a detachable head, two mils, a big awkward monstrous motherfucker. God I hated those things!

The thing about those detachable-head syringes was they always seemed to collect a little blood, down in the neck area, where the replacement head and needle slipped tight over the plastic nozzle of the barrel. You could never fully empty them out into your vein, because the black rubber stopper on the end of the plunger couldn't get down into that bridging neck. This was dead space.

Sure enough, Ronny's syringe was this sleek clear plastic rocket with a band of dried crimson down near the point where the needle began. Not what I wanted to see. A very used syringe. I pointed this out to Candy. We discussed the pros and cons of going home or having a shot here in the Cockatoo toilets.

"I'll see how I go cleaning it," I said.

I went into the men's room. There was a washbasin and a piss trough and four cubicles. My plan was to clean the pick thoroughly, then mix up and have a hit, then clean it again and fill it with a hit for Candy to take to the ladies' room.

I turned the tap on slightly and filled the spoon with

water. I carried it into the end cubicle and placed it on the cistern. There was a window above the cistern, looking out over the back alley that ran behind the Cockatoo. The glass was broken but a security grille of iron bars covered the space. I hoped that if I flushed out the pick several times I could get rid of that blood.

Normally I'd suck up the water and squirt as hard as possible, to jiggle things around in there and dislodge the caked blood. It was a pretty automatic habit. But I forgot to account for the fact that I wasn't familiar with this type of syringe. It you were going to squirt hard, you had to hold the end on with your fingers.

I dipped the needle into the spoon and drew up water until the barrel was full. The window invited. I don't know, I just wasn't thinking. Maybe I was being neat, not spraying water on the walls of that filthy bog. I aimed toward the window and pushed the plunger hard.

The pressure was too great. The needle, like the pod of Saturn Five, came off from the main body at supersonic speed. By the time I heard the *pffft!* of its flight through the cubicle, it had sailed through the security bars, straight out the window and on into the night.

I looked down at the useless piece of plastic in my hand. A syringe without a needle was like a car without an accelerator. You could admire it or polish it but not get that glorious wind in your hair. I couldn't believe this had happened. I couldn't believe my stupidity.

I had to find that missing piece. I couldn't risk getting home to a flat devoid of syringes. I stood on the toilet bowl and hoisted myself up to the window.

The alley was dark. I tried to imagine trajectories, angles of entry, angles of descent. I figured it could only have come down in the Dumpster full of construction rubble that was opposite the window. Then again, it might have been in that huge pile of green garbage bags wedged hard up against the refuse bin.

No question. I had to get out there.

I went back out into the club and explained the dire situation to Candy. I walked around the block and found the alley. I located the Dumpster and the pile of garbage bags, most of which had split open. The place stank of rotting vegetation.

I looked back to the window and figured the bags were the go, not the Dumpster. I trod on them gingerly, using the edge of the Dumpster to keep my balance. Everything was spongy under my feet. Suddenly my right leg disappeared beneath me. I fell knee-deep into rotten tomatoes. A wet squelch filled my jeans. I heard the scurrying of rats.

I pulled my leg out. My jeans and shoe were soaked. Now I stank. I stepped back cursing and shook my leg. From the corner of my eye I noticed movement.

Two figures were walking down the alley toward me. They were in silhouette, but I had no trouble making out the police hats and holsters. My heartbeat picked up a little. It was not cool to run. I could stay and pretend to be looking for something in the garbage. There was nothing wrong with that. For some reason I thought of a tennis ball. I would tell them I was looking for a tennis ball.

Then I remembered the dope. I had half a gram of heroin and half a syringe and a soup spoon in my pocket. It was time to go. Just not my night.

I did the fast-casual walk. I didn't look back and I didn't hear their footsteps pick up. I rounded the corner and ran the half block to the Cockatoo Club. A kind of high-speed limp, a *whoomp-slurp, whoomp-slurp* sound.

Candy was being sweet-talked by some young turks. Wide-lapel types. Good luck to them.

"Big fuckup, baby doll," I said to her, nodding polite hellos to them. "Let's get a taxi out of here."

"Aw, where youse goin'?" they shouted, but we were out the door already.

"Maybe Ronny's got AIDS," Candy mused in the taxi on the way home. "Maybe it was meant to happen."

"That'll be a small fucking consolation if there are no syringes at home." My stomach was doing somersaults by now. When you made the decision, you wanted to act fast.

We got home and my brother Lex was there. The three of us at this time were sharing a flat. Lex had his own little problems, sometimes with heroin, sometimes with free-basing, off there on the sides of our lives. Sometimes our problems intersected, sometimes not. Usually only in cases of emergency. It must have been some Catholic guilt hangover bullshit thing. We generally liked to try to keep our problems separate and hidden.

It blew me out that he could fuck up so spectacularly, one year on heroin, the next on cocaine. I'm talking about solid blocks of dedication. How anyone could use cocaine for even an hour without wanting some hammer pretty quick was beyond me. But there you go. He was always an odd one, Lex. Off on his own obscure path.

Lex had recently done the get-healthy thing too. (I think this was a heroin period for him.) It might have been a week, maybe two, since he'd had a whack. So I'm sure he must have picked up the vibe when we walked in. The anticipation. You don't go to the movies, six days off the gear for God's sake, and come home abuzz with excitement about the late news coming up.

He was suspicious but it was a standoff. If everyone was pretending to be clean, then everyone had to keep up the facade. We sat in front of the TV chatting idly. My pulse was racing and I couldn't concentrate. On anything but the fact that I had heroin. In my pocket and not in my body. On the outside I was trying to be calm.

Lex asked about the bad smell coming from my pants. I told him I trod in a puddle and it must have had something awful in it. He told me it hadn't rained for three weeks. I told him it was a puddle next to a construction site.

The lounge room led into the kitchen. We couldn't search through the garbage bag while he was there, and we couldn't really carry it past him into our bedroom either. Finally he went to bed. Sulking a bit, I think.

We sprang into action. I carried the garbage bag into the bedroom. It was putrid. That's what happens when you detox at home. You don't do normal things like take the garbage out. Everything is a touch difficult coming down off heroin.

I laid out some newspaper on the floor and tried to pick the least rank things out of the garbage bag, one at a time. If there were any syringes, they would be down at the bottom. Finally I created enough room to tilt the bag sideways and shake it a bit, like searching for the surprise at the bottom of the Froot Loops. I spotted the orange lid of a Terumo 1 mil—my kind of pick, Mother Jesus we are home!—in an ashy sludge of wet cigarette butts. Then three more. Must have thrown out a handful.

I threw the garbage back in and took the bag to the kitchen. I rinsed the ash off the syringes and washed my hands and arms. I went to the bedroom and Candy already had a belt tied around her arm. There were times when I loved her enthusiasm.

I took the lids off and felt each needle for the two that were least barbed. These syringes had had a good run in the weeks before we stopped. I took the best two and scraped them back and forth hard on the flint of a matchbox, to try and reduce the barbs. They would do.

We mixed up and had the blast and fell into each other's arms and told each other how very very much we loved each other. How we had such a bright future, all this abundant love, this intense thing, and how very stupid it would be to throw it all away and fuck up on dope. How we would stop again tomorrow. In that bliss, in that love, in that confidence, in that melting, you couldn't doubt it was true.

A CHANGE IS AS GOOD AS A HOLIDAY

But when tomorrow came, it was always so hard. We decided that moving to Melbourne would make the process easier, that if you couldn't change in small increments then you could maybe do it with a big bang.

It seemed like a good enough adventure to me. Anyway, I was sick of Sydney's summers. All that sweat when you're so sick.

Like all junkies, I guess I'd thought for a long time that my environment was the problem. My situation. The people I knew. I must have figured that somehow in Melbourne the desire to use heroin would miraculously go away. We started with high hopes, and for a while we almost got to find out what it might have been like, being in love, being in a relationship, without drugs. I wanted so much to treat Candy with respect, because she was beautiful and incredible and deserved it. I always thought that heroin was a temporary thing, an obstacle on the other side of which lay the real future. I continued to believe this long after it was obvious that heroin had settled in for the long haul.

Candy hadn't used smack in Melbourne, and of all her friends, O'Brien was the only one who was really into it. So I suppose it's not really strange that O'Brien would soon become our main Melbourne friend. He was thin and hyperactive, pale-skinned, with dark circles under his eyes and a shock of black hair that he was endlessly flicking out of his face. I liked his nervous intensity from the moment we met.

For a while, for a few weeks, I was on my best behavior. I was in a new town. I was Candy's boyfriend. I was under the spotlight. Certain rumors had preceded me, and it was known that Candy had started using while in Sydney. Such a promising young actress: there were people who cared and worried about her. I wasn't exactly seen in a favorable light. I was the guy who introduced her to heroin. When you're typecast, when you're pigeonholed, it's an uphill fucking battle.

So our PR campaign involved getting clean. When we moved to Melbourne we hadn't had a hit in at least four days. We intended to keep it that way. It seemed most of Candy's friends just drank a lot. I was doing a Visa card at the time, a Mr. Irving J. Gibbon, that I'd stolen from a bedroom at a party in Sydney. I tried to ingratiate myself by showering everyone with cases of Heineken and bottles of Stoli. Maybe it was appreciated. I was generally too drunk to notice.

We were taking these heart-condition tablets called clonidine. The word was they made it easier to come down off the hammer. They lowered your blood pressure, so they reduced the sweating and palpitations and a few other things. I don't know about that. They made me faint a few times. Which was not a great introduction to Candy's circle of friends.

You hit the ground hard on a clonidine faint. After a bit of bruising, we decided it was better to be drunk and take lots of Valium. Then we wouldn't stand out so much in Melbourne.

We stayed with Candy's friends Anne and Len in the beginning, across the bridge at Yarraville. Len was a wild drinker, so our foibles were insignificant. He made it comfortable to lie around and be self-indulgent. We really tried hard to stay away from the smack those first few weeks.

We got over the hump and were beginning to feel all right. I stopped using the Visa card because I figured I'd been pushing my luck after six solid weeks of trivial shopping under the limit. We started to settle down into a more low-key life: pulling bongs, drinking beer, watching videos, and thinking about our future. Melbourne was okay. The nervous edge was a result not so much of the city itself as the unfamiliarity of a heroin-free life.

We tried. One day we even woke up and decided to have a picnic, just the two of us, in the Botanical Gardens. We started the day with a cup of coffee. No clonidine, no Valium, no beer. We sat in the morning sun in Anne and Len's backyard and planned our picnic. We were light-headed with possibility. The day seemed to invite. It was exciting, getting prepared, buying food, catching the train to the gardens. By one o'clock we were spread out on our blanket, throwing morsels of food to the small birds who twittered around us on the grass. I lay with my head in Candy's lap and she stroked my arm. A soft breeze blew through the park and the light came dappled and swaying through the trees that arched above us. We talked about everything. I said, "You're more important to me than anything in the world." We decided it was time for Candy to try and get pregnant soon. I'd always liked books, so I was going to start looking for a job in a bookstore. We drank some cheap champagne and didn't even finish the bottle, and I thought, How debonair, how civilized. *This* is what people do. We packed up and walked arm in arm to the train station. It seemed that it wasn't just love, but romance too. Later, at home, we kissed ourselves into a white heat.

It was good, too, getting into some nonfutile sex. Candy was the juice, I tell you. I took a leap forward in the kind of stuff I knew.

But then that night came when I met O'Brien and, you

know how it is, that fucking hammer thing dominates like a thick presence in the air. Like a smell. Like a viscous fog. Just the vibe of heroin is all I'm talking about. Its unspoken absence.

We were trying to be social. "How have you been, Candy?" and "What do you do, O'Brien?" All that kind of stuff. Five minutes later O'Brien grins and says to Candy, "So, I hear you've been a bit naughty in Sydney." I know where this will head. My heart starts going. I swear to God I can't recall the next three minutes of conversation. Then O'Brien is saying, "Do you want to?" Candy looks at me and grins and says, "What do you think?" We've all got the wicked eyes and suddenly we are the thumbs-up buddies. Let's go!

We got revved up and then we scored. O'Brien took our money and went into a block of flats in St. Kilda and came out with a small tinfoil packet of pink rocks. Jesus, what a pleasant surprise. We all got stoned and relaxed and then O'Brien started explaining to me about the dope situation in Melbourne, how to score, who was good, what kind of prices, how it worked. So I learned a bit. It was damn good gear that first night. We were pigs in shit, the three of us.

Why does it seem so absurd to explain all this now? From there it was just a hop, skip, and a jump. Some weeks later our dope-buying forays had increased. The St. Kilda scene was all right and we soon had a couple of phone numbers too. We were sniffing our way up the ladder. As you do. It didn't seem dangerous at first. Once or twice a week, how could you go wrong?

Suddenly it was two months later.

One day we woke up and realized we'd just been using for nine days straight. It was one of those mini periods of beautiful smack. We were pinned from dawn till dusk. On the tenth morning we had no money. The churning was back in our lives, in our stomachs.

There was a pawnbroker on Acland Street. It didn't

matter who we went to, they were all just as fucked as each other. Candy had some jewelry, not much. There were a few nice things. Some silver and gold. The wedding ring her grandmother left her. Some knickknacks we'd bought on credit cards. Antique lacquered Chinese goblets. Odd stuff. We got a little money. Enough to use for a few more days.

Then we decided to stop.

"We're just going to have to put up with it," we said.

"It hasn't gone too far this time," we said. "A few days sick, and then we'll be all right."

"Tomorrow," we said, "we wake up and act as if the last two months haven't happened."

Tomorrow was a Saturday. We woke up at nine. By eleven we were feeling the cold front of anxiety moving in.

"There must be something we can do," I said.

Candy was wearing a silver necklace, something she said she'd never sell. It was important to her, fuck knows why. Time has a habit of making things special.

She fingered it. "I suppose we could try this," she said.

"Sure," I said.

She bit her lip and frowned. Her eyes were sad.

"Look, Candy, you're only hocking it, you're not selling it. We'll get it back. We've got three months. Or more if we keep paying the interest."

It was half past eleven. The hockshop shut at midday. We jumped in the car, an old bomb Len had given us, and sped across the Westgate Bridge. I knew to expect disappointment from pawnbrokers. We were hoping the necklace would bring maybe seventy bucks. Surely it was worth a couple of hundred.

Acland Street was crowded. Saturday morning madness. Bad traffic. We pulled up outside the pawnshop at five to twelve. Candy double-parked and went in. Cars backed up and honked but I ignored them.

She came out at one minute to twelve. She got in the car.

"Twenty-five bucks," she said.

My heart sank. It was not enough. She started the engine.

"I have to move the car," she said. "Just wait a minute. Maybe he can work something out."

It didn't make sense, or I didn't want it to. I looked at her to make eye contact. She didn't let her eyes meet mine.

She made a U-turn across the tram tracks and parked the car.

"I'll be back soon." She got out quickly. I sat in the car. A cog turned a notch in my stomach. The future was beginning.

It was bright and sunny. There were people everywhere. I hated them all, since it was so hard to hate myself or my own life. I wished I could stop time and take the money from their wallets.

I sat in the passenger seat staring at a ladybug crawling across the windshield. It was hard to avoid thinking about what Candy was doing across the road. But somehow I managed to avoid it for a little while.

After about five minutes I craned my neck around and looked across the road. The pawnshop door was locked. The Open sign had been turned around to read Closed. The security grille was pulled across the window, protecting the jewelry and cameras.

I told myself that Candy was not fucking the guy in there. The inside of the shop was an unreachable space. My mind went pretty blank. I watched the ladybug. Then it flew away. The sun beat hard on the car hood. Everything was glare. We needed the money, I told myself. It was a sensible world of supply and demand.

After about fifteen minutes she came back. She opened the door and climbed into the car. I was watching her for every small signal. Maybe I never knew a lot about Candy in all those years. But I knew at that moment that her heart was beating fast, that she'd just been through a new kind of fear, through a dark tunnel into new territory.

With her right hand she turned the keys in the ignition.

With her left hand she threw a pair of scrunched-up panties on the floor.

We pulled out into the traffic and I looked at the panties among the crumpled cigarette packets and chocolate wrappers.

"What happened?"

"I fucked him."

"Shit."

My body released something into itself. I was flooded with a substance that might have been adrenaline. It was deeply unpleasant. For an instant I had the sensation of falling. This cannot happen again, I thought. This is not a good thing.

I looked across to see what she was thinking or feeling. Her face dealt with the traffic and nothing more.

"Are you okay?"

She shrugged her shoulders.

"I'm sorry," I said.

"Don't be," she said.

There was a pause. An old lady struggled through a zebra crossing.

"Well, what happened?"

"I told you, I fucked him."

"How much?"

"Forty bucks."

I sat in silence. It seemed a pathetic amount, not that I really knew the going rate for a pawnshop owner's Saturday morning poke. We had sixty-five bucks. It was more than a fifty, but way too little for a hundred, which was what we really needed. Forty bucks for a fuck. It didn't seem right.

"Are you okay?"

"You asked that already."

I could read the subtext. I was not a stupid guy.

For a moment I wanted to stroke her, to comfort her, to turn the clock back fifteen minutes. Fifteen measly minutes. To say, "Not that. We will never go there." But heroin was its own special hunger, and clocks ran in one direction only.

"That's it. We're going to stop using, Candy, once and for all. Fuck it. Fuck it all."

"Yeah right," she said.

What we did with the sixty-five was, Candy sweet-talked Fat Nick in the café into giving us a hundred. Nick said, "With beautiful lips like that asking me, how could I refuse, darling? You owe me thirty-five. I trust you."

That was the hop and the skip. Somehow after that the jump into prostitution didn't seem so big. We'd been around at Victor and Maria's, friends of O'Brien's, a few days after the hockshop business. Victor was all right, a little pretentious in his "I am a vampire" sort of way. He was a junkie and a musician, one of the cotton-fields-and-chain-gang-boys from Melbourne Grammar School. He was okay. He was pretty honest in the dope-dealing sense.

Maria was always a glowing angel, the softest junkie I ever knew. She was pure Italian art gallery stuff—the translucent skin, the dark curls. Victor and I chatted while he divided up the dope, and Maria took Candy into her room to show her some clothes or something.

Later Candy told me that Maria told her about working at the Carolina Club, about money and conditions and what went on. So we knew someone from our world, the normal world, who worked, and suddenly it didn't seem so foreign or so wrong.

"Would you ever do it?" I asked, a little hesitantly, not quite sure of the danger inherent in the question.

"I don't know," Candy said. "She earns a lot sometimes."

The thing, the concept, seemed to hang in the air, in the gray cloud that had formed between need and unease.

A few days after this we were driving near the Carolina Club and Candy stopped the car.

"I just want to talk to them for a second," she said.

She went inside. I didn't feel as bad as the Saturday morning at the hockshop. Just a couple of flutters in the stomach.

She came out in five minutes. "Well, I've got a shift if I want it. Thursday night. Start at seven. Finish at three or four. What do you think?"

I didn't answer.

What I thought was, Do it, we need the fucking money. How I felt was, nauseous, just a little, as I stared at the gear stick and shrugged my shoulders.

"Look, if it's horrible, I won't do it again," she said.

"I suppose so," I said. "I suppose it's just money."

And it was, and would be. For all the years to come, in the quest for hammer, it paid for Candy to fuck other men, but it didn't pay to think about it.

Candy told Anne and Len she had a job doing phone sex. It seemed an acceptable alternative explanation for her dusk-to-dawn absences. I doubt they believed it for a minute. But it was convenient for all of us to pretend.

On the first night, Candy was nervous. She got dressed and put makeup on and picked a fight.

"I don't want to do this," she said. "What the fuck am I doing? Why don't you earn some money?"

For fuck's sake. I was hanging out for some dope. This was not what I needed at six-thirty P.M.

"Baby, it's temporary. I'm going to earn heaps one day."

"You're fucking pathetic," she said.

"Listen," I lied, "don't go, then. It's not important."

"Okay, good, then I'm not going."

"Okay, fine."

"Fine."

"Good."

She sat down and lit a cigarette. I was lying on the bed.

"It's probably better this way," I said. "We'll be sick for a little while, then we'll be okay." I was panicked by the prospect but I tried to sound calm.

She smoked the cigarette in silence. She stubbed it out in the ashtray. She stood and picked up her coat.

"You're a fucking arsehole," she hissed.

She slammed the door as she went out. The car started and she drove away.

I went out to the main part of the house and pretended nothing was happening. I drank some beer with Anne and Len. We watched a video. It was *The Man with the Golden Arm*. Maybe they were having a dig at me.

Anyway, it was not the best movie to watch when you were hanging out for heroin. I went to bed and took some pills and fell into a restless sleep at about one.

At four-thirty in the morning Candy shook me awake.

"Hi," I said with a croaky voice.

"Can I turn on the light?"

"Yeah, sure."

I was blinded for a second.

"How was it, Candy?"

"Good." She smiled. "Guess how much I earned?"

"How much?"

"Five hundred and sixty dollars!"

"Shit!"

"And I've found a new dealer. He's good."

She fanned a wad of hundreds and fifties and twenties across the bed. She held up a small foil package.

"I've had a bit already. It's super-strong dope." I could see that both statements were true.

She leaned over and kissed me on the lips.

"I'm sorry about shouting at you earlier," she said. "Anyway, it wasn't too bad after all."

"That's all right. I'm sorry too."

It was a good generic statement. It covered a lot of ground.

"Well, can I?" I asked, pointing at the dope.

"Sure," she said. "I'll get you some water. I'll have some more too."

That's how it started. We had a hit and went back to bed and Candy described her night to me. How the men came in and had a drink and selected the girl they wanted. How they paid the house portion at reception, and the rest to her in the room. How extra money seemed so easily negotiable on top of that: twenty dollars to touch her breasts, thirty dollars for any serious change in position, like, say, doggy-style. How surprised she was at the way the money poured in all night. How clinical and unsexual it all seemed. I listened in rapt attention. With every word it seemed that Candy was describing either a world we could live with or one that was unacceptable. But the men sounded sad, and it all sounded like the joke was on them. As dawn came I thought, Maybe it's not so bad.

We went to sleep and got up about eleven or midday and had another hit. The new dealer's name was Lester, and he would figure in our lives, on and off, for a while.

Two Saturdays earlier, Candy didn't know about her market value. The hockshop owner had taken her for a ride. He would get his later, when an overwrought methamphetamine addict in the throes of speed psychosis shot and crippled him in an argument about the value of a lawn mower. But Candy learned pretty quickly about market value. For a while, for a few years, she was the hotshot money tree and we lived, like royalty, in the kingdom of invincibility.

FOURSOME

The hotshot money tree. At the peak of good things financially, we actually rented a nice flat, out along Queens Road. The building was designed by some Swedish architect back in the thirties. It was a deco number, full of curves and whiteness and railings and round windows, designed to give the impression of being on a ship. It was full of yuppies too, nine-to-fivers in suits, with nice cars; and then there was us.

It made us feel so full of hope, to move into such a swish place. We felt a kind of duty to keep the place clean, to empty ashtrays, stuff like that. Perhaps we felt that our lives would change just by being there.

But not necessarily change as in making the decision to stop using dope. It was that time when things subtly shifted, when we began to accept that we were devoted to the cause, when the point became not how to stop, but how to use well. Candy was beginning to get good at working, at the way to do it without feeling, at how to get the most money for the least effort, to be in charge of johns so danger never happened. It hadn't been long, but we'd done that mental somersault where we reasoned that it was all for money and therefore it didn't affect our love.

We were on a roll. The money came thick and fast and

it seemed the wonder of a comfortable life would be endless. We weren't sick for months at a time. We felt instinctively we were in the middle of vast good fortune.

Candy was doing escort. It was less restrictive and less boring than brothels. We got to drive around together all night. There was some comfort in that, some comradeship.

Mostly things went smoothly. Occasionally Candy could earn a thousand dollars between six in the evening and six in the morning. We were stoned and happy all the time. Even when the money was bad it was good.

I didn't have a license, of course, couldn't really drive, having never done it much, but at least here I was able to give a kind of moral support. We had a deal with Jesse, a cousin of O'Brien's who worked a day job in computers. We'd take his car every night on the condition we always filled it with gas when we returned it, and once in a while we'd give him a free taste. He was that rare breed, a casual user. They belong in nature documentaries.

We'd drive all night from job to job. Probably my greatest contribution to the whole deal was doing the street directory. I'd always liked maps. We'd park, Candy would get out. Sometimes I'd go to the door with her, to check that the place seemed all right. Then I'd sit in the car with the seat reclined back and the radio turned low, and wait for her to finish. There were times I felt a sadness, bored and restless in a quiet street in Doncaster or Heidelberg or Brighton. A kind of dull sadness about being tied by flimsy strings to this life, in the middle of nowhere in the middle of the night. About my part—there must have been one—in accepting that a relationship could be like this. An ache of guilt, occasionally, that I could have the gall to call it love. But mostly I thought I wouldn't swap my life for anything, that Candy was in it and heroin was in it and what more could you possibly want?

It was hard to score good dope at six in the morning. Generally we'd try and have that kind of shit wrapped up by midnight or one. Sometimes we'd still have a small whack left at dawn, and then sleep for a while. Other times we'd go to bed a little ragged. Then we'd wake up wired at midday, but with lots of money, so we could score straightaway.

The afternoon was the time of love, when things were bright and busy, when it didn't feel like it sometimes felt when I sat alone in the car at night. We would wander and eat, or smoke a little grass and watch TV, or look for clothes in Salvation Army shops. We would often hold hands as we walked, and even in winter we'd feel warm in the sun. The supreme body furnace was in us, spreading its warmth through our veins.

We spent a lot of time scoring and organizing deals, doing all the drug stuff. Then in the evening the calls would begin to come from the agency.

One night at about eleven, Candy went to a job at some tacky motor inn in St. Kilda, and the bitch at reception had the nerve to say, "No. Not here you don't. This is a clean hotel." Candy ranted and raved, but she didn't want to lose the guy. He'd booked for an hour, but once he saw her, he went a bit gaga.

Candy sensed this, which was what she did well. She told him that for eight hundred bucks he could spend the whole night with her, back in the apartment on Queens Road. He loved the idea. But he said he only had two hundred on him, he could get the other six hundred in the morning. Candy looked at me and said, "What do you think?" I shrugged my shoulders. I sized the guy up and thought it was worth the punt. He was as straight as they come. He was drunk and sincere. A Western District farmer down in the big smoke for a couple of days.

I was the minder, obviously. It couldn't have been my physical size, but often in these circumstances people treated me with some deference. Or more likely, some wariness. It must have been the mere fact of being a pimp. As if we weren't just a fucked-up boyfriend and girlfriend putting on a big front. As if Candy, being so beautiful, would have selected me as the toughest and the meanest from some pimp employment bureau.

His name was Keith. I shook my head and looked to the ground, trying to show a form of sympathy tempered by doubt.

"I dunno, Keith. Six hundred is a lot of money in a situation of trust. You sure you've got this money?"

"There's no problem with the money. I swear, first thing in the morning. As soon as the banks open. No problem at all."

"Because you cannot fuck around in a situation like this. You understand that, don't you?"

"Of course I understand."

I could hear the dryness in his throat, his nervousness at dealing with me when Candy was the object of desire.

"What have you got to give me for the night, Keith? I'll be in the same flat, don't worry. I'm not going anywhere. Driver's license?"

"No problem."

He pulled it from his wallet. I looked at it. He was thirty-six, a ruddy-faced farmer acting completely out of character for a night.

"It's not much security though, is it?" I added. I looked at his wedding ring. "Tell you what. Give me the ring and I'll feel good about this."

"Oh come on," he pleaded.

"Keith." I cut him short. "Two-way trust. The ring's not going anywhere."

He slipped it off his finger and I put it in my pocket.

"And the two hundred," I said. "You give me that now, as a deposit. Because I have to pay the agency at the beginning of an all-night job."

It was bullshit, but only Candy and I knew that. We had several dealers to choose from, but we could hardly make Keith wait while we paged someone or drove all over town.

The closest dealer, a door knock away, was Ellie May the transvestite. Her dope had been all right lately and I could just turn up without ringing; she was always there.

We drove the short distance to Ellie May's flat and parked.

"What are we doing?" Keith asked as I got out.

"This is the office," Candy said. "He's dropping in your deposit."

I got a two-spot off Ellie May and we went back to our Queens Road digs. Keith looked impressed and seemed to relax. We'd cleaned the flat immaculately in an afternoon smack-fiddling binge.

Keith went to the bathroom. Candy went to the lounge room and made a call to the agency. She told them the job had fucked up, that there was a big scene at the motor inn, that the guy had gotten freaked and canceled. She told them also she'd come down with some kind of *thing* and was vomiting a lot and wouldn't be able to work anymore that night. It was only midnight by now so they weren't pleased. Still, they had no real choice but to buy it.

Keith came out of the bathroom and Candy told him to go into the bedroom and make himself comfortable. I was in the kitchen mixing up on the counter. Candy came in, looked over my shoulder, and checked out the amount of dope we'd gotten.

"Hurry up," she said. "I've got to get in there."

I was almost ready with her syringe when Keith appeared at the door and gave us a fright. Our backs were hunched away from him.

"What are you doing?" he asked, a genuine curiosity in his voice. Candy swung around and guided him back to the bedroom.

"He's just fixing a tap," I heard her say. Sometimes the most absurd things make the greatest sense.

She rushed back into the kitchen and had her shot. I had mine and settled down to watch TV for the night. From time to time my conscience would wander into my body, and

I'd think about what they were doing behind that wall at just that moment. I was never usually this close to it. But there's a paradox about taking heroin and feeling anything, and it was easier to be blank and watch the screen.

After about half an hour Candy came out of the bedroom. When the door opened I could hear Keith's loud snoring. Candy looked at me and grinned.

"He's out for the night, I think," she said.

We watched TV together and occasionally Candy went in to check on him. At about four A.M. we had another blast. Candy went back to the room then and everyone slept for a few hours. Jesse wasn't working in the morning, and he had said we could keep the car until later in the night, as long as we gave him a nice taste.

I woke when Keith, hungover and pale, staggered to the bathroom at about nine. Since I was still dressed I was ready to go.

"Let's hit that bank, then," I said.

The three of us drove to the National Bank on St. Kilda Road. Candy waited outside in the car and I went in with Keith. There was a fuckup. As in, they wouldn't give him his money. He didn't have the funds. His credit card was over the limit too.

We stood in conference away from the counter. I tried to look angry but restrained.

"Keith, this is a serious problem. I'm sure you know that. It's not that *I'm* heavy or anything. It's just that the people I work for, the people above me, well—they are. And they won't stand for this. It's six hundred dollars. I have to have the money."

"Listen, I can send it to you," he pleaded. "I really didn't expect this to happen. You can hold on to my driver's license."

"Keith, that's not the way it works. I have to have the money before we part company, and I want to part company soon. I'm busy. I've got things to do."

"I understand that."

"Now think. How can you get the money? Ring someone, get someone to put it in your bank account. It doesn't matter how. If you don't get the money I have no choice but to make life difficult for you."

"There is one thing," he said.

He was a creative thinker. He got the St. Kilda Road branch to ring his hometown branch. They handed him the phone over the counter and he spoke in familiar tones to the manager. I moved away to give him room, but I heard him say things like "urgent" and "a spot of bother, I can't explain now."

Finally I saw the look of relief on his face. He gave the phone back to the teller, who spoke to the country manager for a moment. In a couple of minutes Keith had his six hundred dollars. He walked outside the bank and he counted the notes out to me. I gave him his ring and driver's license. Suddenly he was not important in my life.

"Well, I'm glad that's all ended okay, then." I tried to smile pleasantly. "We have to go now, Keith. Enjoy the rest of your time in Melbourne."

I jumped into the car and pulled my seat belt over my shoulder. Candy leaned across me.

"Bye, Keith. Nice to meet you!"

And we drove away. Keith stood there, unshaven and uncertain, and then walked off in the opposite direction.

Later in the afternoon we lashed out and scored three grams off Lester. Lester was best when you bought the bigger amounts, but sometimes he took a little arranging. We returned the car to Jesse and gave him a little hit. He was happy.

We caught the tram back home from Jesse's place at Carlton. We decided we'd ring the agency and take another night off, lie around and have lots of dope and watch TV and then get a big sleep.

But at about nine the intercom system rang. We weren't expecting anyone and we looked at each other. Candy answered and I saw her eyebrows rise as she buzzed the security door open.

"It's Kojak," she said.

"Kojak? I wonder why."

Kojak was a dealer Victor had put us onto. We hadn't asked him to come around, so it didn't really make sense. We didn't owe him any money, we didn't owe him any favors. We weren't in any trouble with him, so we hoped his visit meant good news.

He came in with a pretty girl. Her eyes were lowered and she scowled at us by way of introduction. We could see she was hanging out for some gear. Her name was Lucy. She had short red hair and pale skin. Lovely green eyes, even with her huge pupils. She wasn't all skin and bones, so she probably hadn't been using for long. No more than a year or two. She was about twenty-five, a late starter.

Kojak didn't use the dope he sold. He was in his mid-thirties, came from Malta or somewhere like that. Shaved his head, God knows why, drove a brand-new blue Commodore. Nonusing dealers, of course, were the scum of the earth, but Kojak was okay as far as nonusing dealers went. He was reliable, the deals were big, the dope was pretty good. The main reason he wasn't high on our list of priorities was that he often didn't respond to his pager for an hour or two.

"So how are you, Kojak?" I said. "What brings you here?"

"Can Lucy use your place for a shot?"

"Of course."

"And after that, can we use your bedroom?"

I looked at Candy. She shrugged.

"Sure. Go right ahead."

Lucy hit up and suddenly relaxed and became friendly and talkative. Obviously she had no cash and the deal was a hit for a fuck. We chatted for five minutes. Kojak asked us if we wanted to buy any dope and we said no, we had plenty, but maybe tomorrow. Then Kojak said to Lucy, "Let's go," and they went into our bedroom.

This hadn't happened before.

"She seems nice," Candy said.

"Yeah . . . yeah, she does."

We stared at the TV for a few minutes. Then from the corner of my eye I noticed Candy's head tilt toward me.

"Maybe we should go in there," she said.

"Go in there? What do you mean?"

"Go in there. Join them."

I looked her in the eye. I was trying to see if I understood her motives. There was no real reason to do it or not do it.

"I guess so," I said.

"Lucy's cute."

I nodded agreement.

"Anyway," she added, "it might be a good idea to get in good with Kojak."

She was right about that. It was our duty, really, not to let an opportunity pass. In some strange way, if Kojak got an extra thrill, then he would owe us something, even if only a particularly good deal or leeway with credit sometime in the future. Besides, I felt a stirring of horniness for the novelty of the situation.

We tiptoed to the bedroom door and knocked. There was a pause.

"Yeah?" Kojak sounded surprised.

Candy opened the door and stuck her head around. "Would you mind if we came in and joined you?"

"Sure," Kojak said.

"Sure," Lucy said.

We went into the room. Lucy was lying on her side propped up on one elbow. She looked even more gorgeous with no clothes on. Kojak was sitting at the head of the bed, one leg tucked under him and one stretched to the floor. Obviously we'd interrupted Lucy sucking Kojak's dick. Kojak was holding his erection in his hand. I had a quick glance and was glad it didn't seem any bigger than mine.

We took our clothes off. Candy was naked in a flash. I took my time because I wasn't exactly sure what I was going to do. What would be appropriate. How things would pan out. All I knew was I felt tingly about Lucy and Candy, and nervous about the presence of Kojak. I just wasn't into men; it seemed stupid to force anything.

Candy climbed onto the bottom end of the bed on her knees. From my point of view, everything was sexually charged. Candy's butt was smooth and white and pointed up in the air toward me. When she moved her left knee forward to crawl toward Lucy, the curve of her pubis and the soft flesh of the inside of her thigh were exposed. It was an angle I hadn't often seen. Anyway, all angles looked good when looking at Candy.

Lucy spread her legs and stretched her arms out. She clasped her hands around Candy's neck and pulled her forward. They started tongue kissing. I was curious to see what Candy looked like kissing someone else. It was a luscious heroin-stoned meeting of wet lips and tongues. They writhed on each other's bellies and their legs became all intertwined.

Kojak got his hands between them and was rubbing Lucy's breasts. He moved his erect dick closer to their faces. Candy lifted her head away from kissing Lucy and started sucking Kojak.

I was naked by now and up on the bed. From above it would have looked like this: the two girls in the middle, Candy facedown on Lucy; Kojak in the vicinity of Candy's right shoulder; me down around Candy's left foot. The two men diagonally opposite.

Lucy had red pubic hair. I put my hand on her cunt. My arm from wrist to elbow was rubbing on Candy's inner thigh. Candy cocked one leg over Lucy's belly. Things were beginning to melt. I moved up to the left of the girls, level with their waists. I kept my hand on Lucy's cunt, my fingers exploring, feeling how different it was from Candy's. Lucy took her right hand from Candy's breasts and started playing with my dick. I leaned forward and started kissing her. It had been a long time since I'd kissed anyone else. It was a delicious shock.

Lucy's breath, Lucy's lips, the smell of her—it all tasted different. I really wanted some time to get down there and check out her pussy, but even though our bodies were moving slowly and wetly, everything in my head was happening at a delirious high speed. From one second to another I had no idea what would happen next. Being a drug addict basically meant trying to control your universe at all costs; for me, then, this business in the bed was a novel experience of vertigo and abandon and free fall.

Kissing Lucy was like being lost in a dream. Six inches to my right Candy was sucking Kojak's dick. Everything was cool. As in okay. I watched for a moment, intrigued by what Candy looked like doing that from an angle I'd never seen before. She had the double-chin thing on the downstroke, like in porn movies, but then I guess everyone does.

We rolled around a bit and positions changed. I spent a while licking Lucy down below, and Kojak tried to go through the *Kama Sutra* with Candy. I kept my eyes open because it was nice looking at the color of Lucy's pubic hair up close, the way the red seemed to disappear against her flushed and swollen skin.

Then things changed again. Lucy was up on all fours and Candy was lying beneath her and sucking her breasts. Candy's body came out sideways from under Lucy's stomach. I couldn't help thinking of a mechanic, the legs jutting out from under a car. A naked female mechanic.

I sat on my knees with my legs spread wide at the groin. I spread Candy's legs and pulled her into position toward me, lifting her up by the buttocks. It was like the docking of the satellites. I fucked her—it felt real nice—while her ankles swayed gently around my shoulders and ears like long stalks of grass in a breeze. All the while she nuzzled Lucy's breasts, hidden under there like she was changing a brake line.

Meanwhile Kojak had gone down the other end, to fuck Lucy from behind.

"Ow!" Lucy shouted. She reached her arm around and pushed at Kojak's stomach, pushed him away from her arse. He'd been trying to stick his dick in her tradesmen's entrance, no lube, no nothing.

"Not there you don't," Lucy said, admonishing him as she might a headstrong child.

Kojak didn't complain. He just started fucking her in the designated area, and then things settled down into a quiet rhythm. Of course I was loaded on heroin and Kojak didn't use, so in the staying-power stakes I wasn't about to be challenged. After a few minutes Kojak grunted a few times and came. His whole demeanor changed then. His clothes were on before his dick had even deflated. He pulled on his shoes.

"I have to go," he said, backing out the door. "I've got business to do. Bye-bye, beautiful girls." He didn't say a word to me. But I felt good about the matter. Kojak had gotten a thrill. I knew that at some point in the future he would probably give us a little dope on credit.

The hall door slammed as he went out. I had a moment of insecurity, as if I had no power here, as if everything would stop now. With Kojak in the room, it might have only been for show and profit. But Candy and Lucy seemed just as into it now as they were before. I decided to take the plunge and keep the momentum going.

I pulled out of Candy and lay on top of Lucy and we started kissing again. Candy and I were both used to each other. I guess in a way we were both fighting over Lucy, who was new and unknown. But it was a friendly kind of rivalry. Candy started licking Lucy's pussy. Lucy said, "It's good now Kojak's gone," and I could hardly believe my ears.

Just the three of us. The situation began to dawn on me.

Really, this was paradise as far as I was concerned. That's not exactly true: *heroin* was paradise. But me alone, naked, in a room with naked Candy and naked Lucy—our sole purpose to have sex, to *do things* with each other—well, I have to say I was pretty fucking happy.

It's funny, though, I did feel a little strange about putting my dick in Lucy with Kojak's sperm so recently deposited up there. But I got over that. We tried a whole lot of positions and three-way variations. There's a chance on heroin that you'll just never come, you'll fuck and fuck and finally give up. But I was stretched to the limit of what being horny could possibly mean. I was sure something was in the offing.

In the end I was fucking Lucy in the missionary position and Candy was down between our legs, doing whatever with Lucy and licking my balls and scrotum. I'd never experienced the luxury of an extra tongue. Being on heroin was always like winning the lottery, but *coming* on heroin was like winning it twice.

My life was a lot like a cartoon, so it wasn't surprising that I actually saw bands of stars swirling in front of my eyes and around my head for five or ten seconds at the peak of things. Then we all collapsed in a pile for a while.

I knew the next thing I wanted was a nice big blast. We had enough dope to keep our chins superglued to our chests for a good few hours. I felt so full of benevolence, I was tempted to offer Lucy some. But I realized that was taking things too far.

"Did Kojak leave you some gear, Lucy?" I asked.

"Yeah, there's a little bit," she said. Then she added nervously, "But only enough for me, really."

"Oh no, that's okay, it's just that we don't have enough to give you any," I lied. "I just didn't want you to feel left out."

The three of us went back into the lounge room and mixed up. We all got completely wasted. For many hours we couldn't even open our eyes to watch TV. We just dribbled a lot and mumbled shit that nobody understood. We burned holes in the sofa and on the carpet when our cigarettes, lit but unsmoked, suspended in our hands, smoldered down to long cylinders of ash as we drooped toward slack-jawed unconsciousness. It was the best kind of domestic bliss, the absolute absence of discomfort.

At dawn I woke to kids' cartoons. Candy was asleep. Lucy had gone, leaving a note that said, "Nice to meet you both, see you soon." Three weeks later Kojak told us he'd heard she'd gone to rehab. We never saw her again.

COLIN GETS LUCKY

Every now and then, despite the money, Candy got pissed off with the hard slog of prostitution. We'd try to make a go of dealing, so she could work a little less sometimes. We never reached great heights. Just kept using all that extra gear.

Lack of foresight would get us into trouble. It's a lack of foresight to use a day's worth of dope in one shot. Equally, it's a lack of foresight to plan to stop when deep down you know that you can't. The best intentions mean fuck all.

At such times you find yourselves adrift in anxiety, unprepared once more for the onslaught of stomach cramps and the hideous sweat, wandering the city with vague thoughts of shoplifting. This was problematic on a midwinter Sunday, when Melbourne was empty and windswept, like a scene from *The Omega Man*.

Candy and I were walking down Little Bourke Street, discussing who we could call and what story we could use to get some money. Then the gods intervened. We walked past a bank of phone booths, and one of them began to ring. We looked at each other. It was an odd event. Candy picked up the phone and I leaned in to listen.

"Hello?"

"Hello? Who's that?"

"Who's that?"

"This is Colin."

"Hi, Colin."

"Who's that?"

"This is Candy."

"Is that Lifeline? I want to speak to a counselor."

"No, this is Candy. I think you've got the wrong number. What number did you try to ring?"

"So this is not Lifeline? Who are you?"

"I'm Candy."

"Oh . . . So I guess I've got the wrong number."

"What's the problem, Colin? Why do you want to ring Lifeline?"

I gave Candy the thumbs-up. Someone in distress, or in an erratic state, could mean someone erratic enough to part with some money. Candy was thinking the same way. We almost always did.

"Oh, I'm just not feeling too good. I don't know . . . Where are you?"

"I'm in a phone booth in Little Bourke Street."

"A phone booth . . . no, you're kidding me."

"No, I'm not. You called a phone booth. Listen." She held the phone outside the booth. "Hear the traffic? I'm in a phone booth. I swear."

"That's incredible," he said. "Wow."

"So, Colin, what is there to be so depressed about?"

"Well, everything, really. My wife hates me, I hate my job. I hate my life."

"Where do you work?"

"In a pie factory in Preston."

"Do you have many friends?"

"No, not any, really."

"Maybe you could be my friend."

"Why, what are you like?"

"I'm really nice." She oozed such confidence when she said it.

"How old are you? What do you look like?"

"I'm twenty-four. I've got long blond hair. How old are you?"

"I'm thirty-two."

"Well, maybe we should meet! I mean, what a bizarre coincidence, me walking past just at this moment and the phone ringing like that!"

"Sure, that sounds great. I can't believe it. It *is* a coincidence! Well, when could we meet?" We could feel Colin's mood, his day, his life, changing.

"I don't know. I'm not doing anything . . . I suppose we could even meet today."

"That'd be fantastic! I can't believe it. One minute I feel like killing myself and the next minute I've met someone really interesting."

"Oh, now you don't want to go killing yourself. Otherwise you'd miss out on interesting meetings like this. But listen, I've just remembered something. I'd *love* to meet up with you today, but I'm desperately searching for some money to help a friend out. It's a bit of an emergency. Something's come up. It's difficult to explain. But I tell you what, if *you* could lend me some money, then we could meet up today, and I could pay you back tomorrow."

There was a short silence.

"What, you want to borrow some money off *me*?"

"Yeah. That way we'd have an excuse to see each other twice in two days. What do you think?"

"I'm not sure . . . how much do you need?"

He was faltering. Candy had to act fast.

"I need two hundred dollars. Listen, you could come straight into town now. Where do you live?"

"Coburg."

"Right. You could just jump on a tram, be here in half an hour. We could go for a walk through the park, or a tram ride, go to a café. It'd be loads of fun."

"Well . . ."

"Listen, the money's not a problem. My friend, the girl who needs it, is giving it back to me tomorrow. So as I said, we could meet again tomorrow."

"Why does she need it in such a hurry?"

"It's really hard to explain. It's personal. I promised her I'd help her. But trust me, it's very important. A one-day loan. How can that hurt you?"

"Well . . . I guess I could. . . ."

"Yeah! It'll be great. I'm dying to meet you already. You sound really interesting."

"Okay, then, where shall we meet?"

Candy smiled at me. I punched the air in silent joy. I couldn't believe she'd pulled it off. One minute we'd felt like killing ourselves and the next we'd met someone really interesting!

The plan was this: Candy would meet Colin at the Bourke Street Mall. She'd take him on a get-to-know-you tram ride, one circuit around the city center. Have a quick coffee at the very most.

We'd done a flit from Queens Road after we didn't pay the rent for a couple of months, and now lived in the middle of the city, in a decrepit warehouse in a back lane. Candy would get rid of him within the hour. Then we'd leave straightaway to score. It was my job to arrange for the drugs.

Everything was perfect. Within two hours of the phone ringing we'd gotten two hundred dollars from a perfect stranger, got loaded, and prevented a suicide into the bargain. We felt good.

Candy told me about Colin. He was short, and he wore shorts, with white socks to the knees. A zip-up green parka kept him warm. His hair was greasy. He had dandruff and acne scars. He wore thick bottle-lens glasses that magnified his eyes disturbingly.

"It was so cruel," she said, not knowing whether to laugh or cover her mouth.

"We got the money. That's the point," I said.

"He said he'd never met anyone like me."

"Well, that's got to be worth two hundred dollars," I said. "Is he worth more?"

"Maybe just a few times. I mean, it's not like he's rich. I think he just saves his wages. I'd better play it careful. String him along. He's pretty thick. Not all there."

Over the next couple of months, somehow, unbelievably, we continued to get money out of Colin. Candy never fucked him. She never did more than meet him for a tram ride or a coffee. She never allowed him to see our place or know our address.

Somehow, the previous debt would be wiped, and then it was just the new problem of trying to get money out of him today, as if it were the first time.

I think Colin was falling in love. Candy told him she was an artist and that she lived in a complex of studios shared by other artists. Our phone, according to Candy, was the communal phone for all these bohemians. Candy said she lived alone in her studio and she didn't have a boyfriend.

I was therefore the gay friend who lived in the adjoining studio. That's why I answered the phone so often. Colin tried to have long conversations with me, digging for information about this incredible girl he had met. I fueled his curiosity with praise for her uniqueness. I sprinkled my praise with hints about her availability. I insinuated that she was unlucky in love and was really just looking for that "special man."

I would ration her. Just to make him tense. A little bit of edginess and anticipation can go a long way in a guy like Colin.

We'd be having a good day. Lots of dope. Lots of money. The phone would ring.

"Hi, Colin!" I'd say warmly and loudly, looking across the warehouse floor to Candy.

She'd motion to me with her arms, No way!

"Mate, what a shame, you've just missed her. I heard her go out a few minutes ago."

I mean, the guy worked in a pie factory. He'd probably saved a thousand dollars in four years. We really had to reserve him for emergency days. Other than that, we didn't want him invading our lives.

Just when he thought his princess had left his life forever, she would call him, trying to act casual. He'd given Candy his home number. God knows what his wife thought.

Candy would keep the excuses coming, stories of misery. He was the only one who could help her, she'd say. On three or four occasions over two or three months, she got a couple of hundred out of him. And then eventually, as happens with johns, his patience began to wear thin.

When that time comes you bring out the secondary ammunition: tell the truth and see what happens.

On a dark, despairing Sunday, Candy changed tactics. I put my ear close to the phone.

"But I don't understand," Colin whined. "You're always in trouble with money."

Candy sighed. The sigh said: You are about to be the recipient of momentous news. You'd better be grateful.

"Colin," she said, "there's something I've been meaning to tell you. I'm having a lot of problems. I'm a heroin addict."

"A heroin addict!"

I don't think Colin had ever experienced such drama in his life. I imagined his heart pounding with this new excitement.

"I know," Candy said. "It's terrible."

"A heroin addict! Well, that explains so much! Why didn't you tell me?"

"I was so embarrassed. I've been trying so hard to stop, so we can have a better relationship together." She chose her words carefully. "You know, a better friendship."

"Well, why don't you just stop?"

"It's not that easy, Colin. It's not that simple. There are some very heavy people chasing me for money. Once I get the debt out of the way, then I can start to think about stopping."

"But how much money do you need?"

"Look, I need thousands. But, darling, it's not your problem, it's not your concern. I have to deal with this myself. I wouldn't dream of asking you to help me with thousands. It's just that today, it's a real emergency. They want two hundred as an installment."

I was scribbling furiously on a pad: "To show good faith."

"You know, to show them my good faith. Or they'll hurt me."

"My God," Colin said. "What sort of people are these?"

"You don't want to know, Colin. You really don't want to know. Will you help me, Colin? *Can* you help me?"

She sounded like some helpless heroine in *Gone with the Wind*. I would have laughed, only trying to get money for drugs was no laughing matter.

And somehow, yet again, we pulled it off. She pulled it off.

But once you'd gone into the reserve plan, you knew the end was in sight. You could now hustle someone like Colin without having to hide your sheer desperation. This was quite a relief. But it could only work a few more times, because now you were expected to take some kind of action, like going to a detox or drying out in the country. And of course you never did.

Some weeks later the thing came grinding to a pathetic halt. The final thing you do in the face of adamant refusals is get nasty.

We were sick. I sat on the couch listening to the conversation with a sinking feeling in my gut. Who else could we try?

Candy was hissing things like, "Surely you've got *something* in your house you can sell!" I knew the cause was lost.

I picked up my pocket phone book. I opened it at ABC. I ran my finger down the page. Greg Anderson. Who the fuck is Greg Anderson? As I began to concentrate on the new task at hand, I tuned out of Candy's lost battle.

The last thing I remember her saying was, "Listen, we'll come around and pick up your washing machine."

But Colin drew the line. Colin had more dignity than that. About household appliances, at least.

FREEBASING

Colin was a freak occurrence. I mean, the public phone, the way it all happened: the odds were remote. Still, when you open yourself to the possibility of weird money or quick money, it's bound to happen every now and again. That's how we got into Tucker's coke deal.

There was a time when cocaine was a drug I liked. I was young and full of beans. I was eighteen, nineteen, twenty years old, and selling lots of hash and pot.

The money began to roll in. The amounts I was dealing got bigger and bigger. I was like a small business, expanding from the ground up. The kind of thing the government would have been proud of. It was a vibrant, golden time, full of excitement and unlimited opportunity. There wasn't a single sign on the horizon of imminent downturn.

As I started doing bigger amounts of grass, I started making connections with people who were older and better-traveled down the drug path. Cocaine appeared, and before long I was buying it by the ounce and selling by the gram. Along the way I learned to freebase. It was a necessary business practice. If you weigh a given amount of cocaine before and after turning it to base, you can work out its purity.

Eventually things got out of hand, as they do with the yip-yap drugs. I succumbed a little too much to the unstoppable madness of freebasing and ended up owing a couple of people a lot of money. But that was a few years earlier, and Candy hadn't been in the picture then.

With Candy and me, hammer was the all-consuming thing. We were both firmly of the opinion that cocaine was a serious pussy drug, or at least among people silly enough to snort it. Freebasing, of course—crack, as it was coming to be known by the time I met Candy—was a different matter. A very fucked-up way of life, for those who like their pleasure hard and fast and endlessly repeated rather than our way, hard and slow and endless. A fucked-up way to fuck up.

But a lot of people liked coke, and there was market value in that.

Candy and I looked bad enough that yuppies wanting to rough it for a while in coke dealing could believe we had some cred; but not so fucked-up and tattooed and toothless that they didn't trust us.

I never actively looked for cocaine business, but occasionally something would pop up that warranted some middlemanning. Some shifty coke brokering.

Tucker was a muso who sometimes bought our smack. He was one of those types who had been the drummer for Dragon or John Farnham, some shit like that, fifteen years earlier, and was stupid enough to boast about it.

Tucker was like a gun for hire at cheesy club gigs now. Once, I'd delivered some dope to him at the Starlight Club. The band was dressed in frayed but matching baby-blue tuxedos with flared trousers. Tucker was listlessly attacking his drum kit to a rather haunting version of "Girl from Ipanema" as boozy seniors bored with bingo stared into their drinks. I guess I would want some heroin too, under such circumstances. But he was a little sad, the way he hadn't had a habit in ten years and tried to hold things together in that pathetic I'm-not-on-methadone-but-I'm-not-going-to-let-things-fuck-up way.

Anyway, there was some big pie he had his fingers in. Or maybe not so big, but big enough for us. Ten ounces of coke at a good price, and everyone could make a little cash. I knew a keen buyer, through O'Brien, and one thing led to another. But everything was subject to the purity of the coke. And Tucker, who had freebased before but didn't actually know how to cook it up, wanted me to be the tester.

He also wanted to use our warehouse. Fuck it, we couldn't say no to a quick cash injection. It was worth a thousand bucks, just to be there and test the coke. Tucker was pretty nervous. There was more in it for him. He even came around to the warehouse earlier in the day. He swept and dusted and put flowers in a vase.

I didn't like the two guys selling it, but then those coke and heroin worlds didn't intersect a great deal, not down at our level. The buyer was some film guy, some pansy fucking producer or something, and I felt sorry for him, because he was extremely nervous and not doing a good job of hiding it.

He brought his girlfriend along, like he was confident and casual and did this kind of thing all the time. But I could see the way saliva, what little of it there was, kept sticking in his throat. And the way he licked his lips, and the way his voice came out croaky or high-pitched a few times. It reminded me of what happened to my own voice and my saliva whenever I got arrested.

So there was me and Candy and the two Richmond gangsters (semi-gangsters, at least) and Film Boy and his babe (he'd met her when she was the talent in a yogurt commercial he shot) and Tucker, who was frantically introducing everyone and cracking dumb jokes which are not worth recalling.

The scene was not unpleasant but it was not really relaxed either. We all just wanted to get the deal done and get back to our normal lives: Candy and I to hitting up smack; the semi-gangsters to extorting money from cheesy nightclubs or whatever they did; Film Boy and Babe to showing off to all their filmic friends and learning how to turn a potential profit into a disastrous septum-corroding loss; and Tucker, king for just an evening, to being the sad ferret he was.

Because I was testing the dope, I was this kind of neutral link who both sides were looking to for assurance. Film Boy, in particular, was relying on me to give the okay.

Everyone sat down and Semi-Gangster One pulled out the bag and plonked it on the table. Film Boy looked at me like I was going to tell him how pure it was just by looking at it. He had no fucking idea.

"Go ahead, it's your deal," I said. "Check it out." I was giving him a heavy prompt. I had to help the poor bastard out.

He reached over and took the bag. He dipped his finger in and tasted it on his tongue and teeth.

"Tastes all right," he said. "Let's have a line."

He pulled a razor blade from his pocket and scooped out a couple of mounds. He laid out seven thick lines on a mirror. He rolled up a fifty-dollar note and snorted a line. Then he passed the mirror around. It was really just a ritual of politeness. Probably only Babe was genuinely excited, in a positive sense. As opposed to edgy, like the rest of us.

The coke tasted all right on my gums. I woofed down the snort. I hated that jerky little nyang-nyang thing it did in your brain. Anyway, it had been so long since anything had gone up through my nose, I didn't really know if this batch was any good or not. What the fuck was a snort supposed to do?

Snorting was silly when you were about to buy ten ounces. The base test was the only way to go.

The conversation sped up for thirty seconds, as it does when people are snorting, and everyone seemed to be speaking at once. Film Boy was weighing the coke on his brand-new electronic scales and being a real suck about how good it seemed. The semi-gangsters were relaxing a little and lapping it all up. Tucker was agreeing with everything everyone said. Candy just sat there smiling.

I really wanted these people out of my house.

"Let's get testing," I suggested.

We all moved over to the far corner of the warehouse, where there was a sink and a stove, a space that vaguely resembled a kitchen. We sat around the table. There weren't enough chairs. Film Boy perched on a milk crate so that only his head was visible above the table. He probably felt as awkward as he looked.

I'd gone out and bought a little glass pipe from a bong shop and some gauze from the hardware store. I'd made myself a good-looking base pipe. No use wasting the test rock.

I set up my diamond scales. Everyone watched the process. There were some nice rocks in the bag but basically it had been powdered pretty well, and it's the powder that you want to test from, because that's where the sugar will be.

I dug deep into the bag with a teaspoon and stirred it around. I pulled out a few small amounts from different parts, what I thought was a representative sample. I weighed out exactly a gram.

I poured a couple of teaspoons of water into a little Master Foods spice jar, which earlier in the day had contained oregano. I'd cleaned it and removed the label. I tapped the cocaine into the jar and swilled it around. The water went a little cloudy but it didn't look too bad.

I filled a frying pan with an inch of water and put it on the stove, scooped out about half a gram of bicarbonate of soda and added that to the mix in the Master Foods jar. If the coke was any good, I wouldn't need much more bicarb than that.

When the water in the frying pan started to boil, I stood at the stove with the jar and said, "Okay, let's see how we go."

I screwed the lid on tight to the little jar and dropped a teaspoon into the frying pan, with the underneath of the spoon facing up. I lowered the jar into the water, resting the bottom of the jar on the mound of the teaspoon, to conduct heat away from the jar and along the teaspoon. The last thing we wanted was an exploding base test.

I swirled the solution and it quickly went clear in the heat. I pulled the jar out and untightened the lid for a second, to release the pressure. Then I lowered the jar back into the frying pan.

For about thirty seconds the solution stayed clear, and then a film of oil began to appear on the surface. The cocaine hydrochloride—a salt that dissolved readily in the blood vessels of the mucous membrane—was now becoming pure cocaine base, or freebase, or candy rock, or crack. The bicarb was reacting with the hydrochloride, and the cocaine was being separated from the other diluents.

As the layer of oil thickened, it became too heavy to support its own weight and began to form an almost perfect sphere. As I shook the jar gently, the oil drop fell to the bottom of the jar, where it bounced and wobbled.

More balls of oil formed, and dangled, and fell to the bottom of the jar, until the main ball grew larger and larger and there was no more oil on the surface.

"Well, it's definitely coke," I joked. I knew now the deal would go through. "I think it's okay too."

I'm sure Film Boy's shoulders loosened up a little in relief.

When I was certain I'd extracted all the coke, I turned the stove off, moved over to the kitchen sink, and turned on the cold tap. I flicked some water on the jar to cool down the glass. Then, with the jar tilted sideways, I gradually moved it under the flow of the cold water. As the gray oil began to harden, it turned an off-white color. This was the right color, this or a dirty yellow gray; pink suggested the presence of procaine or Xylocaine or some other inferior substitute.

One second the oil was wobbling around, the next it was beginning to lift off the bottom of the jar as I shook it gently, and the next it was a hard white rock tinkling and pinging as it hit the glass. I held the jar up to the room and smiled.

"Tinkle tinkle! We have lift-off."

"So is it good?" Film Boy asked.

"It's okay," I said. "We'll know exactly how good when I dry it and weigh it."

The rock was completely solid now. I tipped out the water and dropped the rock into the palm of my hand. I sat down at the table and placed it on a paper towel, bouncing it around to dry it.

When I could hold the rock without getting any moisture on my fingers, I knew it was about as dry as it was going to get. I dropped it onto the diamond scales. It weighed .73 grams.

"There you go," I said as I fine-tuned the milligram arm. "Your cocaine is seventy-three percent pure. That's my job done. Apart from beam me up, Scotty."

Film Boy nodded his head like he was trying to ponder his options.

"Seventy-three, eh? That's a pretty heavy step-on."

He was talking through his arse and he was bluffing some slick Greek boys who, while not out-and-out frightening, were tougher than he was. I myself was pretty impressed they'd done this well. I'd seen—and sold—a whole lot worse than seventy-three.

"Listen, seventy-three's okay," I said. "I've never seen a return better than ninety, ninety-one, and that was rocks. You're doing okay. Just don't step on it any more and you've got a good product."

I was a fucking facilitator. I should have been in industrial relations.

"You've got a deal," Film Boy said, and the semi-gangsters grinned, but still in character, and everyone shook hands. Tucker was smiling broadly. No wonder, I thought. Apart from his cash cut from Film Boy, he was probably all set to get a little bag as a prearranged cut from the semi-gangsters. The coke might have been eighty percent pure before that deal was made.

The semi-gangsters counted the money, which took a good while, but was not the kind of thing an outsider could really help with.

I cut the rock into smaller chunks with Film Boy's blade. Candy and Film Boy and Babe had never based before, so we decided the experienced users would go first and they could watch and learn. I was pleased to be showing off an old and dormant skill.

Being MC, I was first diver off the block.

The pipe I'd bought was ostensibly a pipe for smoking buds. I'd filled the upturned end of the pipe—the end you light—with about twenty circular gauze filters, which I'd cut out painstakingly with nail scissors and pushed down until they were wedged tight.

I placed my little piece of rock on the topmost piece of gauze and clicked on the lighter. It was a model that didn't need to be held down with the finger to keep the flame going. You could melt your thumb trying to freebase with a Bic disposable. I adjusted the flame until it shot out a good four inches, yellow at the tip, then blue closer in, and invisible just near the nozzle.

I held the blue part of the flame above the rock, close enough to heat but not touch. The surface of the rock began to turn to oil, which oozed down through the filters. When most of the rock was liquid or semiliquid, I took a deep breath and blew out, emptying my lungs as completely as I could.

At the point where I could exhale no more breath, I turned the flame onto the gauze filters, and at the same time put my mouth over the stem of the pipe and began to inhale. The freebase sizzled and the glass pipe filled with a thick curling smoke, which rapidly disappeared down the pipe and down my throat. The extraordinary thing about the sensation of freebasing was that, aside from all the other wacky things it did to your head, the cocaine acted as a local anesthetic on the throat, so you never felt any pain from inhaling so much hot smoke. Unlike, say, pulling hard on a bong full of really harsh pot.

I held the smoke in. For as long as possible. That roar of the blood vessels began, that luxurious and over-the-top pounding of the heart that I hadn't felt in a couple of years. My head was going boom boom boom. This was buffaloes and death compared to snorting's aggravating fleas. A goddamn stampede, an intrabody, extrabody, out-of-body experience.

"Fffffffhew!"

I blew the smoke out and sat stock-still, staring at a spot on the table, hoping my head wouldn't explode. About thirty seconds later I felt I could begin to talk. "Jesus," was what I said. Strange, the expressions we use.

It *was* a good rush, freebasing, just as blasting coke was okay too. But that's all it was, all rush and no tail, and you wanted it all the time (I mean *all* the time, every two minutes; I could get by for a good four hours without heroin, eight in an emergency), and it made you feel real juddery and jumpy and, ultimately, just plain nervous. Also, cocaine made dickheads into bigger, louder dickheads.

The pipe did the rounds. Everyone was pretty happy, especially the novices, though Film Boy got his first pipe wrong breathing out when he should have sucked, and blew his melting rock and a few of the gauze filters all over the kitchen. We gave him a second go, of course. A born goose, that one. Someone should have said to him, early in the game, "Film Boy, don't even *think* about dealing."

Candy and I got our thousand bucks and said good-bye to everyone, and it was a good feeling to close the door. We stood in the silence for a moment and hugged, pleased with the ease of the earn. In the middle of hugging I realized that there was this other stuff, that I loved Candy and felt some enormous warmth, for her, for us, for the situation, for the way we were in it together, for better or for worse. Then we rang Lester and organized to meet him. To go get some *real* drugs. To get rid of these jitters from the coke. To come home and get a big one on board.

I DO

We thought a wedding would fix us. We thought we would go through the motions of normality and then normality would arrive for real.

We knew that we were in it forever. When we banged up a warm hit of smack, our love seemed infinite. All that we knew then was the world of bliss, that clean, polar realm of narcosis where the liquid psyche resides. We were, as they say, as one. We'd found the secret glue that held all things together.

"I love you so fucking much, Candy." There was no eloquence necessary beyond that delivered by heroin.

"You're my beautiful boy," she'd croak back, sometimes running her fingers through my hair.

We'd be lying on the couch in the warehouse, drifting in and out of conversation. In this state, the idea of marriage was a given, an absolute—the culmination of the momentum of deep love and loyalty.

But waking up sick, or waiting for dope, it was hard to feel anything other than awkward. Talk was kept at a frigid minimum. Eye contact was avoided. We chewed our nails and waited for phones to ring, for Lester or Kojak or someone with money. We couldn't touch each other. We couldn't help each other. It was like love went on hold.

Then when we hit up the dope at last, we'd fall into each other's arms, and it was as if the terrible tension had never existed. In this way we were like dogs, who in the bliss of being patted forget completely the stress of being recently hit.

In between these two extremes were the medium times, which was most of the time, the day-to-day stuff, neither sickness nor bliss. Heroin was the oxygen that fueled our bodies through the days. Sometimes the idea of marriage carried over, like a kind of leakage, from the bliss times to the medium times.

We were at Candy's parents for dinner. It's fair to assume we were putting on the bullshit fronts about how good our lives were; it's what we did in such situations. I was always working on some big plan or project. It was pleasant, like a dream, going to Candy's parents' place and eating nice food and drinking real wine, expensive wine.

Candy's father, a gentle man in favor of a quiet life, would often bring the conversation around to the grandchildren he was so looking forward to.

"When's that half forward coming?" he said. "We'll have him playing for the Saints."

Candy and I would look at each other, and what with the red wine and the meal and a little bit of heroin and the real love between us, it was easy to smile and feel real emotions.

"I think soon would be good," Candy said.

"Me too," I said. "I really want a baby."

The four of us seated around the table were engulfed in a mixture of hope and belief—that the arrival of a baby would, must, clean up the mess we were in. The mess was generally unacknowledged and unspoken at gatherings like this, but if you concentrated, you could sense it in the air, like a faint smell.

"I must say one thing, though," Candy's father said. "I know it must seem old-fashioned for you younger generation, but I'd like to think that no grandson of mine will be born a bastard."

I had no intention of ever not being with Candy. Deep in my heart it was inconceivable that we would ever separate. The mess our lives were in: that was the thing that would end.

"We've talked about getting married," I said. "We think it's a great idea. It's just a matter of when, really." It was rare to be able to speak from the heart with Candy's parents.

"Exactly. It's just a matter of when," Candy's mother said.

"Well, we'll start planning it," Candy said, and later in the week we really did begin the process of filling out the necessary forms and applications.

It wasn't hard to plan. In the end we opted for low-key simplicity: a registry office wedding, a couple of witnesses, a couple of relatives. Anything larger seemed too daunting, and besides, we knew that money spent on any kind of lavish displays would be money not available to us in times of desperation.

"What about inviting your father?" Candy asked. "It might be a good chance to try to get in touch with him."

"Candy, you know the story: any event in my life is a negative event in my father's eyes. I don't think he'd see a wedding as being any different."

"Things change, you know."

"I don't think so. But maybe you're right. Maybe Lex has got a number where I can reach him."

"And what about Lex? Let's invite him. It'd be great to see him again."

"Yeah, well, I'll definitely do that. That's a good idea," I said.

I did invite Lex, who couldn't make it, and he did have a number where I could find my father, but in the rush of things, I never got around to making the call. It had been so long. It was too hard.

Candy's father had a younger sister, Catherine, who lived in Sydney with her eleven-year-old daughter, Candy's cousin Sarah. I'd met them once or twice back when things were beginning with Candy and me. We'd had leisurely dinners in the late summer dusk in Aunt Catherine's leafy Stanmore backyard. Sarah idolized Candy, and possibly me too. Candy and I might have been, to Sarah, visitors from another world, where style and grace and freedom were the norm, where every drag of a cigarette glowed with a renegade beauty. We invited Catherine and Sarah and they were thrilled to accept.

We were married one winter Saturday. Obviously it was a big dope weekend. You want to be relaxed at your own wedding. But we were caught short of money, so Candy arranged a brothel shift for Friday night. Aunt Catherine and Sarah arrived at six that evening. They met us outside the warehouse and took us to dinner.

"Are you excited?" Sarah asked.

"Of course!" Candy said. "It's my big day."

"*Our* big day," I corrected, and everyone laughed.

It was awkward making excuses—"I still have to go to my cleaning job, worse luck," Candy said—and cutting the dinner a little short. I liked Catherine and Sarah a lot. Catherine probably knew what was going on but chose to operate with a discreet and nonjudgmental compassion. Sarah's innocence and enthusiasm were charming, and under the circumstances, painful to watch. We walked them to their hotel and told them we'd pick them up in a taxi in the morning. Then Candy caught a cab to work and I wandered home and watched the Friday night movie, *Alien*.

Candy came home in the early hours with enough dope for a big morning hit and plenty of money for later. We set the alarm and grabbed a few hours' sleep, allowing ourselves an hour to get ready. I felt a bit fuzzy but it wasn't too hard to get out of bed on such a momentous day. I sat in my underpants, hunched over the coffee table as I squirted the water into the spoon. Some kind of speech welled up in me, a rare event but a sincere one.

"I don't know about you, Candy," I said, "but I'm doing this today, above all else, because I love you. Today really *is* special." I pulled out the plunger from the barrel—it made a tiny, lovely *pop*—and languidly stirred the water to dissolve the heroin. "Today we're making it formal. I want to be with you forever. I don't want to use dope forever."

Candy was naked, exquisitely beautiful. She walked across the room and straddled my lap, facing me. She stroked my temples and cheeks and kissed me once, a dry sweet kiss, on the forehead. "Forever and ever," she said. "We'll be together forever."

She wrapped her arms around my neck and squeezed me to her chest. I sat there with my ear pressed against her skin, at the boundary between the world outside and the inside world of Candy. After a moment I pulled back. I grazed my fingers back and forth across her left breast, until her perfect pink nipple began to rise. My hand was swaying like seaweed in a rock pool washed by a gentle change of tide. Then I leaned forward and cupped her breast in my hand and wet the nipple with my lips. It was a fairy-tale kiss.

"Come on," I said, "let's have this dope. We don't want to be late."

We whacked up and then made some coffee and Candy had a shower while I lathered and shaved. I was well stoned, so the long slow rasp of the blade on my skin was at that moment the noise of all pleasure condensed.

I showered and dried and gelled my hair back and dressed in the tuxedo I'd rented. I felt wonderful.

"The ring," Candy said, "have you got the ring?"

I felt for it in my pocket. "No worries," I said, "the ring is safe."

It was a plain rose gold band we'd bought for eighty dollars in a hockshop during the week and which, a few days after the wedding, regretfully, we would end up hocking for twenty dollars.

Candy had found a magnificent Spanish lace dress in a secondhand clothes shop. It was old and some of the white had yellowed, so she'd dyed it black. By chance, in another shop, she'd found a pair of elbow-length black lace gloves. Her long blond hair hung wildly, and bright red lipstick defined her pale face. She stood in the middle of the room and twirled around.

"How do I look?"

She took my breath away, a kind of Gothic flamenco baby doll.

"Amazingly beautiful," I marveled. "I wish we owned a camera."

She smiled. "Tonight, you will be my husband."

I nodded my head a few times, savoring the wonderful thought. "And I guess that means you'll be my wife."

When we pulled up in the taxi to collect Aunt Catherine and Sarah from their hotel, Sarah's eyes nearly popped out of her head.

"Your dress is black!" she said, climbing into the back seat beside Candy, and Candy smiled and said, "I know." Sarah grinned in astonished delight.

"It's different," Aunt Catherine said, deadpan. "But you do look beautiful."

The registry office was in the Old Mint building, a musty colonial relic with an air of decaying grandeur, incongruously nestled amid the skyscrapers of the business district. Anne and Len were our witnesses, or bridesmaid and best man, if you could call them that in such a reduced ceremony. They were waiting out front with Candy's parents when our taxi pulled up.

I saw Candy's mother's jaw drop as her daughter emerged from the taxi in her black Spanish dress. Her face seemed to ripple for an instant as the battle between the need to be angry and the need for composure took place.

"It had to be something, didn't it?" she muttered to Candy as we all gathered around and made pleasantries.

Candy's father kissed her and said, "You look like a princess, darling."

"The wicked princess, yes," Candy's mother said, but she smiled and shook her head, as if accepting defeat, and we all went inside in a fairly good mood.

It was all very nonbaroque, the civil ceremony. There was a little spiel from the celebrant guy, the "in sickness and in health" stuff, and then the "Do you take this woman, do you take this man?"

"I do," I said.

"I do," Candy said.

I slipped the ring on her finger. I made a little prayer to the powers that be: Make this real. Make it a moment of change. Then we kissed and there were flashbulbs flashing. We signed our names a couple of times and Anne and Len did some signing too. We went outside into the overcast day and everyone took a few more photos and we smiled lamely and Candy's mother said, "Well, back to our place for some drinks and a bite to eat." It all seemed a strange letdown. I really just wanted to be alone with Candy.

But we went back for the tiny gathering. It was a little stifling, with classical music turned way down low in the background and the eight of us milling around sipping champagne or lemonade and nibbling at cheese on crackers. After a while I found that trying to make small talk was becoming difficult. I was the safekeeper of the dope and I had our syringes and a spoon down my socks. I figured it was time for a visit to the toilet.

I was trying to find a vein and had been in there for a few minutes when Candy came to the door.

"What are you doing in there?"

It wasn't that I was trying to hide it, it's just that I wanted to be alone for a minute. It wasn't as if we *both* could have disappeared into the bathroom. But I could hear from her tone of voice that she didn't like the idea of me being in there alone, making biased decisions about how to divide up the dope.

"I'm doing a shit."

"You fucking liar," she hissed, trying to keep her voice down. "Open the door!"

"Candy, go away." It was hard trying to talk with my belt looped around my arm and held between my teeth.

"Open the fucking door!"

I could see the handle jiggling, the strain she was putting on the lock.

"I'll be out in a minute," I said, trying to sound pleasant.

Bingo! I got the spurt of blood into the syringe and pushed the plunger in. Candy was whispering, "If you don't get out right now," but it really didn't matter. I cleaned the syringe and flushed the toilet for effect, out of habit.

"There you go," I said, opening the door and smiling widely. I handed her the packet of dope and the spoon and a syringe. "There you go, wife. Have a nice blast."

"You prick, husband." She laughed and took the stuff off me and went into the bathroom and closed the door.

I went back out to the lounge room to be social. The next thing I knew, I was sitting on the couch, hopefully only a couple of minutes later, and Candy was shaking me awake.

"You must have fallen asleep," she was saying, trying to gloss it over. "A little too much champagne, I think."

"I'm so sorry," I exclaimed, jumping up, straightening my suit. "It's all the lead-up to the wedding. I haven't had much sleep."

The others halfheartedly entered the convenient fiction, mumbling, "Of course," and, "Yes, I'm sure it must be nerve-racking," but it was really time for us to make our excuses and good-byes before things got any worse.

"Thank you for everything," we said to everyone.

We weren't going on a honeymoon, and a wedding is a seminal event, so we figured we'd go get lots more dope, lash out more than usual. We'd talked Candy's parents into giving us cash for a present—"We're right for everything else," we'd said—and Aunt Catherine had slipped us an envelope at the last minute too. There was also Candy's money from the night before. We made the taxi driver stop while I got out and phoned Lester from a booth. Lester said come over, and we directed the taxi across the Westgate Bridge.

"You were fully nodded off back there, you idiot," Candy said.

I cringed at the thought of it. "Shit. That's a bad look. I remember sitting down and talking to Aunt Catherine. I must have just closed my eyes for a moment. Do you think they would have noticed?"

"Oh, of course not. They were only all standing there gawking at you like they'd just seen a snow leopard. Of course they didn't notice, darling."

I bit my bottom lip and shook my head slowly and looked out the window, almost groaning in embarrassment. Then I caught Candy's eye and we both burst out laughing.

We made the taxi wait across the street from Lester's place. Lester thought it was hilarious, us turning up in our wedding gear like that, and he gave us an extra hundred on top of what we bought.

"I like to see old-fashioned commitment," he said. "Good on you both."

We were hungry now. The taxi took us back across the bridge and we got off at a McDonald's in the center of town, not too far from the warehouse. We attracted a few curious stares, and I guess maybe it *was* a bit strange being dressed like that at McDonald's. We didn't give a fuck.

I had a Quarter Pounder with cheese, a chocolate shake, medium fries, and an apple pie. I liked taking the lid off the shake and dipping the fries in. You got the salt and sugar tastes at the same time. Candy had a cheeseburger, a strawberry shake, and a large fries.

We sat in the smoking section. Normally we bought Horizons since they were the cheapest, but today was our wedding and we'd splurged on Stuyvesants, the international passport.

We were the coolest people in McDonald's.

We had a lot going for us. We'd found the secret glue that held all things together. We were young and beautiful. We were married now. We were about to go home, get out of our monkey suits, get naked, and get wasted.

WALLET

"Eh, Nick, how you going?"

"Hello, my son," Fat Nick replied from behind the counter. "What you like today?"

"Chocolate milk shake, thanks, Nick. Extra chocolate." This was not a code. I had a sweet tooth, and for a long time sugar was the mainstay of my diet. Just being in the café was the code.

Nick busied himself making the milk shake. Candy waited in the car outside. I sat on the stool in front of the cash register, tapping my fingers on the Formica. Nick's short-order cook, Little Nick, threw hamburger patties onto the grill. It was a beautiful Melbourne Sunday, and I almost felt that I didn't really hate all the straight families who'd come down to St. Kilda for a gelato and a stroll.

Nick took the ice cream scoop from its milky rinse water and lowered his arm into the freezer. He looked at me and raised his eyebrows in a question.

"A one-spot," I murmured.

He nodded, no worries, and the day became even more beautiful than a moment before. There were other people, of course, *better* people, really, but this was quick, convenient, and reliable. Candy had gotten home from a night shift at about four A.M. and we'd shared the last of the dope and gone to sleep. Now it was midday. We had oodles of money, so we could ring Kojak on the pager later. We weren't really sick, but it was always nice to get the day started as soon as possible after waking up. So Nick's café was it.

Fat Nick hitched the milk shake onto the stainless steel blender and left it frothing as he leaned down to the fridge door. He rummaged around and popped back up, pulling the milk shake off and placing it on the counter. He took a straw and speared it into the shake.

"Anything else?" he asked, ever the normal milk bar proprietor.

"That's it, thanks."

"Two dollars twenty," he said.

I opened my palm to show him a folded hundred-dollar note. As he took it he dropped the small packet into my hand. It was wrapped in foil first, then tightly bound in Glad wrap. I put it in my mouth, lodging it up the back between my cheek and my lower teeth.

The hundred went into his pocket. He pressed some buttons on the register and pulled out a random selection of small coins and gave them to me. He always liked to make a show of giving you your change. I liked the way I never actually paid for the milk shake.

Among those of us lucky enough to be okayed by Fat Nick for heroin purchasing, the urban myth went around about how the dope was actually kept in the hamburger meat, and how once an unsuspecting (real) customer had bitten into a nest of foilies in the middle of his cheeseburger.

"What's this?" he'd exploded, spitting a mouthful of meat and bun onto his plate and holding the burger open for Fat Nick to inspect.

Fat Nick hadn't missed a beat, merely stepped around the counter, swooped up the plate, and ordered Little Nick to make another burger. "With the works, hurry up!" Pulling fifty dollars from his pocket, he'd thrust it upon the hapless customer.

"For the inconvenience," he said, as if it were a hair or a fly and not seven hundred dollars worth of heroin.

Personally, though, I thought the story was merely the product of the wishful thinking of our small but motley circle of privileged buyers. It was certainly a hamburger I'd like to buy.

"See you soon, Nick."

I took my chocolate milk shake and walked out into the bright sunshine.

"Okay?" Candy asked as I slipped into the car.

"No problems." I smiled, balancing the milk shake and pulling the seat belt over my shoulder. "Do you want to go home, or find somewhere near here to do it?"

It would have meant the difference between fifteen minutes and five minutes. Normally I liked to get home and safe, but it was a beautiful day and it felt kind of friendly.

"Let's find a park," Candy said.

We drove along Albert Park Lake and pulled into a small parking lot next to a public toilet. Only one car was parked there. I gave Candy the remainder of the milk shake and went into the toilet to get water for the syringes. As I walked into the cement gloom, I heard a shuffling sound coming from one of the cubicles.

Then it clicked. The car outside. The noise from the cubicle. This was a gay beat. I'd interrupted something. I could hear the strange silence of someone trying not to breathe.

Don't worry, guys, I thought. I'm out of here.

I turned on the tap in the basin, cupped the palm of my hand, and trapped a small pool of water. I sucked up a syringe full. Better from the palm of my hand than barbing the pick on the bottom of the basin. I mixed up the heroin with the 1 mil of water in the spoon. It expanded to about 1.5 mils, which I split into two syringes, each three-quarters full.

I left the toilet block, and as I passed the other car I noticed that the passenger-side window was open. A brown leather wallet was on the seat. What a stupid place to leave it. I looked around quickly. The thing was, contemplation was never good in these circumstances. I leaned into the car and took the wallet.

Candy was busy doing her lipstick in the rearview mirror and didn't notice any of this. I hopped into the car.

"We've got to go," I said. "I nicked a wallet."

The beauty of our partnership was that we knew never to be surprised. Candy heard the urgency in my voice. She merely dropped her lipstick, started the car, and drove off quickly but calmly. This was what true love was. Implicit understanding.

I looked back but nobody emerged from the toilet block. Cool. I opened the wallet. Five dollars.

"Five dollars. Five fucking dollars!"

I was a little pissed off. Something so easy happens, and then it doesn't seem worth it after all.

Then I unzipped the other compartment of the wallet. I smiled and turned to Candy.

"Cards, baby. Cards!"

The trick with credit cards was acting fast—not for shopping, I mean for the big cash hits. Shopping was hard work—a little nerve-racking, a little boring. But to walk into a bank and try withdrawing cash, you wanted to know that card had not been reported stolen yet.

I chewed my lip and studied the cards. Roger P. Moylen. The signature was tough. Smart Roger. It would take several hours to get this one. Most signatures were a breeze, so basic that even the most rudimentary resemblance passed people's inspection. But some were so full of the most precise curlicues and flourishes that it stood out like a dog's balls if you *didn't* get it exactly right. It took a lot of practice to make that happen under a teller's watchful eye. We discussed the signature.

"It's no good anyway," I said to Candy. "As soon as he's had his dick sucked he'll know his wallet is gone. He'll ring and cancel his cards tonight, for sure. I don't want to risk the banks. Maybe we can just keep them for a little low-level shopping."

Unless, I thought. Unless. My mind got to thinking as we found another park and had our blast. Roger Moylen. A National Bank MasterCard. A Westpac Savings Account Keycard. A State Credit Union Savings Card. A Grosvenor Insurance Company Flexicard. I'd never heard of the Grosvenor Insurance Company but the card looked pretty snazzy.

Four cards. How much money? I rifled through the rest of the wallet. No driver's license. The only other item of interest was a borrower's card from the Video Shack in Collingwood. Good. A clue. Now if only he was in the phone book, I was in with a slim chance.

We got back to the warehouse and went through the phone directory. He was there. It was not a common name. There were four Moylens in Melbourne and only one R. P. Moylen and he lived in Collingwood.

Time to scam. I figured he'd finish his business in the toilet and find the wallet missing and be pissed off and go home to Collingwood to take stock. I waited an hour and called. A young male voice answered.

"Hello."

"Hi. Is that Roger?"

"Yes."

"Roger Moylen?"

"Yes. Who's this?"

"Um. Look. This is hard." I was trying my best to sound guilty and a little pathetic. "I'm the guy who stole your wallet."

"Fuck. *Fuck!*" He was really pissed off. "And you have the audacity to call me!"

"Hey, listen!" I jumped in. "I'm calling you because I feel terrible. I'm sorry I did it. I'm really sorry. I was just after some money, that's all. I want to give your wallet back. I feel awful. I feel stupid. I don't normally do this kind of thing."

He was softening. I could feel it on the phone line.

"Well, why did you do it?" He was trying to sound mean. But he was intrigued.

"I told you. All I wanted was some money. It was stupid."

"It sure was stupid," he agreed. Roger was reveling in his chance to act tough, to expel a little anger. Fair enough too. I would let him kick me while I was down.

"I'm lonely," I said. "I was hanging down at that park because . . . because I'm lonely, you know what I mean?" Roger was hanging down at the park too, so I *knew* he'd know what I meant. "I'm really confused at the moment. I've got no money. I've come from Adelaide. I've got no friends, and . . . and I saw the wallet on the seat. I just took it. I—I wasn't thinking. Now I feel bad about it. I'm not interested in your credit cards, and I want to give it back to you."

"Phew," he said. Young Roger was really chewing over this one. "How did you get my number?"

"Phone book."

"Where do you live?"

"Footscray," I lied.

"All right, when will you give it back?"

"Now wait a minute." It was important to be plausible. And to use a bit of reverse psychology. "How do I know you won't call the police? I'm giving your wallet back here, I'm doing the right thing. I don't want to turn up to meet you and get arrested."

"Listen," he replied. "What's your name?"

"Mark," I lied.

"Mark," he said. "You have my word. I just want my wallet back and we'll forget about the whole thing."

The real guilt I felt was not that I had his wallet but that doing this was so easy.

"Well, it's too late now," I said. "I can't get over to

Collingwood until tonight, and I want it to be daylight. In the open. So that I can see you're alone. You've got to understand. I'm nervous about this."

"Mark," he sighed, "I won't do the dirty on you."

"Okay, then. Okay. I'll meet you early in the morning. Let's say around nine." I described a park near Collingwood Town Hall. He knew the one.

"Right, then. Nine o'clock. How do I know you're going to be there?"

I put on my best indignant voice. "Roger, do you think I'd go to all this trouble of calling you if I wasn't going to meet you? I told you, I feel guilty. I'm not actually a thief. That's why I'm doing this. Otherwise I could just throw your wallet in the garbage."

Or empty all your accounts before nine, I thought.

But Roger's mind seemed to be put at ease by that, and anyway, he sounded not a little curious to be meeting someone under such unusual circumstances.

I got off the phone. Candy had been listening to the arrangements.

"Well," she said, "what do you think?"

"I dunno. I'm not sure." This one really needed pondering. I was searching back through the conversation, feeling for the nuances in Roger's voice. Had he bought it? My gut said yes.

"I think I can do it," I said.

I spent the evening working on the signature. By midnight it was looking pretty good. The important thing was getting the speed up. I couldn't afford to labor too carefully over Roger's fucking baroque trimmings. Confidence and speed. That was going to matter in the banks.

Most banks opened at nine-thirty, but a handful of the central branches—all of which were within a few blocks of our warehouse—conveniently opened at eight-thirty.

Roger didn't sound like the kind of guy who had ever needed to be aware of this kind of information. Not the kind of guy who works in the city. That was my gamble. If I didn't turn up at that park by about twenty past nine, then he'd call the banks and cancel his cards. If all went well, by twenty past nine he'd be welcome to cancel them.

I woke up a little nervous. I shaved and got dressed in my scamming clothes: a tatty but neat suit and a conservative tie with some kind of crest motif. Definitely way out of fashion. Dark colors, everything muted and somber. Browns and navy blues. Nonmatching coat and pants. Nothing flashy about this commuter. I parted my hair at the side, the way I hated. I combed it back and stood there looking like just the right kind of Mervin. Candy straightened my tie like the loving wife. My mouth was dry.

We'd scored during the night and used the last of our dope at about three A.M., so I'd had about four hours sleep, but the dope wasn't exactly out of my system. Enough so that I felt okay—only just—but my pupils weren't too small. You didn't want pinprick pupils when you were scamming. It tended to unnerve people. On the other hand, you didn't want to be hanging out, with those big black saucer pupils like neon signs announcing, FEAR AND SWEAT! SCAM IN PROGRESS.

You had to find the balance. Just the right balance. A little bit of heroin and a little bit of adrenaline. And the carrot-on-the-stick of the rewards to come.

It was twenty-five past eight. I wanted to be at the first bank when the doors swung open. When the tellers were still half asleep. When no one was expecting a scam.

I pecked Candy on the cheek. "Should be back by nine, baby. Nine-thirty at the latest."

I walked out into the bustling morning throng, swinging my empty briefcase, heading toward Swanston Street. I arrived at the doors of the National Bank at 8:29. I was third in line, which felt better than being first. A security guard came and unlocked the doors.

My eyes scanned the tellers and I chose the youngest girl I

could find. She was making eye contact, waiting for her first customer of the day. I was locked into the mode now. There was no turning back. I smiled and strode up to the counter.

"Hi, there!"

I was beaming.

"Good morning," she said, like a chirpy sparrow. "How are you?"

"Fine, thanks." I handed her the MasterCard. "I just want to know what my current balance is on this."

"Okay. Just one moment. I'll have to call the branch to find out your credit limit. Let me see." She ran her fingers along a list of branch numbers. "That's the Collingwood branch. I won't be a minute. Let's hope someone's there. They don't open for an hour, you know?"

Well, this is where I find out if my gut instinct is right, I thought. I tried to make my body look relaxed. My eyes drilled into her as she talked into the phone. Some keen teller was working early. I was looking for a sign that something was wrong. Looking for that confused expression a person's face takes on when told, "Try and keep him there while I phone the police."

But she wrote something on a piece of paper and put down the phone and walked back over to me and smiled.

"Your credit limit's two thousand dollars," she said, "and your debit balance is currently $1,096.55."

"Right." I nodded. I wanted it to look like this was approximately what I was expecting. "So that means I can withdraw . . ."

She took the cue. "You can withdraw . . . nine hundred, let me see, about nine hundred and four dollars."

I rubbed my chin. "Better make it eight hundred and eighty," I said decisively.

She didn't even blink, and I knew at that moment that Roger had believed me and was expecting to meet me. Probably eating his Rice Bubbles right now with nervous anticipation. She pulled out a form and filled in the details.

"Just sign here." She pushed the form toward me.

I bent over the paper and went into a four-second trance. The signature looked fine. She barely even glanced at it.

"How would you like that, sir?"

"Hundreds will be fine, thanks. And four twenties."

She counted the cash and gave it to me. My stomach eased. I wished her a nice day and smiled and left the building. It was 8:37. I walked around the corner to the Westpac branch for transaction number two.

With the Westpac Keycard it was easier. I went over to the withdrawal slips and pulled out a few. I was happy with the second signature I did. I filled out the other details such as date and account number but I left the withdrawal amount blank.

I was in the swing now.

"Could you tell me my balance, please?"

It was four hundred thirty dollars. I started writing in the blank space.

"I'll make it four hundred. Better leave a little in there, eh?" I chuckled. I was trying to be charming. This teller was a little stony-faced and she didn't chuckle back. But she didn't call the police either.

"How would you like the four hundred?" she asked. It was music to my ears.

I had $1,280 now and it was two down and two to go. The State Credit Union, next institution on the list, was one of those smaller operations, just two or three staff members working there. I preferred the anonymity of the bigger banks to the intimacy of this setup, but there you go. I had a job to do. I walked in and I was the only customer, so all three staff members looked at me and smiled.

"And how are we all this morning?" I asked, as if I was a regular customer. I filled out a withdrawal form again and left the amount blank.

"Could you tell me the balance, please?"

She ran the card through the machine.

"Three sixty-five," she said.

Again I started writing. "I'll take out three hundred and forty," I said.

"No," the teller said. "I mean, three dollars and sixty-five cents."

My heart skipped a beat. My head said, "You are busted." I could feel my whole face flush red and then scarlet. But I tried to continue.

"Ah. Three dollars. And sixty-five cents. No worries. Well, I'll just take three dollars in that case."

She did the rigmarole and gave me three coins. I think she felt more embarrassed than me, because she thought *I* was turning red at being so poor and pathetic. I was glad to get out of there.

There was only one office listed in the phone book for the Grosvenor Insurance Company, over on King Street. I walked through the revolving door of a stainless steel and glass office tower. A display case in the lobby listed Grosvenor Insurance on the second floor. That was good. Not too far down the fire exit if things got hairy. I took the elevator, all mirrors and soft lights. I looked really pasty.

This place was not like a bank, more like the foyer of any old company. I didn't really like the idea of doing an unusual transaction in a place like this, but I was in the middle of trying to be a man, to redeem myself, to be a breadwinner, and what I liked or didn't like was hardly the issue.

"Can I help you?" A smartly dressed receptionist looked me up and down like I was a tramp who'd somehow become separated from my park bench.

"Yes, please. I hope so. I've found a car that I want to buy—lovely old Alfa, you know—but I don't have all the money, so I'm wondering if you can tell me what my policy's worth."

She took my Flexicard and studied it like it was a used condom. "Just one moment, sir."

She walked through a door and into the abyss, where

Interpol were no doubt giving her instructions. In a minute she returned. I was looking out the window, down at the street. I wanted to get a good view if a police car arrived.

"Mr. Moylen?"

I swung around and smiled sweetly at her. I got the feeling she would do this quickly to get me out of there.

"The current value of your policy is standing at $949.11."

"Can I withdraw from it?"

I was trying to feign stupidity. I wanted to appear like the dandruffy type. To send her the vibe of an innocent nerd.

"No, sir, you can't withdraw from an insurance policy."

"Hmmm. But I need that money. It's such a lovely car. A *lovely* car." I breathed deeply and sighed. "Ah well, then. I suppose I'll just have to cancel the policy then. Will that take long?"

"Not too long. I'll just get the necessary paperwork."

I stood there slightly incredulous that this too could be so easy.

She came back with some forms and a file marked MOYLEN.

"Do you still live at Dempsey Street in Collingwood, Mr. Moylen?"

"I certainly do," I replied. It seemed like the right answer.

She filled in some forms and I signed Roger's name a couple of times. After a while she gathered everything into a bundle and began to walk back into the abyss.

"Now, it will just take a few moments to process that check, Mr. Moylen."

"Check! Did you say check?" I stifled a gasp. She nodded. "But this . . . this bloke with the Alfa . . . er, I really need the cash. Is there any chance of cash?"

She was definitely shitty with me. "I'm sorry, Mr. Moylen. We don't handle cash transactions here."

"Are you positive? No chance at all, then?" I was really pushing things here, but the junkie in me was thinking, So close and yet so far. It seemed such a waste to get a useless check.

I waited for it anyway, all the time keeping an eye on the road below. I thought it might be a bit of a lost cause, but I had one more plan. Across the road from Grosvenor Insurance was another Westpac branch. I got the check and walked over, filled out deposit and withdrawal slips for $949, and marched confidently to the counter.

I explained to the teller that I'd just received this check from the Grosvenor Insurance Company, and that I needed the cash right away. I said that I assumed that since it was a corporate check, from the company across the road, made out to my name, and since I had several forms of ID—here I pulled Roger's cards from his wallet—it would be no problem to put it through my account and cash it immediately.

The teller said he'd have to check with the manager. The manager carefully studied my deposit and withdrawal slips, and the Grosvenor check, and the Westpac Keycard. He looked over at me briefly and then, to my great surprise, nodded his head.

I felt like cheering but it stayed inside. It was a time for decorum as I collected my $949 in cash. I said thank you to the teller and left the bank at a moderate pace, but with a spring in my step. It was nine-fifteen and I had $2,232 in my wallet, which was once Roger's wallet.

I was feeling fucking great.

At 9:25 I opened the door to the warehouse. Candy was naked on the couch, hunched over, painting her toenails. She looked up with a hopeful smile as I came in.

"So how'd it go?"

I tried to play a little joke. I pulled a sad face and shook my head and said, "It fucked up."

But a smile broke out on me before I'd even finished saying the words. I reached into my pocket and pulled out the wallet and showered the money all over her. "Only joking," I said. We both started laughing hysterically. Candy jumped up and down and hugged me.

"Baby, baby, baby!" she squealed.

She had her arms around my neck. I was rubbing my hands over her back and buttocks, looking down at the hundreds and fifties and twenties scattered around our feet.

"Let's make a phone call," I said.

"Kojak or Lester?" she asked.

Later in the day we were pretty fucking comfortable. Pretty happy. Fucking stoned. We were on the couch in the warehouse. I was having trouble opening my eyes. My mind was doing that thing, you know the thing, kind of like zooming over landscapes. Gliding through the ether. Never happened much anymore.

In the middle of my immense and exquisite warmth I pictured Roger, sitting nervously on a bench in a park in Collingwood. I knew he would not still be there, but in my mind it was the only way I could picture him.

Lightly built with sharp features and short dark hair. Blue eyes. A few pimples. Wearing a denim jacket. A neatly dressed guy, with white runners, Reeboks maybe. His eyes scan the horizon. And he looks at his watch a lot. Then he starts looking behind him, left and right, trying to work out where the fuck I might appear from. Hoping I'm running late. Forcing himself to believe in his heart that I'm just running late.

So much of my own life seemed to be spent waiting on park benches, knotted with stomach cramps and trying to look casual, willing the dealer to arrive. Roger was no more than a ghost to me. But it was during my own long waits in parks—they say that if you've been a junkie for ten years, you will have spent seven of them *waiting*—that I began to realize that I myself was becoming transparent. That I myself may well have been a ghost, and that I was haunting my own body, just as the image of Roger would occasionally haunt my mind.

CRABS

Let me tell you about the crabs.

Things were fucked up, as always. But not too bad. Candy had a good job in a brothel in East Melbourne—day shift, the boss liked her, she'd been there two months, hadn't caused any trouble, was earning heaps—so I didn't have a great deal to do with my time, except wait for Candy and the money to come home. After that it was my job to get the dope, or do any other drug-related things—credit card stuff, check fraud, whatever came up.

In a way, Candy was like the steady income, the bottom line, and I was on special teams. The bottom line averaged about four hundred a day, but sometimes we had tight two-hundred-dollar days or good thousand-dollar days. Either way, it all went up our arms. Four hundred was subsistence, a thousand was a bonus day. This is above average for shit-kicker junkies, but like I've said, Candy had the looks.

Sometimes, for whatever reasons, we ran out of money and gear. Candy would go to work not feeling so good and I would sit at home watching *Here's Humphrey* or *The Young and the Restless* and not feeling so good either. Then she'd ring me after she'd done her first client for the day. She'd dress sensibly—put on an overcoat, at least—and go outside the brothel and up the road to meet me. I'd come by in a cab and get the money. Go get the dope. Have a blast. The world feels fine.

When you've been hanging out and you have a hit and get that relief then at last you can think about things like breakfast. A chocolate milk and a jelly doughnut. Buy a packet of cigarettes and you feel like a king.

But I never fucked around for too long in such circumstances because I knew Candy was back there in the brothel doing the hard slog: getting pins and needles and beginning to sweat and touching hairy men.

So I'd load her a syringe and go back to the brothel, pretending to be a customer. They put you in a waiting room and the girls came in one by one.

They'd say, "Hi, I'm so-and-so."

I'd say, "Hi."

Then they'd leave the room. It was pretty appalling.

At the end of it, you go back to reception and say, "I'll have her, thanks." But when Candy came in I'd give her the syringe and say, "How's things?" and "I'll see you tonight." She'd leave the room and then I'd go out to the foyer and say, "Thanks, but I've changed my mind."

Mostly we didn't have to worry about this kind of shit, because, as I said, it was a pretty comfortable time. The main thing I remember from this few months is that I read everything by Graham Greene, Len Deighton, and Robert Ludlum. Deighton and Ludlum—heroin helps you concentrate on stuff like that, helps you settle into the plot convolutions. Greene is good at any time.

Anyway, the crabs. One of the hazards of the job. You got crabs, you went to the pharmacy, you bought the crab lice lotion, you got rid of them.

Not us.

Maybe our lives were a little limited. But to be invaded by such predators was a fascinating thing. These were primeval creatures that lived on blood, as we did. Creatures that pierced the skin and jacked back blood and existed for one purpose only, as we did.

What's more, as a heroin addict I was always happy picking and squeezing and prodding. Monkeys have less going on in the way of higher brain function and more in the way of brain-stem activity than humans. Less neocortex and more cerebellum. At the zoo you can see how happy they are picking nits from each other's hair. This is the primal business. Which heroin reinvents, as it so sensually overwhelms the brain stem.

That's why on heroin you can spend four hours squeezing blackheads that aren't even there. That you wish were there. Not even the monkeys know such sophisticated pleasures.

So you can see how the arrival of the crabs would be an exciting event, like a festival. We all want festivals to last. Through the night, at least.

When the itching gets so bad that you actually notice it through the sense-numbing wall of the heroin, then you know you have a serious infestation.

The first thing Candy and I did was mix up and have a blast. Then we took scissors and cut our pubic hair down to a basic manageable five or six millimeters, a kind of pubic crew cut. I thought this looked pretty silly on me, with my dick looking goofy and exposed, but of course from Candy's point of view it was all the rage and quite a money spinner in the brothels.

We were a tight team, so none of this was in any way embarrassing. It was microscopic and medical and not much different from watching a good documentary on television.

Down to business. With a pair of very sharp nail scissors we took turns extracting the individual monsters from our skin.

Crab lice have eight legs. Each leg has a sharp prong or barb, as on a surveyor's tripod or a whaler's harpoon, for gaining a firmer hold.

Of course they must also have some kind of puncturing

and sucking device for getting the blood, but I couldn't actually see this. I just saw the huge rust-colored bulge of their bodies and the dainty flailing of their transparent legs when we pulled them from our skin.

It was a long night because we inspected each specimen one at a time. I sifted Candy's spiky pubes under my thumb or index finger. I would see something that looked like a tiny freckle or a faint blemish, gently prod its edge with the point of the scissors, and begin to lift. If you listened really carefully you could hear a faint ripping sound as the legs began to tear loose from the skin.

I'd slide the scissors in between the legs and under the body. Then lift straight upward, with a finger hovering to trap the creature gently on the flat blade.

As the crab came loose from the skin, we would inspect it. There weren't really any criteria of excellence other than size.

"Look at that, that's fuckin' huge!"

We worked a wide area around each other's groins, shining the lamp in close. They were everywhere. I worked downward from the top of Candy's pubic hair and along the lips of her cunt, outward to her upper legs and around to her arse. There were crabs on the rim of her sphincter. I'd never seen a sphincter at such close range, under a hundred-watt bulb. I was surprised at the reflex action it made—a kind of puckering—when I touched its edge carefully with the point of the scissors.

We killed them between two thumbnails, watching the body distort. Then a clear cracking sound, and the body was flat, surrounded by a small field of red.

In a way it was sad to be so thorough, to know that before the night was over we would have them all. So we left the eggs alone. These were tiny white dots laid on the base of a pubic hair. To get rid of them you had to clamp them tightly between two fingernails and pull upward along the hair. But this was nowhere near as exciting as the crab-lifting.

At any rate, our theory regarding the eggs was like good

fisheries management: you don't kill the young, so you've got plenty of adults later on. We imagined we might still be interested in doing this the next day, maybe even the day after.

But after a few hours we got bored of the killing. We began to collect them. This was more fun. Soon we had a herd of them, all fighting over each other on the arid glass stretch that was the inside curve of one of the lenses of my sunglasses.

From the crabs' point of view this must have been a bloodless wasteland, a place of utter desolation. What did the crabs need to live? Blood. What did we have regular access to? Our blood. It was three A.M., time for a little nightcap before bed; time also to feed the crabs, to succor them in their last hours.

We mixed up again and shot up. Normally I liked a 1 mil Terumo syringe (nondetachable head, of course) to be filled to about 70, and after I'd plunged the shot right in I would jack back once or twice to 20 or 30. The idea was, you get all that blood back in there, rinse out the barrel, don't miss the skerrick of heroin that might be left in the tiny steel cylinder of the needle itself.

This time, after I'd injected the heroin, I jacked all the way but didn't push back in, so I pulled from my arm a syringe of thick crimson.

"Hey, Candy, check this out."

I was worried about those crabs. Maybe they'd become addicted to the heroin in our blood, and the blind tumbling and clawing and frenzy that could be witnessed in my sunglasses was actually the insane and absurd pain of withdrawal.

I isolated a crab from the main pack. I started with just a drop of blood, protruding from the needle of my syringe. It hovered like a holy balloon, the single drop bigger than the crab's entire body. It touched the broad back of the crab but maintained its globular shape. Then it burst.

The crab was instantly saturated. You could see its legs

buckle beneath it and imagine it was experiencing something similar to the bliss of overdose.

With the scissors I pushed the other crabs around the outer rim of the lens. I squirted some more blood, and a small lake formed in the middle, where the lens reached its lowest point. Candy watched all this intently and gave suggestions and strategies.

Within twenty minutes we had created a scene of bucolic bliss. All around the edges of the lake of blood were gathered like cows a hundred docile and happy crabs. Traumatized by the ordeal of the scissors, they drank in bliss from the healing depths.

As I said, things were fucked up, but not too bad. There were moments soon after a shot when the whole world seemed at peace.

We joked about breeding a race of monster crab lice, about joining the circuit and entering them in all the shows. But in reality I didn't want to go to bed with the thought of those things climbing over the edge of my sunglasses and going off to explore other parts of the warehouse.

The game was over and the time for death had arrived. We killed them quickly, crack crack crack for half an hour, and went to bed.

In the morning we got up and had a hit and Candy went off to work. I started reading *Our Man in Havana*, which was a pretty interesting book.

BOOKS

Here's the kind of trouble I could get myself into by myself. This is just a three-week period. Something like that. Maybe only two.

Candy hadn't been feeling too good in the stomach. She'd had diarrhea for about a week, which didn't make sense, given the amount of heroin we were using.

One night she came home at five A.M. from a Sultan's Harem shift. I woke briefly and we organized the morning activities. Candy counted out two hundred fifty dollars from her earnings and I set the alarm.

I woke when it went off at nine. I paged Kojak and he called me right back. I caught a cab out to meet him on Dandenong Road, at Caulfield. As usual I sat in a tram shelter and waited for fifteen minutes. At least once you got onto him and made arrangements, Kojak was reliable. He was never more than half an hour late. I got a two hundred off him and caught a cab home. At the café beneath the warehouse I bought two ham and cheese croissants and two take-out coffees.

It was the way Candy liked it, and fair enough too. It was the least I could do, considering I did fuck all. I came in the door at about ten-thirty.

"Coffee's up!"

I was in a good mood. The dope in your pocket, how could you not be?

Candy stirred. She sat up and stretched her arms and climbed down from the bed alcove. A new bright day beginning. I was mixing up already.

"How are you, baby?"

I leaned across to kiss her as she sat down. Suddenly I gasped.

"Shit, Candy!"

Candy was bright yellow. I mean, electric yellow, fluorescent yellow. Her whole face. Her eyes, where they should have been white, were neon yellow. I'd seen the jaundiced tinge of hepatitis on many people, but I'd never seen anything like this before.

"What is it?" she asked. She saw the alarm in my face.

"Oh fuck. You should see yourself. Bright yellow. You've got hepatitis."

She ran to the mirror, inspected herself. "Shit."

It happened just like that. It came on that fast. One day she was marble white, the next, canary yellow. There was no way she could work. After we had a hit we went to the Fairfield Infectious Diseases Hospital. We figured we'd find out what to do to knock the hep on the head as quickly as possible, to get back to our normal lives.

But they took one look at her and put her into a sealed room. Candy was under quarantine. It might as well have been house arrest.

Two weeks at least, they said. She's not going anywhere.

They grabbed me too, took blood, asked if we'd been sharing needles, told me I'd be lucky if I didn't have it myself. When they'd finished, I asked if I could go say goodbye to Candy. They said, "Just don't be long. She needs to start resting." Candy looked gaunt and emaciated in the dimly lit quarantine room.

"This is a nightmare," she said. "How am I going to get dope?"

"I don't know, Candy, I don't know. I'll try and bring you some."

"Please try, baby. Please help me." Her eyes were wide with fear.

"I'll see what I can do," I said. "But make sure you stress that you're a heroin addict. They're a public hospital. I think they're obliged to give you methadone. I'm not sure, but I think so."

"Yeah, I'll do that. But still, try and bring me a taste."

I stroked her yellow hands. By the time I left the hospital in the afternoon, she'd entered a kind of delirium. She would stay that way for two weeks. Luckily, they did give her methadone, which was a blessing, since I was hardly the man on the spot to be bringing in the grams of pure. It seemed to be all I could do to look after myself, and that very badly.

It was such a hostile universe: I got arrested twice in the next few weeks. They were both dumb events, but the first one was particularly dumb. It was just a pair of ten-dollar earrings from Sportsgirl, something to make Candy feel better. But I walked outside the shop and felt the shop detective's hand on my arm. "Can you come with me?" All that crap. I couldn't believe they even bothered with the police. The cops were bored, took me back to the station, did the paperwork, let me go with a date to appear.

Most days I stole books. This was a labor-intensive form of crime, long hours for low rewards. I was always tired and never stoned enough. But in the second week I got hold of a credit card from O'Brien—plastic wasn't his thing—and it's how I got arrested the second time.

I acted quickly when I got the card. I had a good Saturday buying books from various places and selling them to a second-hand dealer in Carlton. Recent-release hardbacks, biographies, "serious" novels—stuff like that was always the best for resale, and that's what I concentrated on.

I lulled myself into a false sense of security, telling myself that card cancellations don't get run through the computer on the weekends. I used all my dope on the Saturday night, thinking Sunday would take care of itself. It did, but not how I expected.

I was in a discount bookstore in the middle of the city, one of those places that seemed to be full of remaindered art books. The cashier ran the card through the machine and something must have come up on the screen. But she was good and didn't even bat an eyelid.

"It's a more than hundred-dollar purchase," she said. "I'll just run out the back and get the manager to approve it."

Where the fuck was my radar? I was only faintly suspicious, but I figured I'd give it three minutes, then bolt. The cops were there in less than two. This is better-than-average response time.

I was leafing through a magazine, trying to look casual. They were two uniforms who must have been near the shop by sheer coincidence. A beefy man, the usual mean-lipped woman. She blocked the door while he sauntered to the cashier, who was just returning from the back room.

She pointed at me. "That's him."

The male jack was overweight and I was thin. The female was in a dress, and I couldn't picture her running fast. I was sure I could get away from these two clowns, up some alleys I knew, the back way to the warehouse. If I couldn't, then my afternoon would collapse around me.

I didn't have much choice. There was no time to stand there and regret my stupidity about waiting too long in the shop. It was time for action. I jumped a John Grisham display bin and landed, accidentally, in a somersault tumble that took me out through the door and past the grasping arms of the policewoman.

I was on my feet and flying. I couldn't believe I'd done it. I ran into the street and into the path of a car. It screeched to a halt and I rolled across the hood and kept running.

I was aware that the city was pretty deserted, I was aware

that the weather was cold. I could hear Beefboy's footsteps close behind me and I could hear Meanlips huffing into her walkie-talkie about male suspect in pursuit and shit like that. Everything else went by in a blur. There was nothing but my feet slamming on the footpath.

Then I became aware of how tired I was becoming, of how hard it was to run fast. It was like the oxygen had been sucked out of the air by a nuclear blast. I was gasping, heaving; I felt I was being strangled. My adrenaline stocks had been depleted in about thirty seconds, and now my legs were about to collapse.

And the motherfucker wasn't losing ground. Let me rephrase that. The motherfucker was gaining ground. I knew this because his puffing was becoming louder, as were his footsteps. I could hear a siren in the distance, then another, and at one point I thought I could feel his breath on my neck.

We'd come about a kilometer. I was braying like a sick donkey now—whee-haw, whee-haw—but the warehouse was close. I needed to beat him around the corner. There was a fire escape I knew. I could disappear up that, leap across a small gap between buildings, and pull myself onto the little rooftop courtyard that adjoined the warehouse. From there I could slip into the warehouse the side way, unseen.

But it all depended on my beating Beefboy around the corner by at least five or six seconds, so he wouldn't see where I went.

It wasn't going to happen. We rounded the corner stride for stride. I ran straight past the fire escape. My last hope was that I could work up a second wind. But I was slowing down, and the next thing I knew, he'd dive-tackled me. It was a high-speed, full-body embrace. His power seemed enormous. We hit the ground hard in a heap. I felt the skin of my knuckles graze off. Only the padding of my overcoat prevented me from serious injury.

It was delicious, in a sad way, to stop running. He pulled

himself up. He was breathing so hard he couldn't speak. I was breathing so hard I couldn't hear anything. He pushed me onto my stomach and pinned me down with his knee in my shoulders. He twisted my arms behind my back and handcuffed me tight. I lay there thinking my lungs were about to explode. Within a minute there were sirens and police cars and lots of other coppers. It was like a little street party. They threw me in the wagon and drove me to the lockup. Same old shit.

Eight hours later. Released from custody with a date to appear and sick as a dog. I didn't even have the tram fare to get home. I was supposed to visit Candy earlier but that was out of the question now.

I walked through the cold. Sunday night, midnight, midwinter. The city was deserted. Stomach cramps were beginning to cut in, and I held my stomach tightly through my overcoat pockets.

A vacant taxi passed, slowed, the driver peering at me. I waved it away. But it stopped. The driver leaned across and wound down the passenger window. Sweet Jesus, it was Schumann! The nicest junkie in the world. The sweetest fucked-up person of all the fucked-up people I knew.

"Schumann! Am I glad to see you!" I climbed into the taxi. "Man, you wouldn't believe what happened to me."

And I told him the story.

Schumann was tall and gaunt, with a fine aquiline nose and lank brown hair swept back over his ears. He'd seemed to attach himself to Candy and me, and the three of us often scored together. Everyone chipping in. Schumann always the gentleman, always waiting to use the spoon last, or the tourniquet, or whatever. In any situation of dual purchase, the story was usually that one person divided the dope while the other chose. It kept the divider honest. But Schumann would always shrug and say, "Just give me what you think. Whatever's fair."

I would have trusted Schumann with my life. Well,

almost, you know the way it is. He carried with him an air of great nobility. Schumann had been riding high on the crest of a beautiful scam for a year or two. It had all come undone, through no real fault of Schumann's, and now he was reduced to driving the taxi, grinding the slow wheels of his habit seven long nights a week.

The scam had been simple but effective. Schumann had a trusted friend, Pok, in Bangkok. Every time Schumann wired thirty U.S. dollars to Pok's bank account, Pok would send Schumann two weighed grams of very pure Lion Brand No. 4 Thai white powder—the best that money could buy. The two grams were spread out evenly under a mildly adhesive tape, inserted between a folded letter, and sent in a normal airmail envelope. So there was no discernible bulge. It was just a standard airmail letter, delivered to your mailbox, not a "Please pick up from Post Office" slip.

The dope was so pure that when you squirted the water into the spoon, the powder dissolved and there was no need to stir, let alone heat. Clear liquid. It was awesome gear. It made you realize how heavily cut most street dope was.

Schumann didn't sell much, just enough to keep the Pok bank deposits going. Over a period of a few months he found that he was actually stockpiling, and at any given time he had ten or fifteen grams put away for a rainy day.

Candy and I had met him at the tail end of the scam. He let us into his life because he liked us. We had the pleasure of doing business for a couple of months only. It was the funniest thing, Schumann so gentle and so wasted, always talking about how he had to stop, how he couldn't *do* anything on this stuff.

That was an understatement. It was a local joke, Schumann and the radio. Schumann had such an abundance of heroin that there were absolutely no ups and downs in his life. He was meandering through his days at the level of terminal and unwavering saturation.

What had happened was this. The heroin had slowed

down his metabolism so much that almost everything in the world was too fast. The smallest act represented a kind of sensory overload.

He couldn't read. He couldn't muster up the effort to focus on the page, and besides, at any given point in his reading he couldn't remember the preceding sentence. He didn't feel like walking. He found it hard to talk; when he went to the corner shop for his daily supplies of cigarettes and cookies and orange juice, he merely grunted and pointed at the desired items.

When visitors came, such as Candy and I, he was forced to engage in conversation for a few minutes, as he made up the deal of dope. This speech act probably represented the high point of his day.

Even television was too fast for him. He'd tried to lie all day and watch whatever was on. It spun his brain too much, he said, and he'd wound up feeling tense, which kind of defeated the purpose of the heroin. But he felt he needed to do something. He found it impossible to just lie there and drift.

And then he'd discovered the perfect thing. Schumann lay on his bed, day in, day out, face toward the ceiling, and listened to a community radio station called 3RPH. The RPH stood for "Radio for the Print Handicapped." It was for blind people. What 3RPH did was read the newspapers—all day long, very clearly and very slowly. Schumann was deeply satisfied. He told us he felt like a part of the world, like he knew what was going on. He said it was really the perfect radio station for heroin: stimulating, but not too fast.

We'd turn up to buy some smack and we'd hear the clear, precise tones of the announcer, moving along at a snail's pace. "The—Local—Government—Remuneration—Tribunal—has rejected—requests—by—local—councils—for—pay increases—of—up—to—one hundred—percent—despite claims—that—some—mayors—are—working—up—to—seventy-eight—hours—a week—on—council—business."

We'd tap on the window and look in. There would be Schumann, spread out on his bed, a glass of water beside him, the radio in the corner, the fan gently whirring.

Unfortunately for everyone, Schumann gave the Pok system to one other friend, who was a touch more greedy than Schumann had bargained for. Pok opened a second bank account so he could differentiate between who was wiring him money. Schumann's friend Tony had visions of an empire, which is hard to build on two grams at a time. He did have a glorious ascendancy, but it all fucked up within two months. Tony finally got arrested after seventeen airmail letters from Bangkok, all addressed in Pok's spidery handwriting to Tony's place, arrived at the mail exchange on the same day. Pok had integrity as a businessman but not necessarily any common sense; he merely sent the corresponding number of letters to the amount of money that showed up in his bank accounts.

Evidently the only really smart thing that Tony did was keep his mouth shut about Schumann. But some Australian Federal police visited Pok in Bangkok, hassling him for names, and later Pok phoned Schumann, semihysterical: "I'm fleep out, man, I'm fucking fleep out!" Schumann decided enough was enough for that scam. It was a bummer when it all ended.

Nowadays he didn't want to risk things anymore. He'd had quite a tough time trying to reduce his habit from such good dope, but he'd gone back to the hard slog, driving taxis all night and using only as much smack as the money he earned would buy.

When I'd finished telling him what had happened with the credit card and the chase, I leaned my head back and sighed.

"Mate, I need a hundred bucks. Can you help me? I need a little for tonight and a little for the morning. I'll do a day of stealing tomorrow, I'll pay you back at the start of your shift."

"I can't do it," he said. "I'm really sorry, a hundred's all I've got right now. But I'll shout you a taste."

I felt a surge of warmth in my chest. "Schumann, you're a living wonder. You're saving my fucking life, man."

"It's all right. I know how bad you must feel. I'll buy us a hundred and we'll go halves. I was just about to score anyway."

That was just like Schumann, to give away dope even though it meant he might not be sure how much he'd have in the morning. I could never have done that myself. We went to St. Kilda and scored. We had a hit in the cab and Schumann even drove me home.

"Look after me if I ever need it, okay?"

He was a gentleman to the core. He tooted the horn and drove away.

I walked up the stairs to the warehouse, feeling better about my change of fortune. Of course, I still had the problem of no dope in the morning, but that was tomorrow, and right now I could zone out on TV and try and enjoy the stone.

Life struggled on. I tried to make ends meet. I visited Candy in the hospital, still delirious in a darkened room. I held her hand weakly and said, "You'll be better soon. Cheer up."

She said, "Please bring me some dope. This methadone's not enough."

I said, "I'll see what I can do," and near the end I actually got it together one visit to bring her a loaded syringe.

When I picked her up to go home, they said to us, "Your lifestyle has to change, you realize?"

I thought, What the fuck would they know? How could they understand anything?

We got back to our normal lives for another while longer. It wasn't really pleasant but it wasn't a nightmare either. The yellow didn't fade from Candy immediately, but after a couple of weeks you could barely notice it, and a month later you couldn't even tell she'd been sick.

The test came back from the hospital, and for some weird reason I didn't have hep. It was a world that made very little sense.

I went to court twice. The first time, I got the Legal Aid solicitor to defer both my cases and get them heard together. The solicitor seemed like a nice guy. He must have been fairly green, though, because he left his bag in the briefing room when he went outside for a moment. I had a quick look through and pinched the biography of Jack Kerouac he was reading. It would fetch me about six bucks. Every little bit counted.

The second and final appearance, I was well wasted. But I wore a suit and thought I looked like the ant's pants. Candy was with me, looking like a blond vampire, and all the detectives in their beige sport coats were checking her out. The judge said you are a fool, words to that effect, and fined me four hundred dollars. I went straight to the county clerk's office and applied to pay it off in installments. Twenty bucks every two weeks. I made a commitment to myself to try to keep out of trouble. I sincerely believed that this terrible momentum was a thing I could impose my will on, something that could be slowed down.

In Schumann's case, it slowed down a little too fast. At four A.M. one freezing night, police were called to a taxi parked in a dark street in Richmond. The engine was idling and the driver was slumped over the wheel. Schumann had been dead for more than two hours already. He hadn't even managed to untie the tourniquet. I imagine this means that the dope was excellent, so I imagine, and good luck to him too, that Schumann died happy.

LIFE AND DEATH

Somehow at some point we thought that a baby would change things. It gave us something to aim for. It was easy to focus on an outside solution. The theory went like this: we would stop using, and then Candy would get pregnant.

But we got caught a little unawares. Candy discovered she was pregnant and we both had big habits. We had to readjust our way of viewing things. This is the baby we wanted, we said. This is the baby that will change our lives. So now we have a reason to stop using.

Of course, I didn't really have to stop. The baby wasn't in *my* body. But it was the ideal opportunity for both of us to grab hold of the change of direction that we figured would set us on the course of our future. Schumann's dying had shaken us a bit; it seemed that even the generous weren't exempt from the bad flow of events.

In the early weeks after Candy found out, we realized we were going nowhere in the stopping department. We tried and tried, and kept saying tomorrow, tomorrow. Or we talked about a quick methadone reduction program: start on just 40 mils, go to zero in two months, something like that.

Time flies. We managed to miss the ultrasound, the birthing classes, the prenatal appointments. Suddenly Candy was twenty-two weeks pregnant, and one night there was blood in the bath.

"Oh shit! I think this is bad," she said.

"It'll be all right," I said.

We got a taxi to the hospital.

They took her into the room to check her out. I waited where the other men were, in a waiting room with blue plastic chairs and a TV chained to the wall. The men were excited and talkative.

After a while, maybe an hour, a nurse came and called me in. Candy was crying.

The doctor looked at me and I could tell she didn't really like me.

"The waters have broken. The cervix is dilated. There's no going back now. This is what we didn't want to happen. This is a premature birth. As I've just explained to Candy, she's going to have to go through labor. Whatever that takes, however long. But you need to know, at twenty-two weeks, the baby's not going to survive."

The words were clear, but nonetheless I stared at her for a while. Tasting the sour meaning on the back of my throat.

"Ahh," I groaned. "Ahh, shit."

I felt the future drain away from me, like a rush of blood to the toes. It was physically painful.

Candy sobbed more and I moved across and held her hot hand. She squeezed my hand tight. For a moment it felt like we weren't really junkies, but two people who loved each other, in the middle of pain and loss, in the real world.

A nurse took us to the room where it would happen. It was a delivery room, just like the ones where the live births arrived. The nurse made Candy comfortable.

"I'll be in and out," she said. "You should be okay at the moment." Then she left.

There was not much for us to do or say. Every so often Candy groaned. Sometimes I held her hand. She wasn't sobbing, not in a rhythm. But the tears kept streaming down her face for more than an hour, until the pain began to heat up.

When she looked at me, there was not the toughness there that I knew so well. Her forehead creased and her soft lips quivered and her eyes were saying, "Help me, help me."

And I was helpless, or unable to help. What the fuck could I do for her?

"It's all right, baby, it's all right." I stroked her forehead. "We're just going to have to get through it. I wish it could be me instead of you."

Words were really ridiculous.

For a long time Candy stared at the ceiling, crying, and I sat on a chair beside the bed, hunched over with my head in my hands. I heard the plastic doors swing open and closed. I heard the shuffle of feet on linoleum, people probing Candy and asking questions.

They must have thought we looked pretty bad. At one point a counselor came and talked to us for a while. It was good to talk to anyone. She told us how it wasn't the end of the world and how surely we'd be able to have a baby sometime in the future. She told us that even though it was going to die, it was *our* baby, and when it was born we should hold it, look at it, touch it, say good-bye to it. She said that when it happened they would leave us alone for a while with our baby.

The counselor left and Candy held out her arms and we hugged. I could feel her hot tears on my shoulder, soaking into my shirt.

The doctor came back. I asked if there was any chance the baby could live.

She shook her head. "I'm sorry. It's just too young. Another few weeks, you never know. I'm very sorry."

"Well, will it be dead when it's born?"

"It might be alive for a minute or two. But unassisted, it can't live for long. And we won't do anything to keep it alive."

Candy's contractions were becoming more frequent. It seemed like she screamed for hours. Time went by in an antiseptic blur. The smell of the place was bugging me, something I couldn't put my finger on. Then I remembered that hospital smell, the smell of the corridors, after the car accident.

I am sixteen years old, rushing to see my mother in the emergency ward. The nurse says go in. I walk into the room full of machinery but I can't find my mother. There's an ugly lady with a huge purple head but I can't see my mother anywhere. For a moment I think this must be the wrong room. The lady with the swollen head—it's big as a watermelon—is hooked up to all sorts of tubes and screens. Then she smiles weakly and raises her hand. I move toward her and say, "Mum," but my legs buckle under me. I know I am fainting and can't stop it. I taste vomit and hospital disinfectant at the back of my nose, and then I black out. When I wake up the nurses are fanning me and they have wheeled my mother away somewhere else. "Where's Mum?" I say. "They're just working on a little problem, love. There's been a bit of a blood clot. They've taken her down to surgery." The next time I see her, two hours later, she is already dead.

I shook myself out of the memory and went back to mopping Candy's brow with a wet towel. For the next nine hours I felt I was an inconsequential sidetrack, branching off the freeway of Candy's ordeal.

I hated the world so much when the world went wrong. A whole long night of blood and screaming, and I hadn't had smack since early afternoon. I remember feeling guilty—an unusual emotion—because I wanted so badly for Candy's pain to end, not just because of the pain itself, but more because of the way the clock ticked on the wall, tick tick tick, the hands moving away from my last blast, or toward my next. That's an essential truth of the night. Even then I knew the guilt would be the kind of guilt that would bury itself for years. Still, when you need a hit you need a hit.

A lot of the time I couldn't watch. I stood at the window and looked down nine floors. The park was down there, a dark rectangle around which the traffic edged. At one point Candy's screaming shook me out of my trance.

"What the fuck is that! Nurse! What the fuck is that!"

She was sitting up, her legs spread, lifting her butt off the bed, covering her bloodied cunt with her hand.

The nurse on this shift had been a bitch.

"That's its foot. Take your hand away! Leave it alone!"

I did not want to see the baby's foot.

It seemed like hours later that the baby was born, but it probably wasn't long after the foot appeared. It was nearly dawn.

The smack thoughts and the guilt kept growing. I was in the middle of a tragedy, Candy's and mine, and the longer the night stretched toward dawn, the less I could think about the thing at hand, the more I became obsessed with the thought of my next shot. The need for smack. All I could picture was the syringe, the pulling back, the spurt of blood. An image of myself in great relief, slumping back on the couch.

But Candy was going through labor and, pethidine and epidural aside, there were no shortcuts.

The baby came feetfirst. The doctor and the nurses tugged at it. Candy was screaming and I held her hand. Now I had to look down. For a moment only the head was still inside Candy. Then they pulled it free.

Candy was delirious and I stroked her face. They gave the baby to me for a moment. It was just like a real baby. Its arm moved up and down.

"It's alive!" I shouted.

The doctor had a look. "It's probably just a spasm," she said.

But I knew I had held it when it was alive. Sometime in the next minute it died. They cut the cord and cleaned it, wrapped it in a soft white blanket. They cleaned Candy and changed the sheets and propped her up in bed.

Candy stroking her dead baby. Everything white and clean.

Candy wasn't screaming anymore. But she was crying again. The endless tears of Candy. She was moaning softly and I tried to kiss her tears. My eyes welled wet and red. I looked down at the baby boy and rubbed his soft warm head.

Finally I began to cry. Then I realized, It doesn't matter if I don't rush out of here. The heroin can wait. We lay there crying together, touching the baby and crying. I hadn't cried in so long, my chest was tight with the very fear of it. A foreign experience invading my body. A kind of surrender for a terrible moment or two.

The nurses left us alone.

We said things like:

"Look at his little hands, his fingernails."

"Look at his lips, his beautiful lips."

"Look how perfect he is."

After a long while the nurse came back, not the foot bitch, a different one, a soft one.

"You two should sleep for a while," she said.

It meant she wanted to take the baby away now.

"There's a chapel here," she said. "We'd recommend you have a funeral service in the morning. It's a ritual. It's the way to say good-bye."

She took the baby. Candy and I fell into each other's arms. Five hours later, at eleven A.M., they woke us.

I felt so empty by now, I hardly even thought about heroin, even though I was sicker than I'd been in a few months. Under normal circumstances it would have been my focus. I was wired as if I was speeding—definitely not my favorite state. But my welfare check was due in my bank account today, so there was something to look forward to in the gloom.

I felt that something dark and important had happened, but I knew I couldn't really pause to think about it. I was trying to get through things, a minute at a time.

The nurses helped Candy from bed into a wheelchair. I wheeled her though the corridors to the hospital chapel.

The counselor from the night before stood with a generic-brand hospital chaplain at the door to the chapel. They welcomed everyone who arrived. I guess it was their job to be sincere, so it's no use being sarcastic about it.

The chapel was pretty sterile. The same hospital smell, the same linoleum tiles, a few rows of seats, a big cross on the wall, a vase of abundantly colored flowers on a table. I tell you, the flowers made me feel sad but good. They were beautiful things to look at. Staring at the flowers seemed to help me not cry.

Candy's parents were there; I had called them during the night to give them the bad news. Candy was always at them for money, so things were not good when it came to the subject of their daughter and drugs. But here they were, downcast, upset, everybody comforting everybody else.

There were a couple of nurses and cleaners. White uniforms and green uniforms. I don't know if they were just Christian types who loved to pray for the passage of the souls of the dead, or if the hospital had a policy of forcing staff along, to beef up the numbers. Some kind of funeral roster.

Candy was paler than I'd ever seen her. She had been drained of the boy who now lay dead, wrapped in a white shawl, in a tiny open casket not much bigger than a shoe box, on a stainless-steel meal trolley at the front of the seats.

"Wheel me up there," Candy said.

She had to stand up to look into the casket. I held her under the arm. She looked up at me and her eyes were erased of everything but tears. No color there, just liquid. She reached her arms around my neck and hugged me and cried. I looked down at the baby. The sleep of the dead, as they say.

The chaplain came over. "He's gone to a better place, you know," he said.

I suppose that had to be true, wherever he'd gone, us being junkies and all.

Candy slipped her finger into the baby's hand. "It's so beautiful," she said. "Why can't he be alive? Why?"

"We just can't know the whys and wherefores of God's will," the chaplain said.

I touched the baby's face. I rubbed its cheek with the back of my index finger. It was stone cold now. It had been in a fridge since dawn.

We all sat down, except the chaplain. He stood at the front and said a lot of stuff. I'm sure his words were good.

They wheeled the trolley away. We all stood outside the chapel, where a trestle table had been set up with sandwiches and cordial. A nurse drew me aside. She carried a clipboard and had papers for me to sign.

"Burial or cremation?" she asked.

"Does it matter?" I said.

"I'm sorry, it's a legal requirement if death occurs any time after twenty weeks of pregnancy." She was awkward.

"Can't you just . . . throw it out?"

"It's a registered death. I'm sorry. You have to choose."

"Cremation," I said, and signed the paper, knowing I would never pay the bill, or collect the ashes.

Candy was staying in the hospital for a couple more days. She asked could she have some more pethidine, and the nurses said they would find out if it would be all right. I knew she would work the system. I knew she would do fine in there, hopefully not feel anything.

"I want to sleep for a week," she said.

I kissed her and hugged her good-bye and said good-bye to everyone else. Then I went out into the day, my shirt still stained with blood and placenta, to look for a bank and withdraw my welfare check and find someone to score off.

PART TWO

The Kingdom of Momentum

"Some of the evil of my tale may have been inherent in our circumstances. For years we lived anyhow with one another in the naked desert, under the indifferent heaven. By day the hot sun fermented us; and we were dizzied by the beating wind. At night we were stained by dew, and shamed into pettiness by the innumerable silences of stars. We were a self-centered army without parade or gesture, devoted to . . . a purpose so ravenous that it devoured all our strength, a hope so transcendent that our earlier ambitions faded in its glare . . ."

T. E. Lawrence, *Seven Pillars of Wisdom*

TRUTH 1: DREAMS

Sleep. The place where a deeper unease can penetrate through sick bone and aching muscle, an unease so fine and lightweight it can settle even on the atoms of oxygen in your lungs, coat them with a dread silt, weigh them down, so you puff restlessly all night and whimper into the dawn.

When I'm drifting into sleep, sometimes I jolt half awake for a moment, and I realize I feel scared. Then I think about the sickness enveloping our lives. What's outside the mist? Surely goodness and mercy shall follow us, I dunno, it seems such a tall order. So then I think—and I'm stoned, mind you—I will stop this. I can stop this. I will stop using drugs. I will reenter the world: free at last to choose from all its parts. Not just forced to choose only one of them.

Forced to choose. Hmmm. Near sleep the mind throws words around. Compulsion. Independence. All that shit.

On any given night I dream of horses, car accidents, mental asylums, endless train journeys, storms. One night in a dream Candy points to an island in the middle of the harbor. She is luminous, otherworldly, transparent as a ghost.

"Come with me, in a boat," she says, "across to that island, and we'll fuck over there." As if a dream could prophesy surrender and relief.

Then in the morning, I wake up, there is nothing but fear, oceans of it, no boat to be seen, and how long can I dog-paddle? The water is everywhere, every direction I look. A mean day, the gray water. Nothing is not fear. The day takes place.

In or near overdose you drift in a profound stasis broken up only by the endless falling of snowflakes. But dreams are different from that. In dreams, things happen. This is so unsettling. Things. Events. They just happen, you don't control them.

It's away from the madness of daylight, in my dreams, I find the sadness that my days just can't connect with. Out in the day we can only survive. For every hundred-dollar cock in Candy's cunt, Candy needs a two-hundred-dollar jab in the arm. And I'm Prince Pimp, welcome to the show. I would vomit up my life if I could.

ASHTRAY

Now and then I pulled a scam, but opportunistic and fruitful crimes were really just occasional blips on the gray monitoring screen that recorded the faint pulse of our ephemeral lives. The real money came from Candy. Over the years, as our habits got worse, I guess she began to think about imbalance. That she earned all the money and I used half the dope.

This was some time down the track from the glory days. We were now in the middle years of solid habit. There was a grim determination to our using. The miscarriage seemed to have faded from our minds. At any rate, we never talked about it.

Well, this was what love was, for better or for worse. But when times were tough then the whole world disappeared and nothing existed but bad blood. At such times I discovered a venom in Candy that sat measure for measure with the abundant juice of what she had been before heroin got bad.

It had been a long, uneventful winter. The warehouse was twelve hundred square feet of wooden floors and drafty open spaces, a cold place at the best of times. There were only two ways of keeping warm. One was heroin, the supreme crucible in which all sensation melted to a base level of comfort. This was generally how we did it. The second way, when there was no heroin, or not enough, was a two-bar heater that we huddled around.

There was our bed too, on a raised wooden platform in an alcove near the door. Our clothes hung beneath the platform. We reached the bed, a thin, sweat-stained futon, by climbing a ladder. But invariably we'd end up crashing out on one of the couches, in a jumble of blankets and pillows, in front of the old black-and-white TV, night after night after night.

The couches were in front of the bed alcove. Over the other side, next to the window, was the makeshift kitchen area. In the far corner was the bathtub, which had to be filled and emptied with buckets. This whole section was divided off by a thin partition made of sheets of latticework and Chinese paper. The rest of the warehouse was empty space. The toilet was outside the door, off a small courtyard, across the landing.

I spent my days reading or wandering around the city. Candy was still earning bucketloads, but it no longer felt like enough.

We would always talk of stopping and always find a reason not to. Memory blurs these things, but maybe it was me who found those reasons more often. I'm really not sure. I wanted to stop, but the thought of stopping was an impossible thought to hold down.

Fights could begin for no big reason and stay peaked at a high-tension level for days. One day Candy was pretty pissed off with me because I'd gone to score the dope and I hadn't come straight home in a cab. I mean, we're talking five minutes. The point for Candy was, I came home stoned. Meaning I was caring more about myself than her.

I'd met Little Angelo in a park in Prahran. I know I could have come straight home, it's just that I was hanging out a little more than usual, and I didn't see how a quick visit to the public toilet could hurt. I was edgy. The powder was beckoning. There had been delays with both Lester and Kojak, so we were down to Little Angelo, a long-shot, number three choice.

I went into the toilet. It was a scungy fucked-up place, smelling of stale piss and bad plumbing. However. You adjust. I went to the basin but there was no handle on the tap. Normally I would pour some water into the cupped palm of my hand and suck it up with the syringe.

I swore I'd never get water from a toilet bowl. There was only one alternative. A pipe came down from the cistern into the stainless-steel piss trough. At the top of the trough the pipe ended in a half circle from which the water sprayed out intermittently. I balanced myself and placed the syringe under the fine spray of water.

It sucked in mostly air, and a trickle of water each time. I had to keep tapping the air bubbles to the top and starting again. I was careful not to allow the needle to scrape on the steel of the trough, for fear of barbing the point. Finally I got enough water and hit up in the cubicle as quickly as I could.

But when I walked in the door of the warehouse with a big grin and my soul full of warmth, Candy took one look in my eyes and said, "You're a slimy cunt."

She said the word cunt very hard. I was taken aback.

"Hey, baby, I just had a quick little hit. It was nothing."

"While I was waiting here biting my fucking nails!"

"I got back as fast as I could! It didn't make any difference."

"No difference? Did you have your hit in a time warp?"

"You know what I mean."

"No, I don't know what you mean. Where did you hit up?"

"In the park. Where I met Ange."

"Did Angelo do it with you?"

"No, he left as soon as we did the deal."

"Yeah, because he's decent enough to go home to his girlfriend."

"Candy, he *sold* me the dope. Why would he want to have a hit in a public toilet?"

"Well, why the fuck would you?"

"Look, I admit it was dumb. I don't usually do it. I'm sorry. Okay? I'm sorry."

I went to the dresser and pulled out the bathroom bag that contained our fits and spoons. I just wanted to ease the situation into a lower gear.

"Here," I offered, "I'll make you a nice taste."

"I'll make it myself, thanks, *dickhead.*" She snatched the packet of dope away from me.

I was offended now. "What's your fucking problem?" I snapped.

"You're my fucking problem. You're a waste of space."

"I'm a waste of space?" Repetition. It was the last refuge of the brain dead. "Jesus, Candy." I was searching for a comeback. "I'd think you had your period but I know you never get them these days."

It was a low dig.

"Yeah, I never get my period because my body's all fucked up and out of whack because of this fucking drug that *you've* led me into."

"Oh, right. Like I held a gun to your head, is it?"

She was concentrating on mixing up the dope in the spoon.

"Eh? Held you down and hit you up, did I?"

"Fuck you," she said.

"Fuck you too, Candy."

I didn't want to fight but it was hard to back down. Heroin was not designed to go hand in hand with stress. I slammed the door and walked outside, into the city crowds. I walked for an hour or more. I found myself in the State Library and wandered around for a while. I leafed through a book of photos from *Life* magazine, and another book of photos of houses designed by Frank Lloyd Wright. Picture books were easier. Then I came home. Of course I wanted to sulk. But I couldn't stand the thought of being away from the dope for too long.

But Candy had it in for me that day, and the bickering continued into the night. She wanted a reaction. As usual, I felt nothing but the desire not to have a confrontation.

Something was beginning to give for Candy. A seismograph in Sydney feels the distant rumbling of a profound rupture in the earth's crust a thousand kilometers away, beneath the ocean floor. In the same way, through all the distance laid down by heroin, I was registering a flutter of discontent. God only knows what that flutter was like inside Candy. A deafening upheaval, I suppose. I was sure I loved her, but it seemed that no matter how hard I tried, smack came first.

I was trying to ignore her. I was not a sophisticated unit. "Shhh! I'm watching TV."

"I said, when are we going to stop using?"

"Whenever you like, Candy. Whenever you like."

"What, tomorrow, then?"

"Okay, fuck, tomorrow. I don't care. Tomorrow we stop using."

"Listen to me!"

She stamped her foot. I looked away from the TV and our eyes met. She was crying.

"Don't you see what this is doing to me?"

"Candy," I said, "I don't want to fight. Look, I just don't see what your problem is tonight. We have a life. It's neither good nor bad, okay?"

She laughed an unpleasant snigger and looked around the room as if there was an audience.

"You're kidding, aren't you?" she asked. "Our life is more than bad. It's utterly fucked. And you are evil."

They seemed such heavy words in the cold stark warehouse.

"Oh yeah, right, I'm evil. Now I think you've gone too far, Candy. Goebbels was evil. Adolf fucking Hitler was evil. Put things in perspective, eh?"

"Do you know what I do all day and night to earn the money that we put up our arms?"

I closed my eyes. It was like the question that dare not speak its name.

"Candy . . . I know. You know . . . you know I'm not happy . . . about that."

"About what? Say it."

"Candy, I know what you do all day. Okay?"

"What do I do all day? Listen to this, dickfuck." She stood in front of the TV, blocked my line of sight. She pointed at me and I had to look at her. "What do I do all day? I fuck men. Lots of men. I humiliate myself. I hate my life. What are you going to do about it?"

"Listen, that's it." My arms went up in the surrender sign. "I don't want you to work anymore. That's it. No more brothels, no more escort. We're gonna detox, start a new life. That's really it this time."

The conversation was getting too emotional for me.

"You don't understand, do you?" she continued. "I *want* to keep using. I'm sick of working, yes. But what if I want to keep using? What are you going to do about it?"

It was like I'd been cornered by a series of trick questions.

"Candy . . ."

I gulped. For the first time in a while I felt the fear that was rooted in my stomach, that was always there but rarely noticed, that was beginning to rise into my throat. You sensed it first as edginess, then the vague onset of a panic not yet concrete.

"Why don't you ring Gay Blades?" she said. "You start working for once. You hock your arse."

"Candy, you know I can't do that. I'll . . . you know, I'll get AIDS." It was a pathetic stab in the dark.

"No, you won't," she said. "You'll use a condom, like I have to."

"Baby, I wouldn't know what to do. You're heterosexual, right? So you're just doing what you were good at anyway. Let me fuck women, no problems. If I could do it with women, I'd make us all the money, you'd never have to work, I swear.

"But look at me, Candy. Nobody would fuck me for money, I don't think. Or not very often. Those women, they want muscle chuds, don't they? *Vogue* magazine–type guys. If there was a market out there, I'd do it. But I don't think there is. And I'd be hopeless with the gay stuff. You know that."

"You'd learn," she sneered. "You may not like it but you'd learn how to do it. You'd even get good at it. Then you could find out what it's like, day in, day out. I'd love to see how you'd handle that. And how you'd feel about giving me half your money."

I shrugged. I was trying to look impassive. I was trying to signal it was all too much.

"I'd give you half my money," I said. "You know that. We share everything. That's what we do. You get half of what I do in scams. It's just that you earn more, that's all."

She still stood there in front of the TV with her hands on her hips. I looked at her stomach as if I could see straight through it to the screen.

"On average," I added, shrugging.

"You're pathetic," she said.

It was hideous. Even through the heroin I was squirming.

"Listen, Candy, I go get the dope every day. I organize the deals. I organize the scams. Sometimes I steal books. Who got all the money from that guy's cards? Who took all the risk in the banks? Who does most of the check stuff and card stuff? At least you can't go to jail for working in a brothel."

"Let's get this straight," she said. "If the credit card's a woman's name, I do it. If it's a man's name, you do it. It's that simple."

"Yeah," I retorted, "but when you do it, it seems I help you. I come into the bank or the shop so that we look like a couple. When I do it, I do it by myself."

We were really down to quibbling here. It was time to change tack. I sighed.

"Candy, let's not argue. Listen, I tell you what. Okay, try this. You need to work sometimes, just sometimes, I'm saying. We need the backup money. But I'll start putting more effort into dealing. I'll try and push it a little so it becomes sort of full-time."

"You can't deal," she said, "you always use too much. You're hopeless."

"Well, no I'm not," I said. "That's not exactly true. You wait and see. Kojak said he'd offer me a system. For every five halves I move, I get one free. So I don't really have to cut the deals, and maybe I can get things rolling along."

"Yeah right, we'll see. And in the meantime?"

There was a long pause.

"You don't have to work if you don't want to, Candy."

Another pause. She couldn't believe what she heard.

"You *are* a cocksucking cunt, you know that?"

I was getting pissed off with the personal abuse.

"Oh, for fuck's sake, Candy, get away from the TV. I'm trying to watch a show. I'm not going to talk to you if you go on like that."

It went on and it got more vicious. There were lulls and then the thing would charge up again. There were times when I could settle into the TV for half an hour or so, but there was a bad edge to the night. In the end we reached an agreement of sorts. We couldn't just give up tomorrow. We both knew that. I'd give more serious dealing a shot for a few weeks. Try and get established, try and get a healthy business going. Use Kojak's freebie system and put out the word that I would be available from nine A.M. till midnight (these were Kojak's regular hours) each day. In the meantime Candy would keep working, so we would have lots of cash.

But if the dealing wasn't all that successful, then in a month—we gave ourselves a time limit—we would go down to Gippsland to dry out. We had a couple of friends who lived there, a couple of hours out of Melbourne, in rich green dairy country. Peter and Michael had been on again and off again for a few years. They'd settled into a pretty stable relationship now, and a nice life down there, smoking buds and gardening and painting. Their offer had always been there—if our intentions were good, we were welcome to come down and make use of their spare room and good food and quiet lifestyle.

If that didn't work, if we came back to Melbourne and started using, then a methadone program, we agreed, was finally around the corner. We would get on methadone for six months or twelve months, give ourselves some breathing space, some time to get our lives in order.

It was a kind of relief that there was really nowhere else for the argument to go. Nonetheless a stony silence ensued. Candy sat at the dresser fiddling with makeup and I watched TV, willing myself to be absorbed into the screen.

It was after midnight now, more than six or seven hours since I'd gotten home from meeting Little Angelo. I suggested we have a blast.

"Yeah, okay," Candy said, "but we have to go to bed soon. I've got to get up for work in the morning."

"Don't worry, I don't want to stay up too long."

But of course I loved staying up on a fresh whack of heroin, even if staying up just meant sitting on the couch and nodding off. Maybe Candy just wanted the big hit and the release, the collapse into dreamless sleep. A few times a year I wanted that too. Mostly, though, I liked to fiddle, do crosswords, read, watch TV, squeeze pimples, smoke cigarettes.

I should have gone with the flow that night, but the flow through my veins was always stronger. Such divided loyalties.

We had a nice taste. Candy climbed up to the bed and tried to read for five minutes, then turned off the lamp.

"Come to bed now," she said.

"Yeah, soon."

I was engrossed in the late movie, *The Servant,* with Dirk Bogarde and James Fox. It was a very cool film, with all the British pacing and subtle rhythms that made for good smack viewing.

After fifteen minutes Candy sat up.

"I can't get to sleep with that on. Turn it *off*!"

"Candy, it's a really good movie. I'll turn it right down, okay?"

I turned it down so that even I could barely hear it. I checked the TV guide.

"Anyway, there's only half an hour to go."

But she wouldn't accept that. I watched the last half hour with a blanket draped over the TV and my head, my face six inches from the screen, the pixels of the tube making everything look abstract, the tiny hum louder than the faint dialogue. I assumed that Candy fell asleep during this time.

The movie finished. I switched the TV off and turned on the lamp beside the couch. I was still shaken by the fight, by its intensity, by the evening's events. I had the strange but strong urge to write something just for myself, something private, to dispel the awful emotions and work out how I felt.

I got out a notebook and started writing. *Tonight I had a fight with Candy. I hate that shit.*

After a few minutes I heard a rustling from the bed alcove, and I knew she was sitting up again.

"I can't believe it," she said. "I cannot fucking believe it."

"What? I'm not making any noise!"

"The light," she said. "The light's keeping me awake. Turn if off and come to bed."

I was in the middle of important thoughts, and I wanted to get them out of my head and onto the paper. It seemed at that moment the only way I had of making sense of my life.

"Five minutes, give me five minutes."

"No!"

"All right, I'll cover the light."

I bent the lamp down until its cone almost touched the table. A small circle of light oozed out the sides, but the warehouse was pretty dark.

"There," I said. "There's more light coming in from the streetlights than this. I've got something to write. You can't complain about this."

"Arsehole," she muttered, and rolled over.

Five minutes later it was Candy again.

"The pen. I can hear the pen rustling on the paper."

"Oh, this is ridiculous, Candy. You're looking for an excuse!"

"Turn the light off and come to bed."

"I'm not even discussing it anymore."

"Turn the light off!"

"That's it. I'm not even talking."

"Turn the fucking light off!"

I sat, my back to Candy, and continued writing. Candy continued to snarl at me but I remained silent and tried not to listen.

Violence can be momentarily painless when there is no warning. I felt an enormous thud on the crown of my head. Glass shattered over me and I reeled forward. The pieces of a heavy glass ashtray fell at my feet. I was a little bit confused for a couple of seconds. Then the pain signals cut in.

I reached my hands to the back of my head and cut my fingers on the chunk of glass that was lodged there. I pulled out the glass and felt a stab of pure pain. There was an explosion of blood from my head. I could feel its hot flow through my hair and down my neck. All this, in its own strange way, was less cloudy than the preceding seven hours of arguing. I was in that sweet realm where drama has a resolution in violence.

I leaned forward on the couch with my hands still holding my head. I felt the blood on my wrists and in my ears. I watched it splatter on the floor. I didn't really feel like fainting yet, but I staggered forward onto one knee. It seemed like the thing to do.

Candy was pushing a towel into my head. She was in a panic, fingers fumbling through my hair, searching for the source of the blood, her words spilling out.

"Oh God, oh God, oh God, I'm so sorry, baby, I'm so sorry."

There really was a lot of blood.

"I think we'd better go to the hospital," I said, acting stoic.

She had some warm water in a bowl and was trying to sponge down my head and my face and my neck, all the while trembling and smothering my forehead with kisses and saying she was sorry over and over. I kept groaning like I was losing consciousness.

I just felt relieved to be treated so nicely. So lovingly and warmly. Things would be okay for days, maybe weeks now. I just knew it.

The words came tumbling out while she mopped me. She said she'd been so angry, she just wanted to scare me. She'd wanted the ashtray to smash near me, to show how serious she was. But it was a heavy ashtray and she was a bad aim and things had gone wrong. She'd never meant to hurt me. I believed her.

We walked up to the hospital. Candy held one arm around my shoulder and pressed the towel to my head with her other hand. By this time I actually was feeling a little wobbly. But I was buoyed by the thought that there might be some good drugs in the hospital.

As it was, the emergency room doctor was sharp. I told him I was in a considerable amount of pain. Was there any chance of some morphine? He smiled gently and looked at the size of my pupils.

"I don't think you need any morphine," he laughed. "I don't think you're in a great deal of pain."

It was worth the try. There were no hard feelings. It was a

pleasant atmosphere in the emergency room at three in the morning, everyone loving and friendly.

The doctor shaved a patch of my hair. He injected a local anesthetic and sewed sixteen stitches into my scalp. He gave me a strip of Panadeine Forte and a prescription for some more tomorrow.

"Go easy on these," he said. "Not that I really expect you to."

We walked home slowly, arm in arm through the empty fog-filled streets. We went to bed and Candy stroked my face, and we even ended up fucking softly just before dawn.

TRUTH 2: HOW IT IS

Looking at it closely, things aren't that good, but there are cuddles, a certain comfortable feeling in the coolness of the bed, smiles, admissions of love. And this despite the constant breaking of taboos: only the guy in the hockshop; only a brothel; only to save money; only escort work; never on the street; then on the street, but only this once. The sharing of sex. The feeling of unease, unspoken. But always a condom with the others, so that things still feel all right with us, that way. And there's some laughter into the bargain, along with the touching. Still that intimacy. The other is only work, yeah?

It's the middle of the day, we're sprawled on the couch, a little bit sick, watching TV and waiting for Lester or Kojak to call back. American talk shows. Anything is more interesting than fidgeting. Then without any warning, with barely a sound but the tiniest pop! *the screen shuts down to blackness. And that's how the TV dies. From now on we can hear it but we can't see it. We will need a new one soon—a new old black-and-white one, I mean—to stop us from going crazy.*

We will need a new TV to while away the time, make out nothing's happening, make out nothing's wrong. In the meantime, turn up the radio, reread yesterday's paper. The form guide.

Races that are already over. See how you might have done. You're not feeling sick, that's only queasy. Try not to feel it. You're not feeling it. You feel all right. You've got integrity. Oodles left. The fucking TV's gone.

The weather will verify all this. The morning started fine. Then it's hot—too fucking hot. Lester calls back at last and we get on, then relax. We browse through a bookstore, I steal a book on the Vietnam War.

You lose track of time, you know what I mean? After a few weeks, listening to the TV gets frustrating. It's a visual medium. Finally we wrangle a replacement from Victor's cousin for fifty bucks, a set so old that the screen seems to bulge like a bubble. Summer drags on. The air is heavy, sweet, hypnotic, hazy, like musk. Aesthetic effects suffuse the screen: on The Brady Bunch *you think you see Peter Fonda in the dust. For a moment you think you're in a Holiday Inn in West Texas, and the loose screw in the ceiling fan pops every 360 degrees, beats like a heart. The endless late-night movies you watch. Abstract tragedy. Kris Kristofferson in* Cisco Pike. *Robert Redford and Michael J. Pollard in* Little Fauss and Big Halsy. *Peter Fonda with Susan George in* Dirty Mary, Crazy Larry. *People you never knew. Anything to avoid what's happening: Melbourne, heroin, now.*

The afternoon clouds over. The rains come, yes. But wait for what's in store.

Winter comes around again. On the odd occasion when we take time to think about it, we are ashamed, perplexed. Nothing, it seems, has changed. The same awful struggling for money, the scars grow daily up and down our arms. It becomes harder to find veins. My arm swells; I have to take my wristwatch off.

We watch the all-night music video show. Candy is drawing. I finish a book I've been reading about the Crusades, then I start The Spy Who Loved Me *by Eleanor Philby. But my eyes are beginning to droop. At six* A.M. *we watch the morning news. Soon after that we fall asleep for a few hours.*

It's good to wake up knowing there's some dope left. It helps you sleep better. At ten o'clock the day is dark and wet. The rain bleeds down the windows. We hug in front of the heater, listening to the downpour. We take a bath together, leaving the light off. It's dark and steamy and slowly we spread soap on each other. We dry and make tea and toast. In front of the heater we mix up and have a blast. There is nothing like the morning blast.

Adrift. At times it seems that I am floating in the beauty of docility. Pulling the needle from my arm, I succumb again and again to the luscious undertow of the infinite spaces between atoms. My arm an estuary of light in which all rivers gather.

There's no real chronology. Things happen in units, one after the other but entirely unrelated, dislocated. Each day's about the same. Maybe the weather differs. Or the way certain television programs do not appear on weekends.

During the night, stoned, we promise each other we are going to give up. Then in the morning we wake up sick, and the fear is overwhelming. And somehow, the first thing we have to do is score. Later we can think about our promises.

In the streets: the ugliest people in the world. I never notice them behind pinprick eyeballs. But if I'm hanging out, big panic. Now evil pulsates like a heart in the sun. Oh God, shower me with money and I will be good.

We dream of going to India, Thailand, getting properly *stoned on* real *dope at* decent *prices. But we've never got money beyond the next hit. The high point of our life is the moment we plunge the needle. The self-perpetuating fuck. Once upon a time our bodies melted until they were a force field of sweat, the one indistinguishable from the other. Love? We fucked on the rocks at Rye Beach, she scraped her knees, I scratched my back, I tore my shirt. The bright white light of sex—exquisite. And now this.*

When a fight starts, for whatever reason, pride plays a part and we keep it up, we can't back down. Besides, we haven't slept in two days. We fight about working, about lack of dope. Call your parents. Fuck you, I can't do that again.

The Speed of it. Our Death Approaching. What scares me, flaring at the nostrils, is The Speed. Each breath is The Speed. There are Speeds within The Speed. The day goes slow or fast, in our greatest distress we really don't know which.

In the end, life can be seen to be inconsequential, in the way that nothing matters on some vast evolutionary scale. But everything matters, and we know that most when life seems most horrific, when at each instant of time, all the space around us is everything there is.

Suppose this, Candy. Suppose all time was not the way it is with us. Suppose its mellifluous curves and parabolas, its contractions and contortions, the furious or sedate blood of its pulse, were of a different mathematics altogether. Or say the eye that views could view with the remoteness and the slowness of rocks growing, continents being born, galaxies roller-coasting through the universe. Imagine if we could stand above the flow of time and look down on it just as we stood on Mount Dandenong and looked down on the dots of traffic ten miles away and below.

But there is a blackness all around. We can't imagine anything. We can't suppose. We are trapped inside the thickest of boundaries.

GPO

Rohypnol! Jesus, the dumb things that we do. Rohypnol, get this, makes you think that everything you're doing, you're doing at normal speed. Which you're not, of course. Which explains the GPO debacle.

It was after our big fight, and the stitches. Candy was getting burned out, that's the message I got from the fight. I kind of figured I was less than a man, since Candy earned most of the money and I didn't really pull my weight. I was being threatened with industrial action, and fair enough too. These are terrible things to discuss. It was always a nagging thing in the back of my mind, but more and more now it was like a heavy suit that I wore all the time, all the pockets filled with lead: Candy works as a prostitute, and you say you care about her. I knew I must have stunk inside my suit, but I couldn't get it off.

I wanted to be tremendously wealthy, of course. Because wealth would mean more heroin. It's just that prostitution was the quickest way to fast, regular money. I loved Candy. I'm sure she loved me. The question was not, "How do we go fifty-fifty?" but, "What's the quickest way we can get one on board?"

Still, when I did something like Roger's wallet, fuck did I

feel good. It didn't happen much. When we had fights like the ashtray fight, I didn't feel so good.

If I worked really hard, I could get a hundred or a hundred fifty bucks a day stealing and selling books. More like eighty. A hundred fifty, that's a pretty big day. A lot of lugging, a lot of hours. Barely enough dope for the two of us. I could almost get a real job for that kind of money. And there just weren't enough bookstores in the whole of Melbourne to do it nonstop. You had to be cyclical with this kind of crime. Anyway, it was nothing like what Candy could earn.

We were as sick as dogs, seriously edgy and sweaty. It was a Friday afternoon. Candy said, "I just don't care anymore. I just don't give a fuck." The usual stuff. "We'll just be sick, go through it, get it over and done with."

But I felt I was long past tricking myself into that nightmare. In my demented need, I thought if I could redeem myself in her eyes, she would come good again. I always wanted heroin, but in another way, too, I always wanted to make our love pure. Or as pure as could be.

I just had to get some money. I took some Rohypnols to ease the anxiety.

"I'm going for a walk," I said.

"Don't do anything stupid," Candy said.

I had no particular purpose in mind, which was never a good way to do things.

The afternoon sun was pale and weak. I was sweating beneath my overcoat, but still cold in all the shadows. It never ceased to amaze me how much I could hate the world when I wasn't stoned. It seemed such a hostile place. And yet, get a good blast in me, and my love for humanity was abundant.

I walked through Bourke Street Mall, through the department stores, the jewelry shops. Opportunity just wasn't presenting itself. I sat on a bench and watched people waiting for trams. I thought about handbag snatches. Not the glamour activity, but if I could get away with it, it would do. I knew the back alleys to the warehouse, the same back alleys I thought I could reach when Beefboy the cop was chasing me. I thought this time would be different, that I could get around the corner and into that door before anyone would be able to catch me.

I was lost in my thoughts of alleyways and shortcuts when I saw Candy across the street. She'd come down to look for me. You wouldn't think that's easy in the middle of Melbourne, but she knew I was on Rohies, so she knew I wouldn't go far.

She came over to me. "What are you doing, you idiot?"

"Nothing, I guess."

She knew it wasn't a stroll to take in the sights. "Come home," she said. "You're not going to get any money today. Face it."

I couldn't face it. The thought of absence of money filled me with horror.

She sat down beside me. "You know what I've been thinking?" she asked. "We have to get out of this country."

I sat dejected, my head hung low. She held my hand and continued. "The world is out there, sweetpea. We need an adventure. We deserve an adventure. We've got to stop using. We can do it. We can start today. We can stop using, and save some money, and go overseas. We can be there in a couple of months. Imagine Europe! We can work our way around Europe. We can start today. We really can. We can start right now. Let's go into the post office and get the passport application forms."

Hanging out for heroin, it was hard to believe with any conviction. But we went into the GPO. It was an old building, bluestone and pillars and all that shit. The huge main room was filled with the Friday afternoon bustle. Lines led up to the postal tellers at ornate cedar counters.

We waited in line to ask for the forms. A clock chimed 4:45, a deep single ping. Away from the main line, a teller was counting cash.

Maybe it was the lovely color of the twenties that caught my attention through the muted haze of the Rohypnols. But suddenly I realized that I could grab that money, that it could be mine, that it was a heap more than I could get from a bag snatch, and that I could still skedaddle out of the post office and up the alleys and around the corner and home before anybody could catch me.

It was a very thick wad she was counting. She'd fold every ten notes, wrap them in a thin elastic band, then add them to a thicker pile held together by a thicker elastic band. It was clear that the money was mine. I'm sure no one else in the post office was hanging out like Candy and me. It seemed a natural kind of justice, really.

We got the forms and moved away.

"Come over here," I said.

We moved to the bench along the opposite wall, where people could fill out their forms or lick stamps or write addresses.

"That lady. Counting all that money. I'm going to get it."

"What?"

"I'm going to grab it and run home. You go first, go now. When you get to the warehouse, leave the street door ajar."

"You're insane."

"No, no. I'll just reach across the bench. Real quick. She can't stop me. I'll be out the door."

"Listen to me. You're insane. Look at all these people." She swept her arm across the room.

"It'll be too quick. No one will have time to react."

"I'm going. I'm not involved. I'm out of here. Don't be an idiot."

She grabbed my arm and pinched hard, trying to pull me toward the door.

"Candy, don't worry." I took her hand away. "I know I can do it. This is just for today. We'll still stop. We're going overseas. I love you, Candy."

What the hell happens in our childhood, all that TV? I

was Tarzan, off to hunt down some food for Jane. If it wasn't for the way the Rohypnol turned my body to jelly but my spirit to steel, I would have been too nervous to believe I could do this.

But for a mad second I felt powerful.

"Five minutes," I said. "I'll be home with money."

She stared at me. I tried to look earnest. She turned and walked out of the post office. Years later, when someone explained to me that insanity meant repeating the same mistakes and expecting different results, it would be this singular event I would think of—the GPO, a kind of brilliant summary of things—rather than the whole drawn-out and repetitive insanity of addiction itself.

But for now, action stations. I pretended to fill out a money order form. I glanced across the room. The teller was about thirty, a skinny lady with long red hair. She was absorbed in her counting. As I watched, she counted the last of the loose notes, folded them, and inserted them into the thick pile. She opened a drawer and the thick pile disappeared.

She wrote some figures in a ledger, then reached into the drawer and placed on the counter a new pile of loose twenties. It was about an inch thick. A fucking decent whack of busy Friday money. Mine, all mine.

I sauntered across the room. It all seemed so simple in theory. I grab the money, taking her by surprise. I'm out the door before she even screams. People chase me but I'm across the street and into the alleys already. Even the most athletic guy is fifty yards behind me as I round the final corner. I slip out of view into the door that leads up into the warehouse. I slam it shut behind me. I take the stairs six at a time. I fling the warehouse door open. Candy and I hug each other. Candy says, "You're beautiful, I love you." We count the money. I calm down slowly and catch my breath and watch TV and smoke cigarettes and Candy goes off to get the dope. (I have to lie low for a couple of hours.)

But now, despite the brash simplicity, I *was* nervous. I

moved closer to the counter. I was sure I looked casual, innocuous. But when I thought, *Do it now,* my legs wouldn't move. I started counting down.

Okay. In five seconds I'm going to do it. Five—four—three—two—one!

And again my legs wouldn't move.

All right. This time. Five—four—three—two—one!

Nothing.

I looked at the clock on the wall. It was eight minutes to closing.

I sighed. It had to be done. There was no choice. I thought of the spoon, the mixing, the needle sliding into the vein.

Five—four—three—two—one!

I lunged.

By the time I realized how hard it was to move fast, my momentum was carrying me forward and it was too late to stop. I grabbed for the money with both hands.

My fingers clamped on the side of the wad. And hers clamped on her side. What the fuck was she doing? This was not in the script.

She was so strong. I watched in disbelief as our hands did a tug-of-war. She pulled in her direction and I pulled in my direction and our arms rose in the air as we fought over the money.

At the instant she screamed I gave a final almighty tug. But as I pulled hard up and away from her, my fingers squeezed down on the top and the bottom note. The rest of the money exploded in a fountain of color all over me. This was the moment where, had I been able to take stock, I would have realized that normal speed does not occur on Rohypnol. I watched the whole event in slow motion, like I was outside my body.

At the same time, as the notes fluttered around my ears and down over my shoulders, I felt a huge sense of relief, and sadness, that the thing had failed, that it was over now.

I turned my body toward the door. I hadn't even taken a

full step when I was tackled from behind, heavily. I remember feeling thick and slow, but I was grateful for the bulk of my overcoat, just like when Beefboy tackled me. In Sydney, with all that warm weather, these things would probably hurt more.

I resisted. I didn't hit the ground. But in an instant every concerned citizen in the place joined in the show. Citizen's arrest. Citizen's Twister. I was hit from all angles.

I was held tight in armlocks and leg locks and neck locks. My limbs twisted in every direction. At one point I was horizontal to the floor but no part of me was actually touching it.

"All right, all right!" I tried to gurgle. I wasn't struggling. They lowered me to the ground. My arms were wrenched behind me. There was a knee in my back. My face was scrunched into the carpet. All I could see were feet. There was a lot of puffing and panting.

The Rohypnol was really kicking in. I just wanted to go to sleep. There was a bit of a commotion about "call the police" and "I'll get security." It all seemed so normal now.

Two security guards came. The other men reluctantly dispersed and the guards pulled me to my feet. The whole fucking room had gone silent and everyone was looking at me. The guards held my arms really tight. I didn't have to move my legs too hard to walk. They marched me across the vast room to the staff door beside the counter. The customers parted before us. I felt like I was a camera and they were the extras, told by the director to stare intently but move aside. I was a camera. What a nice thing that would be.

I was led into an office in the bowels of the building. They shoved me into a chair. One of the guards remained at the door.

The police came. They took one look at me and laughed.

"You look pretty pathetic," the fat one said.

I shrugged. I was full of regret. I was not happy to see them.

"Can we trust you without handcuffs?" the fat one asked.

"Of course you can," I said. "I'm not going anywhere in a hurry."

"Cuff him," he said.

I walked handcuffed and flanked through the Bourke Street Mall to the paddy wagon, and the camera thing happened again. I would do the same myself, I guess. Stare, I mean. I love a good drama. But I didn't feel good about being Moses like that.

We went back to the station. They didn't see me as any great threat to civilization. They were even kind enough to call it attempted theft rather than theft, since I assured them, and quite rightly, that the money was never fully in my hands.

They bailed me on my own recognizance. I didn't know what the word meant, until the fat cop said, "It means you don't have to pay any bail, which is good, because we know you haven't got any and we can't stand the sight of you." They gave me a date to appear in court. Really, the climax was the money shower. The rest was just paperwork. It took me about four hours to get out of there. By that time even the Rohypnol wasn't doing me any favors.

I walked through the freezing dark city, back to the warehouse. The door swung open as I trudged up the old wooden stairs. I guess at least I felt like half a man. I mean, I'd tried. But now I was seriously sick; that seemed to be the important thing.

Candy was there, really worried, and O'Brien was over too. She'd called him in a panic when I hadn't shown after a couple of hours.

"You fucking idiot," she said, and hugged me.

"I don't want to talk about it," I said.

I collapsed onto the couch.

"O'Brien is going to lend us a couple of hundred. He had a good win at the races."

Getting arrested was a hassle, of course, but at that moment

I felt the purest thrill go through my shoulder blades. I sighed and smiled.

"You're a good friend, O'Brien," I said. "This is really good of you."

"It's nothing," he said.

"I'm serious. I've had a fucker of an afternoon. This is good. If you were a girl I'd say I love you."

O'Brien laughed.

I knew the dope was coming now, to wash away the GPO, so you really could say that love, just then, was the closest thing to what I felt for O'Brien.

But even O'Brien was concerned about us.

"You guys should give up," he suggested.

"We're going to, soon," I said. Or maybe Candy said it. "We're going overseas, you know?"

DRYING OUT

It took me a long time to realize that home detox, like home-delivered food, is not the best way to do things. But of course, mostly you just learn things the hard way. There was an awful long time when I was naive. Candy too, I guess, and everyone else using in our frantic little world, which we thought was the only world there was. A black naiveté.

The problem with home detox was that it felt a little informal. This made the rules loose. You could break loose rules. What would start with the best intentions would drift into that gray area where sickness overrides everything. And there we'd go again, off and running and trying to ignore the hard fact of another failed attempt at coming down.

A few months down the track, we'd do it all again, try and stop. And each time, the using in between became more fierce, more intense. Each time, our dedication grew: use well. Avoid detoxing. Detoxing is bad. Detoxing is more unpleasant than almost anything, and anyway, detoxing doesn't work. You always use in the end.

But then there'd be a bust or a drought or a rip-off or some evil event that would interfere with the flow of things. We'd go through the horror and panic of not having dope for twelve or twenty-four hours, and this would give us some kind of startling glimpse into the precarious nature of our dependence.

After such times, after we finally got some dope and could relax and act like—feel like—we loved each other, the bravado would course through our veins and we'd make our heroic plans to stop.

The real horror was that sometimes we'd actually commence these plans.

We were living in Port Melbourne now. Long since evicted from the warehouse. After one miserable midwinter stretch, we decided to aim for a Thursday afternoon start to a new home detox program. We stocked up on pills, a little something for every occasion—I'm talking sedation here—and the cheapest palatable alcohol short of metho that we could find, which was a few flagons of four-dollar port.

Not for the first time, Candy said, "This one's gotta be it."

We knew it would be a bad, hard stretch of a week.

On Thursday morning we had the last of our dope. We bundled up and went for a slow ramble down around the bay, where the empty factories gave way to windswept vacant fields, and the rusty cargo ships left on their long haul across the water to Tasmania.

Even though we were stoned, our guts were churning with sadness and fear. Mostly fear, which lots of heroin will turn into sadness, which feels like a vague nausea. It's like how purple and green will make brown. We were scared; the thought of not having dope would make anyone scared.

We walked along past the old seamen's mission, a derelict building we'd once broken into in search of furniture. The dirty beach began to peter out and we walked around the point through a field of industrial rubble. We sat on a rock with our backs to the city and looked across the oily water to the distant power plants at Altona.

We were tired as well as sad and scared. I guess we were able to feel our tiredness because, having planned to detox, we didn't have to run around and do the things we usually had to do, all the hard work that goes into maintaining supply. All that was going to stop this afternoon.

We sat on the rock and we were silent for a long while. I was remembering another time, a better time, on a day like this. It seemed like a lifetime ago, when we'd first moved to Melbourne. We were really in love and had oodles of hope. The future was a thing that gleamed.

That day we'd walked out along to the end of the rocks past St. Kilda Pier. They were huge black basalt rocks like the one we were sitting on now. It was a winter's day like this one, sunny and windy and weird. We'd sat on a big rock well away from the view of the crowds on the pier and Candy had buried her head in my woolen overcoat and sucked my cock, gently and slowly. A police helicopter flew overhead and tilted to check us out and hovered there for a while. I didn't give a fuck. I felt secure and warm, and as I came I reached my arm high in the air and gave them the finger.

That was all those years ago. Now here we were without radiance. The air seemed brittle and empty, like it was hard to breathe.

"I really think we can do this, Candy," I said.

She reached over and squeezed my hand. She had her knees drawn up and her head buried in them and I knew she was crying. It made me feel awkward and stupid. The only solution I knew to tears and awkwardness was heroin, more of it, lots of it. Without any gaps that would let things in. Maybe this is why it was so hard to stop.

I rubbed my hand along her neck and tried to massage her shoulder blades through her pullover.

"I know it'll be hard," I said. "But I'm sure it's like a bridge, and once we cross it, it'll be okay."

Candy sniffled and looked up and smiled at me, and the hard sun made her pinned pupils all but disappear. It was like looking into a pale blue mist. I felt so unhappy trying to smile back at her. Even heroin couldn't quell the despondence, the foreboding.

I pulled her toward me and she slumped into my arm. Her head lay on my chest and she continued to cry softly.

"Can you describe what's over the other side of the bridge?" she asked.

I stared at a container ship coming around the west side of the bay from the city docks. The ship was connected to a world that could answer the question, How do men build ships? How the fuck do they bother?

"I don't think I can exactly describe it," I said. "But whatever it is, it's a place where things aren't so fucked up all the time. Bad things don't happen so much. And we'll have money. And we'll own lots of nice stuff. And we can have a baby and this time he'll live. And we can get back to loving each other properly, without all this bullshit in between."

My mind was drifting into the unfamiliar territory of hope.

"Across the bridge I guess it's greener, and more peaceful. And we'll have good friends and we'll know who they are."

"No cops," Candy mumbled through her tears.

"No cops. If the cops come to the door, I'll say, 'What do you want? What the fuck is your problem?' Cops can't push us around across that bridge. Cops can't come into our house and treat us like shit. Maybe you could do some drawing, painting, paint nice things. Maybe we'll live in the country, grow vegetables, feed the chickens.

"Or maybe we'll go live in Thailand—and not use. Live in an Asian country, nice and cheap, eat great food and chill out for a year or two. Thailand would be great if we didn't use. Or the Kashmir, or the Ivory Coast, or Paris. Or all of them.

"What else? I think we could go canoeing, you know, whitewater rafting, stuff like that, mountain climbing, hang gliding, whatever. It'll be nice to get healthy, sleep well, not have drugs in our system. I'm sure it must feel good."

I felt fucking dreadful, in that everything I felt was dread. A bundle of nerves and need. I stroked her hair in silence for a while. "I love you, Candy."

She was really bawling now. She lifted her head from my chest and her makeup was streaked and her nose was blocked and her lips were quivering. Her shoulders heaved with her sobs, and the words came out in short bursts.

"We really have to do this. We have to do it this time."

"We will, baby, we will. We'll really fuckin' do it this time."

The container ship was now passing where we sat. It was only about a hundred yards away and it seemed huge and silent and empty. A lone seaman waved lazily to us from the foredeck. He probably thought we were happy. It was ridiculous but I waved back. He came from the real world, which we were about to try to enter. I felt obliged to return the gesture.

We sat there for about an hour, which is always long enough to feel the heroin begin to fade. The downhill slide, when it starts to creep away from you, and you wind up tight like a coil as the need for action and money grows. Not today. But I was winding up tight with a different kind of nervousness and anticipation. Detox. Dry out. Motherfucker. Motherfucker. Bonebreaker.

"I suppose we should start getting back," I said. I wanted to get home and get comfortable a few hours before the early stages of the misery began.

We trudged through Port Melbourne and spent most of the last of our money on a carton of cigarettes and some chocolate bars and cookies. We knew we wouldn't be able to eat much more than sugar over the next few days.

By three o'clock a bitter wind was howling down Heath Street, and it was pretty much time for another shot and we weren't about to have one. The pits of our stomachs were laden with gloom, and underneath the gloom was a ferocious panic wanting to burst out.

It was time for secondary medication.

We lugged the TV upstairs and set it up on a table at the end of the bed. We had ashtrays and water and cookies, and talcum powder for when we began to sweat. We poured some port, and downed three Valium each.

The children's programs had started on TV. I couldn't stomach that so I propped myself up on some pillows and tried to read a book while I could still concentrate. I drank a few glasses of the port, and after twenty minutes or half an hour the Valium were beginning to come on and I was feeling wobbly and even a little comfortable. The heroin hadn't completely gone away yet.

The first hours drifted on. The day turned dark and we watched the news and occasionally Candy read me a clue from the crossword. We watched a couple of lame American sitcoms. We were a little drunk, but it was not so much the surplus of alcohol as the absence of narcotics that was beginning to invade our minds.

At eight-thirty Alfred Hitchcock's *The Birds* came on. The cars were cool and it was kind of creepy. Apt too. I began to think it was hysterical rats rather than seagulls that were starting to screech and peck at me and Candy.

Dealing with the commercial breaks was hard without heroin, but all in all I liked the way a half-decent movie could make a couple of hours go by a touch faster. Or more to the point, a fraction less slowly.

We had to be careful with our pills, save them for when we would really need them, in a day or two. But at the same time we liked to set up that psychological buffer zone where you overload in case there's a bad patch ahead. Anyway, the port was blurring our judgment a bit. We took two more Valium each at about eleven.

The midnight movie was *A Hill in Korea*, starring Stanley Baker. I was really drunk and pilled by now and I was drifting into restless five-minute fragments of sleep. I wanted to continue this trend and get some sleep the first night, and

I figured a blackout would be the best way to go. We skolled two more glasses of port each and turned off the TV just as the Koreans were shelling the shit out of the temple where the Brits were holed up.

It worked. I slept for five hours. The first night was over. I woke at six to a hideous Friday. The room was cold and my bones ached. My bladder was full and my mouth was dry. My head was thick and fuzzy. The first thing I thought about when I opened my eyes was heroin. That was normal, but usually I had some, or some coming, one way or another.

I knew that only heroin would bring me to a bearable state of consciousness. I thought if I didn't move I would hurt less. I lay there for an hour, willing myself to go back to sleep. But all I got were bad waking dreams flitting behind my eyes.

Candy was starting to breathe shallowly beside me and I knew that soon she'd wake and join me in the day's misery. She rolled over toward me and her face looked unattractive and swollen.

I went downstairs and out the back to piss. We got the house for cheap rent because it only had an outside toilet. My breath made steam in the air. Willy, the alley cat who'd recently adopted us, followed me out, and as I stood pissing she arched her back and rubbed her flanks in and out against my shins in a figure eight. My feet were like ice and it was nice to have the warmth of her fur down there.

In the kitchen I opened a tin and dished out some cat food in Willy's bowl. The smell of it caught me as I leaned down. Cat food. What is that stuff? I retched once, stumbled over to the sink and vomited over the dirty dishes. I leaned with my head on the metal edge of the sink and panted, watching my saliva fall to the floor.

I ran the tap and tried to shuffle the dishes around and get my spew down the sink hole. It wasn't working so I had to take them all out and rinse them one at a time, stacking them on the counter. When I finished, the sink was clear and

I vomited again, and this time it was easy to run it down the drain.

Candy was awake, lying in bed smoking a cigarette. Big black saucer pupils, like I hadn't seen in a while.

"How are you?" she asked. It was clearly a rhetorical question. I answered it anyway.

"Fucked. I just vomited."

"This is bad," she said, overstating the obvious. "This is gonna be fucking awful."

"We'll be all right, Candy," I said. "Let's have some Doloxene and Serepax."

We wolfed down a mouthful of pills. Our skin was starting to crawl so we tried to arrange the sheets and blankets in such a way that we didn't touch each other. It was a bad time for TV, of course. No one should ever have to be awake between six and nine in the morning, unless *Ren and Stimpy* is on. We lay there as the day picked up and the wind began to rattle the windows.

I couldn't get back to sleep. The pills made me groggy but there was a gnawing hole in my stomach. I tried to read but my eyes were beginning to sting and water. I drank a couple of mouthfuls of water and ate a Chocolate Weston cookie. It tasted like cardboard. Mostly I stared at the ceiling, willing the day to speed up and go away.

All this happened in a state of personal pain. I guess it was a similar morning for Candy too.

We tossed and turned in bed as our body temperatures fluctuated wildly. One moment Candy would be buried beneath the blankets shivering uncontrollably, and I'd fling the sheets away and lie there sweating and panting. Five minutes later our roles would be reversed. Every minute seemed like an hour.

At ten-thirty A.M. the American soaps began and we tried to allow them to distract us. It was hard going. Everything was becoming so extremely uncomfortable that it was hard to stare at any one thing for very long, even a TV. Most of all my hands were uncomfortable. My fingertips felt like they were going to burst. I tried to shake them, to get the demons out, but everything was uncoordinated and my arms and hands just went limp.

By midday we were starting to sweat pretty much all of the time. This is when the real tricky stuff began, because we knew we still had a few bad days to go and it was important to keep the sheets as dry as possible. The sweat would come quickly, with a hot flush down the body. It was like wearing a thin layer of slime. A while later your temperature would change and the sweat would turn cold and really fuck you about. It smelled strange too.

Every now and again we'd have to get out of bed, slowly and painfully, and wipe each other down with a towel. We'd wipe off the slime and shower ourselves with talcum powder and sprinkle a little on the mattress where we lay and jump back under the sheets before we froze. Then we'd feel a little warmth and comfort for four or five minutes.

Once or twice during the long delirium of the afternoon I raised myself up from the bed and stared out the window. The street seemed quiet. A workman parked his van. A mother walked by pushing a baby carriage. I found this world perplexing. I sank back down beneath the sheets and tried not to think about anything. But it was now more than twenty-four hours since our last shot. It was hard to focus on anything other than the terrible fact that sat like a stone in our stomachs.

We kept downing pills. They dulled the edges a bit, but by midafternoon the stomach cramps were cutting in. I took a few Brufen to counteract this but I knew from past experience that there was nothing for it but to weather the cramps for a couple more days at least.

The nicest thing in the world would have been a back massage, but we both knew that neither of us could possibly have done that for the other. My joints ached, my bones ached, my muscles ached. There was nowhere that did not ache. My muscles throbbed too, like my head, which was finally following the rest of my body into the pain zone. My skin itched and I was never comfortable, not for a minute.

We tried not to talk about heroin. Lack of. Like water circling toward a drain, this was the natural place the conversation would go. We had to battle against that flow. Say positive things instead.

"Ohh Jesus," I moaned. "This is fucked. This is major league fucked." I rolled over and lifted myself up on an elbow. "Listen, Candy. You know, if we do this properly, we only have to do it once."

"What time is it?" she asked feebly.

"A quarter past three."

"Friday?"

"Friday."

"How much longer? I can't stand it."

"The worst'll be over soon," I soothed. "Maybe if we can get through tonight, it'll start getting better tomorrow."

Of course it was bullshit. But you had to cling to something on that first full day. The second and the third days, the fourth at a pinch, would be the worst.

By the six o'clock news a bad electricity was coursing through my body. I was stretched tight on an invisible rack, a rack of ugly, distorting force fields. The stomach cramps continued, the headaches became more concrete, more defined, and the diarrhea began. Candy was going through a vomiting stage, over in the corner with a bucket.

We didn't sleep for a second that night, despite all the medication. Our eyes watered and our noses ran and we vomited bile and pissed a fruity piss and shitted something rancid. The only holes not bursting forth with poison and crap were our ears, though it felt to me my brain would explode any minute.

We got through another flagon of the port, and a couple of packets of cookies. The drunkenness helped ease the electric torture a little, although it probably increased the vomiting. We were desperate to sleep, since that would pass the time more quickly than anything else.

We had only four Rohypnols left and we'd wanted to save them for Saturday night or Sunday, as a kind of reentry reward, but we figured we needed them badly now. The heavy artillery of the small-stake pills. They fuzzed the edges some more but did absolutely nothing for the central issues of sleep and pain.

By one or two A.M. even the good stuff on TV was unwatchable, but we left it on for the mild distraction it could offer. A kind of background radiation.

It must have been around three A.M. that we began masturbating in the hope of bringing on relief from the tension. Living on heroin was like drifting through endless savannas of superspiritual comfort. Coming off it, your body became acutely physical. So it was easy to masturbate.

There was nothing sensual about it, nor was it about sex. To touch each other in any way would have been merely to increase our physical discomfort and distress. It was about release and the desire for oblivion. Masturbation was a pathetic substitute for smack.

But it was easy to come. We were like two chimpanzees on amphetamines.

"I'm going to masturbate," Candy said.

"Sounds like a good idea," I said.

She wet the tips of her fingers and spread her legs beneath the sheets and put her hand down there. I started stroking my dick and it got hard in ten seconds. I rubbed my hand across my stomach to wet it with the slimy sweat and used that as lubrication. Candy's legs shot out straight and she clenched her teeth and went *"ffff, ffff"* and was still for a second before her body relaxed.

I only had to pull up and down about five times and my body began to tingle and I came. It was a little painful, like something that tickled too much, but I guess it was the nicest expulsion of fluid I'd experienced in a while. We came at the same time, almost. Tremendous fucking effort! I turned the sound down on the TV and we lay as still as possible and closed our eyes and waited for sleep to come on.

We listened to each other's breathing and it didn't change.

Fifteen minutes later Candy said, "You awake?"

"Yep."

"Fuck it. I still can't sleep."

"Me neither."

A sneezing fit came on, one of those fits unique to the heroin detox, seven in a row, painful and wet and disorienting. It rattled my head around and I was wide-awake again. I blew my nose and groaned. I touched my dick again. It felt possible. I was sure that somehow the microseconds of relief after masturbation would offer the body the chance to slip into sleep.

I started masturbating again, and Candy said, "I think I'll do the same."

We came almost immediately. It was functional and grim. Between three A.M. and dawn we masturbated six or seven times, and none of it got us any closer to sleep. In the end I was coming without even a full erection, and Candy said her cunt hurt because the muscles of her vagina were contracting without anything to contract onto. It was more than we'd come in a year or two. Dawn came like a defeat anyway.

We were in the real horrors by nine A.M. Saturday. Not just the physical stuff, but the very concept of where we were. The night stretched behind us and leaked back into Friday: heroinless. Ahead of us a new stretch, infinite, even worse to contemplate. It wasn't that the idea of a life without heroin was bad. It's just that in the middle of pain it was bad. Because the pain seemed potentially endless. And the antidote to the pain was heroin.

By now the street was filled with the usual Saturday morning buzz of activity. Families and shoppers and all that shit. I couldn't bear to look out the window. The only positive thing was that after a day and a half we were getting marginally more used to the misery. Coping with it better. And we were a day and a half closer to it being over.

On the downside, the hideous pain continued without abatement. If only it would just ease into boredom and a little discomfort. Not yet. We were dehydrated and hungry. We were chain smoking when we weren't vomiting or shitting or sneezing. Everything tasted bad and smelled bad. Our sweat smelled like formaldehyde. Our senses were opening up to the world; the world was clearly an unbeautiful place.

I stumbled downstairs to the kitchen and made up a jug of cordial. I found some Salada cookies and spread them with butter and jam. Willy was there hassling, and I realized she'd been inside for twenty-four hours. I emptied the rest of the tin of cat food into her bowl, this time without vomiting. As I bent to her bowl I noticed she'd laid a huge shit in the corner. I couldn't even think of dealing with it. I'd let it harden for another day or two. I put her and her bowl outside and closed the back door.

I took the food and drink upstairs to Candy, my good deed for the day. She asked me to wipe her down with the towel. The talcum powder and sweat stains formed a brown continent on the sheets. There was nothing but sports or children's crap on the TV.

We ate the cookies and drank the cordial and felt a tiny surge of well-being. This is why they invented public detox units. So you can eat properly and take a few vitamins while you're going through this shit. And get your sheets changed.

In the face of despair it was hard to be positive. I must have had a rush of blood to the head.

"You know," I said, "if we could make the effort to have a shower and change the sheets, we'd feel a lot better afterward."

"Okay," she said. "Well then, you have a shower first, then run a bath for me, then we'll change the sheets, then I'll have a bath."

Under the shower I realized it was a bad idea. It was hard

enough getting down to the bathroom and getting my clothes off in the frigid air. I hadn't allowed for the fact that if everything else felt alien without heroin, so would a shower. The water attacked my hypersensitive skin, tiny malicious darts fucking up the already distorted electrical currents. It was too hot, then too cold.

I tried to let it soothe me. I was sitting down because standing up would have meant fainting. I lay down and put the washcloth over my face. I could hear my labored breathing, and the drumming of the water on the enamel surface of the bath.

Soon the shower had made a hot crop circle on my chest, but my feet were beginning to get cold. Temperature control was out of control. I sat up again and pulled myself tight into a ball, trying to get all of me under the jet of water. I closed my eyes and tried to imagine syringes with wings, floating toward me to lift me away on the feathery air. Then I thought I might start to cry and decided I'd better get out.

I dried myself quickly and turned on the taps for Candy's bath. I looked at myself in the mirror. I looked skinny and pale and distraught and it didn't feel like me. I hated seeing my pupils that big.

It was a cold day and I ran back inside and upstairs as quickly as was possible in such a weakened state. I rifled through the drawers and pulled out a completely new—that is, dirty but dry—set of sweatpants and T-shirt and sweater.

"It's worth it," I said breathlessly. I was hot and weak. One more monumental task to go.

We ripped the covers off the bed and changed the sheets, breathing hard and flopping everywhere. We turned the blankets and the quilt upside down, sweaty sides away from us. I fell into bed and Candy went downstairs to have a bath.

It gave us a good hour or so, not much more. By the time it started raining and the day turned dark at four in the afternoon, both of us were lying crumpled and panting in a pool of muddy sweat and talc.

We'd taken far too many pills. Our second sleepless night was coming up and we had no Rohypnol, twelve Valium, six Serepax, six Lomotil, and a handful of seemingly useless Doloxene. Poor management skills and poor preplanning. We would have to be really careful.

Candy had to run downstairs and shit, and on the way back she made four pieces of toast. That would do us for dinner. We watched the Saturday night news, which was mostly sports, and took two Valium each. We tried to ignore the TV and sleep. We were delirious. Short of heroin, either sleep or death would have been good. Of course it was a forlorn hope.

We drifted through a half-arsed attempt at continuing the crossword. The Saturday night movie was *Song of Bernadette*, starring Jennifer Jones. It was another apt movie because it was all about Saint Bernadette having these visions of the Virgin Mary, and we were beginning to hallucinate too. The walls were wobbling and Bernadette was saying weird things and after a while I just lay back and stared at the patterns forming and shifting on the ceiling. It was not really pleasant to see the ceiling mutate like that but it was easier than concentrating on the movie.

Saturday night was a repeat of Friday night. In no particular order, we masturbated, sneezed, blew our noses, sweated, shitted, pissed. And lay awake. There was a late movie, *The Outlaw Josey Wales,* with Clint Eastwood, and I couldn't wrap my head around that one either. We watched it without interest. Every cell in my body was sending messages to my brain that something was lacking, big-time.

After midnight it was all crap on all stations, *The Six Million Dollar Man,* soft cock rock on the music video show, stuff like that. Stuff that might have been bearable, even funny, in my normal life, my real life, back on heroin. Back on heroin. That sounded good.

The least pathetic thing was tennis, live from somewhere around the fucked-up globe, and it would be running till five A.M. There was something comforting about its hypnotic blandness. I watched a couple of sets after each bout of frantic masturbation or diarrhea. It seemed to pass the time, though it's not something I'd ever watch under any other circumstances.

At some point toward dawn I must have fallen into a short, troubled sleep, because all of a sudden a noise jolted me upright and *The Big Valley* was on and Candy was hunched in the corner where she'd been vomiting into the bucket. She was rocking back and forth and bawling her eyes out.

"What is it, baby?"

Given our circumstances, it was a supremely stupid question.

Candy continued to rock and cry. I thought she must have been freezing in the corner like that.

I jumped out of bed and promptly fell over. I pulled myself over to Candy and cradled her in my arms. I stroked her hair.

"What is it, baby, what's the matter?" I had a real limited repertoire when it came to dealing with emotional situations.

"I can't do it, I can't do it, I can't do it . . ." She went on bawling this for a minute or two. I was thinking, I'm with you, baby, I'm with you all the way. I can't do it either. How can we get some smack? I should have said, "We can do it, we can do it," but instead I said, "It's all right, it's all right," which is not the same thing.

"Come back to bed. You'll catch a cold." Incredible the things we say. I put her back under the covers and lay wiping the tears away from her face. I hated seeing Candy crying. Was all this worth it, this detoxing bullshit? Maybe we could just not use *so much* hammer. That was it! Starting today, turn over a new leaf. Avoid this kind of pain, get it under control.

It was Sunday morning, six A.M. We hadn't had a shot for sixty-seven hours. I was angry about the bullshit on TV and angry about the fucked world and angry about why drugs were a problem. I was angry and upset that Candy was crying. It was totally fucking unnecessary. I had no idea what to do with my anger. All I knew was that I felt, or everything felt, fucked and hopeless. So I lay there stroking Candy and saying it's okay it's okay it's okay.

Then all that was on were the religious programs. Some pedophile Yank with a southern accent was saying, "If you will but surrender to Jaysus." Fuck you, Jack. I slammed the off button on the TV and the room seemed to hum with a terrible starkness.

It was probably at that moment that I decided I would use hammer that day, whatever it took. Candy too, I guess. She kept saying, "I can't do this," and after a while I had to believe her.

We lay in misery until about nine and then turned the TV back on to watch some cartoons. The bullshit began, slowly at first, but soon enough fast enough. We started talking about how well we'd done and how using now after nearly getting over the hump wouldn't really be failure, as such, and how nice a taste would be and how the hell could we get some?

We had no money. That was a part of the plan. Now that the plan had changed, having no money was a bit of a problem. But it was something that had never gotten in our way before.

Still, it was Sunday, a bad day under any circumstances. There wasn't much book stealing and selling I could do. Candy couldn't do a trick sick like this. I didn't have any stolen credit cards. We'd told all our friends we were stopping, so they'd dropped us like hotcakes. We weren't expecting any visitors, no smack Santa Claus.

But now that we'd decided we wanted to use, all the despair left us and the day took on an edge of frantic desperation, even enthusiasm. What we did in the end was very simple. We started calling our dealers and telling them the truth. There were five to call and we were sure someone would have a heart.

On the second call Lester said, "All right, I'll give youse a hundred on tick." Candy promised that by getting the dope she would get well enough to go do a shift at the Carolina Club and pay him back by Monday morning. Lester knew that no one fucked with him, so I guess it was easy for him to say yes.

Suddenly we had energy. We jumped out of bed and dressed ourselves and I ran my fingers through my hair to make it neat and Candy brushed her hair and put some makeup on.

We were so fucking excited. The world was okay after all.

We jumped in the car and flew across the Westgate Bridge and got the dope off Lester and kissed his arse, his fat ugly wife's arse, and the very ground he walked on. Lester was a cunt, one of the greatest cunts in the Melbourne heroin scene. Today Lester was Jesus and Buddha rolled into one.

But you couldn't hit up at the Buddha's house.

My stomach was rumbling in anticipation. My saliva kept rising and I tried to swallow it and then I dry-retched once or twice. I needed to fart but I knew I would probably shit my pants. Eleven A.M., Sunday morning. It was exactly three days now. Seventy-two hours, an inconceivably long time.

I held the fart in and we drove a suburb away from Lester's place. The suburbs out here were neat and ugly and I knew that any minute now they'd turn beautiful, or invisible, which is the same thing. The way hammer makes things stop intruding.

Candy stopped the car in a quiet street and I found an old Coke bottle on the floor of the car and went into someone's front yard and filled it with water from their hose. We mixed up on the armrest between us and God was good and I found a vein quickly, trembling hands and all, and Candy did too.

I know how the farmers must feel when the rain finally comes.

Big hammer, God hammer, sky hammer, sledgehammer. I was knocked flying back into the seat, it seemed. I loosened the tourniquet, my head went wham into the headrest. The molecules of the vinyl welcomed, I mean profoundly welcomed, the molecules of my body.

"Oh fuck. Oh fuck." Just like coming.

Candy groaned. It was joy from our toes to our wonderful heads. I was surrounded by light. My eyes flickered. Everything in the interior of the car was as it should have been. This was not transport. This was transportation. State-of-the-art fucking humdinger drug, none before and none since. I would murder for this bliss.

I licked my lips and tried to express my delight. It came out croaky, "Hnnnnn," long and slow and easy. All the pills we'd been taking would have heightened the impact of the hammer. We were probably teetering close to overdose. That was the loveliest high wire there was.

A persistent noise was bugging me a bit. I opened my eyes. Candy had slumped forward onto the steering wheel and her forehead was pressing the horn. It jolted me back into the world. This was not the place to nod off.

"Candy!" I pulled her off the wheel.

"Huh? What? What?" The usual shit. "I'm okay."

"Let's go. Let's drive," I said.

A big Greek family, maybe Italian, had gathered in the driveway beside us. They were getting into their car but they were looking at us with consternation. They were all in their Sunday best and the daughter was wearing a frilly white First Communion dress.

"I don't think they liked the look of us," I said as we drove away. They stood there watching us go.

"They love us." Candy laughed. "They fucking love us."

We drove through Footscray and back toward the bridge and talked about how good we felt.

"I'm going to earn heaps tonight," Candy said. "I've got a real strong feeling about it. It's in my bones."

"It's in the cards!"

I laughed, glad that she seemed so keen about the matter and knowing that money meant dope.

"It's in the stars!"

Candy was laughing too.

"It's carved in stone!" I said. "Big money for Candy!"

"And we'll never run out again!" she said. "Fuck, it's good to be stoned. Now, let's get some food. I'm absolutely starving. We'll steal something from the 7-Eleven."

TRUTH 3: KISSES

Late at night I think that if I could write a list of the things I like, I could somehow write my way out of the mess I'm in. I don't know how this works or even how it occurs to me that it might work. How the fuck could it work? Write a list. It's a bizarre thought. But what would I write? I like reading. I like movies, especially in the early hours, when the rest of the city is sleeping. I like the American football on TV, strange and beautiful sport from another planet. I like Candy, Candy's warmth, Candy's pussy, Candy's eyes, breasts, sense of humor, attitude, legs, voice, laugh . . . I like a lot of things about Candy. I like sex. The list I'm trying to write should not include the statement I like heroin, because that won't help. I sit for a while in silence but the list sort of peters out at this point and my mind begins to wander. I try to concentrate and bring it back to the list but it's hard to think of things. Travel books. I like travel books. Then I give up. I think, Maybe there's a lot of things waiting to be liked, and right now I don't know what they are, but surely they'll be good. Surely, in fact, goodness and mercy will follow us all the days of our lives.

Will I ever stop using?

The list-writing thing never really gets off the ground. Other times I try to tell myself I must accept certain private inevitabilities. I will live a life of continual deep fatigue, for example. I will carry in me, like a poison, like a virus, rancor for most things, and while this condition will not improve, nonetheless I will learn to live with my rancor as if it were a minor irritation. There will be many achievable things that I will not do and then there will come a time when I realize they are no longer even achievable.

Other things seem to be awkward truths rather than inevitabilities. It occurs to me that what I lack in balance I make up for in my familiarity with fear and unease and occasionally despair; and that this itself is a kind of balance. One truth comes to me strangely, out of the blue. It's around two A.M. *one night and Kubrick's* The Killing *ends and* The Wicker Man, *with Edward Woodward, is about to come on, but first there are a couple of cheap ads. For no reason I can think of, the thought comes to me that the outlook of my life is narrowing, that things are closing off. I don't think this truth but I feel it, sourly, in my stomach, and it's as if my breath has been taken away from me, as when a roller coaster begins its plummet. Whoosh. The outlook is undeniably narrowing. The horizon is shrinking. It's hard to swallow, and my heart starts to pound.*

Then again, though I can hardly speak for others, maybe it's also true to say that everybody's lives are narrowing, one way or another. If that's the case, why even bother to try stopping? Certain flashes of clarity come when it seems better instead to stop trying.

But it's best not to trust clarity. Better to welcome and accept the mist that seeps into our life, that clings to our clothes, that soaks us to the bone in this scrapyard we are lost in. The mist.

And where does the idea of suicide come from? If the options are using or stopping using, and you know you can't stop, that's where suicide comes from.

Of course there's despair, when things fuck up and you want to be dead, but that's just circumstantial. That's just bad feeling brought on by the adrenaline of events, by violence or rip-off or arrest. Bad feeling of the imminent absence of heroin. Absence looms like a mountain, I tell you.

But it's entirely different, what's been happening sometimes lately. There I am on the couch, in the serene embrace of heroin, the warm breast of the dove of peace, the feathered graze of mindlessness. The TV is on—it's something beautiful and interesting, a documentary, say, maybe David Attenborough and the great sperm whales. Maybe cheetahs chasing down a zebra. Candy is watching too. I light a cigarette. There is nothing wrong with the world and nothing could ever be wrong. And then I feel—bang! just like that—that it would be better to be dead. What the fuck is going on here? Life is a circle and death will make it a line, snap it suddenly away from repetitiveness, fling it out into the void, beyond geometry, where at least there's relief from the friction of things? What the fuck is going on?

I'm staring at the TV and the images blur to abstract pattern, leaving room for memory to enter, entirely uninvited. I'm seven years old and Lex is five. Why is this coming to me? The past is not a foreign country but a book long since returned to the library. Yet the scene comes to me and I am in the middle of it. We are at the river park. Mum sets up the picnic blanket and Lex and I run down to the water. Dad goes off to see the man about renting a canoe.

It's exciting. We are used to the beach, where everything is aerated by salt and southerlies. But the Lane Cove River is dark and silty and smells different from the ocean. We tumble into the shallow edges of the river. We practice tackling underwater, pretending we are stuntmen in slow-motion replays.

Dad calls us out of the water. "Okay, boys, canoe time!"

We sprint to be with him and he holds our hands and the three of us walk around the bend to the boat shed. The attendant lifts me and places me in my own canoe. I sit wobbling on the water as I wait. Then Dad is in his own canoe and the attendant passes Lex on board. Lex sits between Dad's legs. The attendant gives our canoes a small push, and we drift toward the whorls that ripple and elongate in the hard midday sun.

I try to turn to come back around to Dad and Lex but my canoe moves in the wrong direction. Dad demonstrates with his paddle and I quickly learn how to steer and countersteer. Lex is grinning like the cat that licked the cream. His tiny hands clasp the paddle as Dad slices it through the water. It looks comical, as if maybe it's Lex who's pulling the strokes and Dad who's allowing his arms to be moved. We meander on the river for half an hour.

Later on we stuff ourselves silly on all the food Mum's unpacked. Lex and I wander off to explore the bush over behind the barbecue pits. Mum and Dad spread out on the blanket to chat or doze. The air is wet with the droning of bees and the piping of birds. The light swings in on the breeze and the breeze rustles the willows. It's a dappled picnic afternoon.

Then Mum and Dad are packing up.

"What do you say we end the day with an ice cream?" Dad asks.

I've had a little too much sun. My body is hot. At the kiosk the ice cream spreads down through my chest like a cool balm. On the drive home Lex is curled up sleeping with his head on Mum's lap. I spread out on the backseat. I tilt my head and let the trees and telegraph poles speed past upside down. The radio plays low. Hits 'n' Memories. *I hear "Knockin' on Heaven's Door" for the first time and am entranced by its dreamy sadness. It's a joy to arrive home. Dad carries Lex inside and tucks him into bed. I get into my bed, on the other side of the room. The light enters from the hallway.*

"Did you have a good day?" Dad asks.

"Yes, Dad," I say.

"We'll do it again soon," he says.

He strokes my hair and then kisses me on the forehead. "Sleep tight, sunshine," he says.

And I fall into the welcoming night.

The memory ends there. It seems painful to think of something so pleasant and so far away. The documentary ends too. I change the channel on the TV and get into some telemarketing.

For $89.95 (introductory offer) I can improve my memory one hundredfold.

Somewhere the past changed. I don't want it. I don't want the present. There is no conceivable future. There is only the relentlessness of coping, punctuated by naked singularities of bliss. In the middle of such moments contentment is absolute: there is only heroin, there is only Candy, the three of us adrift on the endless sea of love. We carry the ocean within us and with us wherever we go. Suicide is therefore not so much ridiculous as impractical, since Candy and I are immortal.

The next day, a case in point, we're standing on Swanston Street, in the middle of the city, waiting for the St. Kilda tram to arrive. We are stoned, as in very stoned. We are going to St. Kilda to meet Kojak to get more dope for later because we have a couple hundred bucks and why not? The cars glide by in a harmony of pistons, the peak-hour crowd flows around us with the buoyancy of astronauts on the moon.

I look at Candy and we smile for a moment.

"Hey, baby, hug me," I say.

She reaches her arms up around my neck. She nuzzles her face into my ear and nape, all the while kissing me lightly. My left hand holds the small of her back, my right hand caresses her arse. I squeeze it slowly, backward and forward, the way a cat massages a pillow. Candy continues to kiss me all over the neck. With every splay of my palm I try to allow my little finger to wander closer up into her crotch. She arches her feet a little in response. She shifts her body imperceptibly, spreads her legs a fraction, pushes against my finger each time it completes its squeeze cycle. Then I sweep my hand up her back and slide it into the curve where her neck meets her skull. We tilt our heads from side to side and move in and out and kiss each other; contentment is in our very pulse. The kissing is languid and fluid. I close my eyes and sometimes I open them slightly. Candy does the same. Sometimes our eyes open at the same moment. Her long lashes seem to be reaching toward me. Her eyes have moved into a blueness beyond desire since all desire is satisfied.

This is the business. This is what we're after.

A car horn toots and a young guy in the passenger seat leans out and yells, "Go for it!"

We look up and shrug. When the car has passed by, he no longer exists. We go back to kissing for a minute or so. Then the tram arrives and we climb on board and it moves off toward St. Kilda. We sit in the back holding hands and watching the street go by.

FREELANCING

What we had, continually, in the kingdom of momentum, was each other. We had each other, but there was never time to think. Time always hardened into basic units: what we needed to do to get by.

I guess it would be fair to say that Candy was fiery. Fairer still to say she was beautiful and fiery. And when she wanted to make money for heroin—which was basically all the time—she was good at it.

Sometimes she made so much money in brothels that the other girls didn't like her. This is capitalism, you see: product and jealousy. But the fiery side meant that she didn't take shit from the johns. Nor from the brothel bosses. And even the most tolerant boss had to weigh up a girl's beauty with the more unpredictable aspects of her drug addiction.

Candy, who was always thinking of the future, as in later today and tomorrow, had a bad habit of taking the clients' money and then trying to take some more. Sometimes it worked. More and more often she got the sack. The customer is always right.

She was getting tired. I had no experience of what went on in the brothels, so what the fuck would I know? Maybe after a while she just found it harder to play the pretty porn bimbo thing. Easier to nod off, to say, "Give me the money. What do you expect? Special treatment? This is a fucking brothel." But it meant a kind of downward thing, like my petty crime, like our health, and like the drug itself—the way the more you took over the years, the more it seemed to lose its strength.

A downward thing, as in Candy went inexorably from good escort to bad escort, from the ritzy brothels to the cheesy. Always getting the sack for not toeing the line and for being too stoned.

And ended up freelancing it, on Grey Street in St. Kilda. After which there was really no place to go.

If we'd come down to Grey Street by cab, I would loiter in a shadow or sit on a bench and be useless. On the other hand, if we'd managed to borrow a car, off Jesse, say, or if we owned one, which happened once or twice, I would sit in the passenger seat and be useless, while Candy walked the street and got into other cars. Not having a license, I was there, I suppose, for moral support. Some would find my use of the word *moral* a little quaint.

Sometimes odd or funny things happened on Grey Street. Sometimes it was scary, and for a moment you would question what you were doing. More often than not it was boring. Occasionally we made big money hits, but it was not like the glamour days of escort jobs at the Regent. On Grey Street you made good bucks by turnover only: forty-dollar head jobs or sixty-dollar backseat fucks, negotiable. But they could be over in four minutes, and now and then on busy summer nights it almost seemed like the old days again.

I was never really into the idea of sucking dicks myself, so I wouldn't have been much help on the gay beat down around Shakespeare Avenue. But one night we were going home about three in the morning with a pocketful of cash. We stopped off at Fat Nick's café and scored a hundred, just to go to bed with. We were already comfortably stoned, but whenever we had the money we could never really see the need for thrift.

It was a fucking cold night. There weren't many bodies around by now: even the living dead of St. Kilda had called it quits for the night. We were walking back to our car. I crossed the road and a young bloke glanced at me and I knew he was nervous. It was not the heroin contact glance I knew so well, so I guessed it had to be some other subcultural thing. The gay beat. He didn't want drugs. He was a pretty boy. I figured that made me the rough trade.

He was maybe eighteen. All I knew was, it was dumb to ever miss an opportunity. You had to try your luck at least. I swung my head back as we passed.

"How you doing?" I asked.

Candy took the cue, like I had done so often, and kept on walking. Don't ever interfere when the other is operating.

"I'm okay." It was more of a question than a statement.

"Are you looking for something?"

"I . . . um . . ."

He was obviously new to this game. As was I.

"Sex?" I offered.

He seemed relieved. "How much?"

We were standing in the middle of the empty street during this conversation.

"Fifty bucks, blow job," I said.

"Okay," he said quickly.

What had I gotten myself into? I had no intention of giving him a blow job. Though God knows Candy had told me often enough, in moments of anger, that it was what I should be doing, if I was a real man, a breadwinner.

I was pretty sure I wouldn't even *know* how to suck a dick very well. So I was going to have to rip him off. I knew it was a paltry sum, but I just couldn't help myself, and if I could get money in any way, then I saw it as my duty to get it.

"What's your name?" I asked.

"David."

"David!" I laughed.

"What's so funny?" he asked nervously.

"I'm David too!" I lied.

I was developing a plan.

"Listen," I said, "if you want to be comfortable, we can go back to my friend's flat, spend a bit more time." I pointed to Candy down the road. "She's got the car. She's got a spare room. She won't mind. But it'll cost more. A hundred bucks."

"Eighty's all I've got," he said.

"Okay. Eighty bucks. It'll have to do."

We caught up with Candy.

"Maryanne, this is David," I said. "He's coming back for a while, if that's okay."

She smiled broadly. "Hi. How are you?"

We walked to the car. Candy turned to me so David couldn't see and gave me the what-are-you-doing flicker of the eye. I gave her the nearly imperceptible don't-worry-it's-a-good-plan shake of the head in response.

It was all about talking fast. Throw in some ambiguity about the entrance to the block of flats, and we were in with a chance. All I had to do was split me and him from Candy, so he wouldn't know where the car was parked. Then somehow split him from his money. Then split myself from him. And make it all seem smooth.

As we climbed into the car I whispered to Candy, "I told him my name's David."

Candy drove. David One, that's me, was in the front, and David Two sat in the back. I couldn't understand how a smooth-skinned boy like him would need to pay for sex. But that wasn't my mystery to solve. I spoke to him over my shoulder.

"This'll be nice," I said. "We can have a bit of an extended cuddle."

I heard Candy stifle a giggle, turn it into a cough.

I was trying to make him not so nervous. I was in unfamiliar territory. I didn't really know the lingo for gay prostitutes. Maybe I should have said, "I'm going to lick your little jackrabbit till it's hard, I'm going to belt through your ring with my big fuckstick."

We'd moved again—the usual problems with unpaid rent—and were living along the river in a flat on Alexandra Avenue.

"Maryanne, you should turn here and find a parking spot. We'll go around the front and come in that way."

If David thought this was strange, he didn't protest.

"Oh," I added, "is your flatmate home?"

Candy had no idea what I was talking about, and no idea how to answer.

"Um, I'm not sure," she said.

"Hmmm. I hope she's okay about it. Don't worry, David, if there's a problem we'll think of something. The laundry room, maybe. I'll reduce the price. We'll get out here, Maryanne. You park and come around."

I left my cigarettes on the dashboard. David and I got out of the car. We walked a few steps. Then I slapped my forehead and said, "Cigarettes." I opened the door and leaned in and got them. I whispered to Candy, "Back path." Then I knew she knew the plan.

There was another street nearby, a dead end. Halfway along the dead end was a rock path that led between two blocks of flats to the back of our block. Candy would park and go that way.

I walked around the front with David.

"Right, it's up there." I pointed. "I'll just go in and check this flatmate situation. When you see the light go on in that window, come up. It's number nineteen. First give us your money. I don't want to get ripped off."

"What?"

He stiffened with caution. He seemed a little surprised by this.

"Listen, David," I said, trying to sound reasonable, trying to create a character who was basically nice, with just a hint of threat thrown in. "Listen. You have to show some good faith. You could just run away, change your mind. That would really fuck my night around. This is business. This is give-and-take. I'm trusting you in my friend's flat. You have to trust me with your money for thirty seconds. I can't go anywhere. There's only one entrance. You'll see the light come on."

I'd talked fast enough. Reluctantly, he pulled out his wallet and handed me the eighty bucks.

"Back in a jiff."

I sprinted up the stairs and went in through the front entrance. Then I went straight out through the laundry exit and up the back stairs. Candy was waiting for me on the landing. We crept giggling into the flat, number thirty-six.

"Better leave the lights off, I think," Candy whispered.

We stumbled around in the dark, keeping our heads low and away from the window. We mixed up Fat Nick's hundred in a shaft of light from the streetlight, and banged up a nice blast. Candy crawled down the hallway to run a bath.

I sidled along the wall toward the front window, making sure I stayed in shadow. When I finally leaned forward enough to take a peek down at the street, I was a little saddened by the sight. I may have even felt a twinge of guilt, I'm not sure.

It was four in the morning and David was standing in the cone of light cast down by a streetlight. He was staring up at the block of flats. I could imagine how dark and imposing it must have looked. He'd spent ten minutes waiting for a light to come on. I guess now he was waiting with a rapidly decreasing sense of hope. Not a car slid by on Alexandra Avenue. Behind him the Yarra flowed silently by, hidden in a thick mist.

I stood in the blackness, fascinated for a moment by his pain. Finally he clenched his fists and pounded the air twice, as a child might bang a knife and fork on the table. I saw his mouth say, "Shit!" and he stamped his right foot on the ground. He looked around him, and he looked up one more time. Then he walked away. The cone of light was empty.

We didn't turn the lights on, just in case. Our eyes adjusted. We had a bath together, and kept adding hot water until dawn. The thing I liked most in the vague suggestion of silver light was soaping Candy's breasts, in slow trancelike circles.

"That was cruel," Candy said.

"I know," I said. "I shouldn't have done it."

But what we *really* knew was that we'd both just warded off the demons, by another eighty bucks, and you had to do that if you could. We'd bought the hundred from Fat Nick, and then David came up, an opportunity. So really the hit we'd just had, Fat Nick's hit, only cost us twenty bucks. In theory.

It made it feel special. We would go to bed soon. When we woke up we'd be that much further in front. There was no point in getting lazy. Every dollar counted, always. And David would have gotten home all right, I'm sure, and been more careful, more suspicious, next time.

Not all the nights on Grey Street were good.

Soon after the David episode there was one of those nights when everything went wrong. Candy made some money early and we scored and the dope wasn't great. That didn't seem too dire, though. It was only midnight. Then the weather cut in, serious Melbourne midwinter rain, and in half an hour the cars cruising by had all but disappeared.

I sat in the car—Jesse's car again, borrowed for the thousandth time—and Candy did the forlorn walk up and down the street. Finally a BMW slowed and she got in for the discussion. Normally at this point they would take off, and I would expect to see her back in five minutes or half an hour. Great fucking security system.

This time she climbed from the BMW and came over to me. She got inside the car.

"This guy could be interesting. I'm not sure. He reckons

he's connected to the clubs. Says he can pay me in smack. Says it's good gear too. Pink rocks. Lots of it. But he can't pay me until after two. He's got to get the dope from the Shangri La Club at two."

"What? And we go with him?"

"Yeah, I guess."

"What do you think? Is he straight up?" I was having visions of a new dealer, a step up, a BMW schmooze with the uncut rocks.

"I don't know. I think he's okay." It was funny how wishful thinking could turn into fact if you were desperate enough. I suppose that's what had happened to David.

"So what are you going to do?"

"We'll take him back to the flat," Candy said. "I'll drive this, you'll have to go with him, show him the way. Fuck I wish you could drive. Then afterward we'll go and get paid at the Shangri La."

Candy introduced us and I got into his car. I had no wish to make conversation. He seemed pretty quiet too. He was dark-haired, burly, clean-shaven, nondescript. There was something tense about him that I didn't like. Maybe it was just the way he gripped the steering wheel. But I had to forget about that, since he was going to be giving us the gear.

I waited in the lounge room, and turned the TV on, and Candy and Burly went to the bedroom. After a while they came out. It was past three.

We drove back to St. Kilda the same way, me in the BMW like a standover weed. But this time he put his foot to the floor and we really took off. Candy couldn't keep up in the old Holden. This guy was flying. I gripped my seat.

"Ah . . . you better slow down for her," I suggested, motioning toward the back window with my thumb.

"She knows where we're going."

I thought we'd roll, or crash. It was wet out there. My brain wasn't going too fast. I couldn't work out why he was doing this. I needed the money or the pink rocks but I wanted to get out of the car.

I had a feeling that I hadn't had in a long time. I was scared shitless, and it felt physical. He was getting up to 160 K's in short suburban streets.

"Could you slow down just a little, mate?" My voice sounded high-pitched and silly.

He didn't answer and he didn't slow down. I looked across. All I could see was the clench of his jaws, and I knew then that he was crazy, one way or another. A different way from me and Candy. Speed psychosis? But he looked so straight. Steroid meltdown? Nonspecific fury? The streets flashed by. My whole life didn't pass before me, but I got a kind of edited slide show. The car was taking sharp bends on two wheels only. At one point the back tires fishtailed. I thought, This is related to my heroin addiction. Definitely. I would not be in this car for any other reason.

We came over a rise and left the ground for a second. Then, in a deft display of precision braking, he drew up sharp outside a police station. The engine was still running. He reached under the seat and pulled out a gun. It was silver. It looked heavy. My heart seemed to go quiet. He just flopped his hand toward me, so that the barrel of the gun gently prodded my thigh. Then he uttered the first direct words that he'd said to me. I remember they were slow, precise words.

"Get the fuck out of my car. Before I take you in there and arrest you."

My mouth dropped open and I stared at him. His mouth was clenched and he stared back.

I was about to say, "What about the fucking money? What about the dope?" when I realized that, cop or no cop, he was a little bit disturbed. It definitely looked like too much methamphetamine to me: tight jaws, paranoia. He was not in a good mood and he was pressing a gun into my thigh. Sometimes you have to readjust.

So I said, "Right. Okay. Right."

I unclasped my seat belt and got out of the car, uncomfortable with adrenaline, almost in pain.

He left at the same mad speed. I stood there bewildered. Was he still going to the Shangri La Club, to get the hammer or the cash? Maybe he just had something against me. But something wasn't right. I thought about Candy. I had to stop her. I turned around just as she came hurtling along at the best speed the Holden could muster, following the route to the Shangri La.

I lurched out onto the side of the road, waving to get her attention. It was too late. She was hunched forward and worried and didn't notice me through the rain-drenched windshield.

Now it struck me that he could kill her.

I ran through the rain. The Shangri La was about a kilometer away, down along the Lower Esplanade. I had four dollars in my pocket. A cab came past and I hailed it. He dropped me off thirty seconds later at the Upper Esplanade, from where I could look down into the Shangri La parking lot.

As I reached the railing I saw Candy pull in and park. The place was full of cars.

She got out, looking around her for the BMW, uncertain as to where I might be or what to do.

I cupped my hands over my mouth. "Candy! Candy!"

It must have reached her faintly through the rain. She turned and scanned the horizon. I waved my arms in the air.

"Get the fuck out of there! He's got a gun!"

I don't know exactly what words she heard. But she knew. She got out of there.

Twenty minutes later we sat in the car in the parking lot of the Port Melbourne 7-Eleven. The rain had stopped. Now you couldn't see more than a few feet ahead of you in the swirling mist that had replaced it. It was four A.M. There were no more jobs tonight. No more money. No more dope.

We had enough money for cigarettes. We knew that if we even attempted to shoplift on a night like this, we would be caught. Sometimes you just had to accept the limitations of your bad luck runs.

We were shaken up. Candy was crying and my eyes weren't real dry either. I tell you what else, I hated that guy.

"This is bullshit," Candy sputtered between sobs. "Our lives are bullshit. Do you understand that? We have to stop. Do you see what's happening to me?"

She said a lot of stuff like this, and I said I know I know. We will we will.

It was a highly charged scene, with dawn coming on and all those tears and mist and the cold car and no dope. It was never nice to have bad feelings leak. That's why heroin had to be a full-time career. Anyway, we drove home and went to bed feeling fucked. We took some Rohypnol, but it was hard to sleep more than a restless hour or so.

For a while afterward I found it satisfying to try and imagine what ended up happening to the guy in the BMW. I used to imagine he died in a high-speed crash, but that he didn't die right away. It was a country road, maybe, in the middle of the night, and he was all mangled up around a tree. He was upside down and covered in blood and bent out of shape in all the twisted metal. He knew he was dying. It was getting harder to breathe. He screamed for a good long time.

But no one was around, of course. And I wasn't about to help him.

Grey Street was when things were getting real fucking ugly. So it was like a blessing when Casper, an old friend of Candy's, came back from the States. I saw a chance to redeem myself. To pull my weight and supply the dope for a change. If I could only make heroin—and Casper was the key to this—then Candy and I could live like landed gentry, and all the bullshit would disappear from our lives.

COOKING

When we finally convinced Casper to sell us the recipe, I figured we could begin to live in a kind of self-constructed heaven. A heaven on earth forever and ever, for as long as we both should live.

It wasn't easy to get Casper to yield his secrets. I hounded him relentlessly.

"But, Casper, we don't really know the same people. It's not like I'm going to be taking any business away from you."

"You and Candy every day is not business?"

"Come on, man, be a friend. There's plenty more where we came from. Sell us the recipe. I want to be self-sufficient."

Finally he agreed. Casper was a brilliant chemist gone, you might say, slightly awry. He was tall and handsome, urbane, polite, considerate. He had a massive habit and he manufactured his own hammer, extracting the codeine from Panadeine capsules, converting it to morphine and then heroin. He'd just returned from a Fulbright scholarship in the United States, where he completed his doctorate on a new synthesis of tetracycline and related antibiotics. He was back in Melbourne doing some part-time lecturing and tutoring at Melbourne University.

As an undergraduate, he'd fucked around a little making

speed and ecstasy, and once he even cooked up synthetic mescaline for everyone. Now, with a more sophisticated problem that he'd fine-tuned in New York, he wasn't about to mess around with kids' stuff. He'd gone back through the journals and sourced some of the original papers on the synthesis of codeine and morphine, particularly Gates's 1954 morphine paper.

He was a bona fide fucking genius. Casper read this shit and he worked it out in his head in ten minutes. He was pretty private, of course, so it was lucky that Candy knew him from the old days. He wouldn't see many people. Didn't need to.

Casper had the best smack in Melbourne, no doubt about that. This was not a backyard home bake with bad equipment and inadequate chemicals. Casper became number one on our list. But as a heroin dealer, he was awful, because he was so comfortable, and therefore unreliable.

I knew the story, the terrible vicious circle. When you've got dope, why worry about someone else's pain? But when you're in pain, you wonder how a dealer could not understand. Of course, we got used to taking the shit with the sugar, but it was frustrating sometimes, knowing that Casper was probably on the nod at his place three suburbs away, with all that Yellow Jesus in a jar. The midday movie meandering through his brain and his mum cooking him lunch.

After I'd begged and groveled every day for about three months, he relented and sold me the recipe. Five hundred bucks, which included three lessons and the contents of those three cooks. I had to get the lab equipment and the chemicals myself, from supply companies in the outer suburbs. I got a basic starter's kit together for less than seven hundred bucks, money I begged and borrowed from friends keen to taste the fruits of my industry. I paid Casper the five hundred in installments, after I sold some of the batch from each lesson.

At first it was shaky. I knew nothing about chemistry, and

could only follow Casper's written recipe to the letter. I didn't know how to adapt to unusual situations, to changes in color that Casper hadn't predicted. Gradually, though, through trial and error, I began to get a clearer idea of what I was doing. Within a few months I was doing all right. I was getting better all the time. I even began to enjoy the process.

I thought of myself as the scientist in the cartoon *Milton the Monster*, which I'd watched as a kid. I still had the theme song in my head, and sometimes, laughing, I'd sing it to Candy as I cooked:

"Six drops of Essence of Terror,
Five drops of Sinister Sauce."
"When the stirring's done
May I lick the spoon?"
"Of course! A-ha! Of course!"

What was best about the whole situation was that finally, after all the trials and tribulations, I was supplying the dope, controlling the means of production, as I'd always hoped I one day would. Candy didn't need to work anymore, except in emergencies. Things felt smooth, and why wouldn't they when you always had dope? The occasional desperate need to try and dry out seemed to have faded into the distant but harrowing past. I felt we'd begun a new chapter in our lives.

Suddenly everyone wanted to see us, but we didn't need to see many people to keep the show running. Just enough cash to keep things turning over. It may not exactly have been a perpetual-motion machine, and we may well still have been mice running in a wheel, but suddenly, for a while, the wheel seemed a whole lot bigger. Breathing space—as well as pure heroin—was what it was about.

It was nice to have a bit of cash. It was nice to have food in the fridge. It was really nice to go to bed and know that you had a blast to wake up to in the morning. It was good not to have to hustle so much every day, though buying such large quantities of Panadeine wasn't easy and involved some real logistics; most pharmacies wouldn't let you buy more than one or two packets, though of course we got to know, love, and frequent the ones whose concepts of professional ethics were conveniently loose. But everything was better than before. These were calmer routines than the routines of the street.

There is certainly a kind of beauty to chemistry.

On an average day, O'Brien might call and say, "What's the story?" Candy would say, "We've already got five packets, you bring three." The three grams of codeine in eight large packets of Panadeine would eventually become one gram of heroin. Down at the lower end of the junkie food chain, the place where we were used to doing business, a gram of pure heroin could be like four or five of street heroin. So we were doing all right. Every day now was like the old, rare, thousand-dollar day.

The cooking became a meticulous routine: breaking open the capsules ("shelling the peas"), mixing the powder with water, extracting the codeine with a vacuum aspirator and throwing out the paracetamol, separating the codeine from the water with dichloromethane, then evaporating the dichloromethane and dissolving the pure codeine in a reagent, the heating of which resulted in a morphine freebase. From the shelling of the peas to morphine was a detailed and complicated process, which took the better part of two hours.

At this stage I would have a thick liquid—"Tending toward a viscous state," as Casper had described it, in his strangely formal junkie-scientist drawl—in the bottom of the flask. It was a deep orange-brown, and if it wasn't, I was in deep shit. I had no contingency plans, like Casper did, with his vast brain full of the poetry of molecules.

The feeling now was always that we were on our fucking way to glory. A couple more extractions in the separating funnel with dichloromethane, a little vacuum aspiration with the flask lowered into boiling water—dichloromethane evaporates at 40 degrees Celsius, a long time before morphine—and a light brown foam of pure morphine would begin to form inside the flask, as if from nowhere.

In all those years at school, I'd never realized that chemistry could be so exciting.

I added enough acetic anhydride to dissolve the morphine, then heated the solution over a naked flame until it began to boil. Right now a beautiful thing was happening. The morphine, bonding with the acetic anhydride, was becoming diacetylmorphine, commonly known as heroin. The by-products were being evaporated away by the action of the vacuum aspirator. I disconnected the aspirator, added a couple of pipettes of water, and swirled. Most of the oil dissolved. I could get the rest later with a quick reheat. Finally, since it was alkaline dope, I added a single drop of glacial acetic acid.

It was the Holy Grail. In my tiny 50 mil measuring beaker there was enough liquid heroin—sometimes rich gold, sometimes dark orange, sometimes pale yellow—to make a few friends happy, to make a little money, and to get Candy and me comfortably through the next twenty-four hours.

"Okay, O'Brien," I'd say. "Let's say twenty-five bucks for the three packets. Give us twenty bucks more and I'll do you a nice shot."

He'd give me twenty dollars and his pick. I'd dip the pick in my jar and pull back to .3. On a good cook, .3 would generally do someone more than adequately. Candy and I had heaps more, of course, but that's both the privilege of free enterprise and the necessity of a big habit.

O'Brien had veins you could drive a truck through and was always stoned in about six seconds. He never even used a tourniquet. I'd open new syringes and fill them for me and Candy to .8 or .9. Just enough room to jack back.

O'Brien was one of those people who seemed to be affected by heroin as if it were speed. He became a Mexican fucking jumping bean on the gear. Up and down, up and down, couldn't sit still, scratching his balls and his nose, yap yap yap yap yap.

I was getting pretty fucked-up veins, and the traces of chemicals probably didn't help. I mean, I wasn't Bayer or Hoechst, and sometimes I was in a bit of a hurry, so I often had trouble getting my cargo on board. It didn't help to have O'Brien zipping around the room like a pinball. You needed to be calm when veins were hard to find.

But O'Brien was lovable, so it wasn't really hard for Candy and me to put up with it. Even so, after the cooking had been happening for a while, it would sometimes take a long time to locate a vein. I'd get pretty wound up in that kind of situation. When I found myself feeling nostalgic for the early days of veins, I knew that things were really getting screwed up.

In the early days I took veins for granted. Veins were a means to an end, in the long run.

One night, for example, way back in Sydney, way back in the beginning, Candy and Lex and I had scored. Lex was drinking a can of Fanta. I'd opened the foil package and poured the dope onto the glass surface of the coffee table. It was a nice little mound of white powder, good dope from T-Bar. I don't know what happened exactly. Lex moved to get more comfortable on the couch. His knee hit the edge of the coffee table, which shuddered once and jumped six inches.

The can of Fanta tipped. Before we could grab it, a drop or two had spilled out. Of course it landed on the heroin. The Fanta fizzed and the mound of heroin dissolved.

There was no decision process. The important thing was the heroin. We injected our bright orange carbonated hits. Lex laughed and sang the jingle: "When You're Having Fun You're Having Fanta."

It was all easy back then. There were the veins that stuck out along my arms like ridges. Where are the veins of yester-year? Then there were veins a bit deeper beneath the skin. But after a few years, by the time Candy and I were burning up, finding a vein became like a geological survey.

It had started slowly. I'd begun in the crook of the elbow, of course, like everybody else. I had a good while there, a year or two in the general vicinity. Gradually I moved toward the wrist. When I got too close to the wrist I went around the other side of the arm.

When that method came too close to the wrist again, I changed arms. I wrote with my left hand, I masturbated with my right, but necessity is the mother of invention and I was completely ambidextrous in the matter of syringes.

In the early years this chase around the arms wasn't too bad, because I could always get a round off within a few minutes. It was the bigger delays that began to cause grief, and the delays began to get even bigger around the time of the cooking. I suppose you could pinpoint two reasons for this.

Firstly, once we started cooking, we went from having one or two or three or five shots a day to ten or fifteen or twenty. So frequency was a factor.

But secondly, there's a chemical problem. Casper taught me a method of converting codeine to heroin that took about two hours. A proper extraction and drying of the heroin to powder form removed trace impurities but took another couple of hours. Why bother with that when you were just going to add water anyway and turn it back to the liquid you had two hours earlier?

The price, according to Casper, was minute traces of acetic anhydride left in the heroin. So we corroded our veins with acid. And one day, who knows, we might die of some mutant fucking cancer. But what a sweet Yellow Jesus it was.

I'd swing my arms around and around to get the circula-tion going. I'd dip my wrists in sinks of hot water. I'd prod and pierce until my arms were caked with dried trickles. Sometimes the syringe would become completely clotted with blood. Then I'd just have to give myself an intramuscular injection in the shoulder, and calm down, and start looking for a vein with a freshly loaded fit.

We started buying boxes of a hundred syringes, then five boxes at a time. I had to use a new pick every blast.

I moved down to my feet and ankles. It was virgin territory, gave me some breathing space for a while. There are certain places that hurt more than others, and the tops of the feet near the toes aren't so good.

I was getting tiny veins and they would roll. I'd jack back on the syringe and get the thinnest suggestion of a trickle of blood. I figured after half an hour it would have to do. But as I began to push in, the skin would rise up in a ball, and I knew I was watching my heroin spread out under my flesh. There are many ways to describe frustration; this is a particularly good one.

In winter my feet would swell up. Shoes became too small for me, like when I was a kid and still growing. Eventually my feet were so fucked and swollen, I moved back up my body, to the northern latitudes. But available veins were getting scarcer.

I felt I was standing naked and cold in the middle of a vast forest at night, and wolves were moving in. I could hear my shallow, panicked breath above their baying.

I started making do with the insides of my wrists, the palms of my hands, the flesh between my fingers and around my knuckles. One week I found a good vein running along the back of the thumb. I was as happy as Larry for the four or five days it lasted.

But nothing could be relied on, and I felt that the world was a treacherous place, or that life, at least, was a treacherous thing. The way our bodies work. Candy shared these feelings, I'm sure. It's a common slant on the world when you're in love.

Everything was scarred. That was a way of viewing our lives too, though of course we never did.

The cooking was heaven and then it was hell. It was probably around the time I left my knuckles and went back down to the balls of my feet that Candy said, "We really ought to knock this on the head, go on methadone, you know, do *something*."

But the big problem for me was not so much the veins. The real bummer was that we were using all this dope, more than we'd ever had, and yet it seemed we were feeling it less and less. As our habits rocketed up to new heights, so did our tolerance. Only when we had virtually unlimited dope did we finally get an idea of what chasing your tail means. Cooking gave us distance from the chaos, just a fraction. I stood back from my life and saw with horror that I'd just repeated the same day three thousand times. I vowed to myself that one of these years, sooner rather than later, I was going to stop.

In the meantime I developed the four-tourniquet method. At the end of each cook, when I could sit down at last, ready to hit up, I'd pull my four ties from under the couch. I'd take off my shoes and socks and roll my jeans up to the knees. One tie for each ankle and one for each arm, above the elbow. I'd pull them tight and begin my search.

The drill would be, say, two minutes left arm, two minutes left foot, two minutes right foot, two minutes right arm. Running my fingers softly over my skin, feeling for ridges that were rarely there. Like reading a page of Braille worn down by the years: the most popular book in the Braille school library. Shining a lamp in close, searching for a trace of blue on my white skin.

There were good days and bad days. Sometimes I'd even find a vein on the first cycle.

One night some equipment broke during a cook. This was cause for alarm. I'd just got the morphine up when the inner metal sleeve of the aspirator snapped off. It had finally corroded, from continual high-pressure use. The instant it happened, the flow of the vacuum was reversed. Water gushed into the 500 mil round-bottomed flask containing the morphine. The morph dissolved instantly, despite my lunge to disconnect the flask.

There were three regulars waiting in the lounge room, as well as Candy. I came out holding the flask, now three-quarters filled with the morphine solution. It was the usual strength, but spread through about 350 syringes' worth of water. Being unfamiliar with these kinds of disasters, I wasn't even sure if the stuff would work, or if somehow the morphine had been lost forever. It was the early days of cooking. I'd been getting better, but I was still essentially just a monkey with a recipe book.

I explained the dilemma. O'Brien, with the Eveready veins, volunteered to be guinea pig. I poured some of the liquid into a glass. He had two glasses in front of him: one with what we hoped was the dope, and one with water, for cleaning his fit.

He filled the syringe and hit up. Trains and tunnels. Bang. I watched jealously.

"Anything?" I asked.

He looked toward the ceiling. "Nothing."

He cleaned his syringe and squirted it onto the carpet. He filled it again with the liquid and hit up. Candy and Victor and Yolanda and I sat mesmerized, waiting.

O'Brien's veins were beautiful. He swiftly but patiently ran through his cycle: fill, inject, clean, fill, inject, clean. The same hole every time. After the eleventh hit he stopped for a moment. He looked to the ceiling again. He licked his lips.

"I think I'm feeling something," he said.

There was a palpable buzz of excitement in the room.

"Let's see your eyes," Candy said. She leaned forward and peered into his pupils.

"Look!" she said. "They're going pinned!"

"Shit, that's good," O'Brien said. "I can really feel it now, I'm getting stoned. Shit that's a good fucking cook."

He started to droop forward and scratch his nose.

Then it was a stampede. No one cared about the hygiene anymore. Everyone just started dipping their syringes into the main flask. Of course I knew I couldn't possibly find all those veins, one after the other. I didn't even bother trying. I gave myself fifteen musculars in a row. I spread them around on both shoulders, and Candy kindly gave me a few in the buttocks. I didn't get the intravenous rush, but after about ten or fifteen minutes it was the same as any nice hit. Everyone sat around the lounge room spouting the warm crap that always came with mission accomplished.

One day, near the end, I got a small reprieve. It lasted a few months, until we finally went on methadone and threw away the lab in a moment of mad enthusiasm for an imagined future. I was soaping myself under the shower when I felt a vein on my stomach. I could see it too: thick and purple under my skin. I suppose by now I was so entirely fat-free that new, untapped veins could begin to appear. It was the femoral vein. It would be my friend for a while. I felt a degree of relief to rediscover easy access, like the good old early days. But all relief was temporary now, and time, or the sense of it, continued to shrink.

I'd mix up and fill the syringe. I'd have to stand in a shaft of sunlight, or sideways to a lamp. I'd drop my pants. The femoral vein cast a faint ridge of shadow from the light source. The vein seemed to originate somewhere beneath my rib cage, and ran down the left side of my stomach before disappearing into my pubic hair and groin.

It was a very comfortable position, to be able to operate the syringe with two hands. I'd cup it in the palm of my left hand with the needle facing back up toward me. I'd place the back of my left hand in the palm of my right hand, then rest my right hand on the flat of my stomach. I'd slide into the skin at a shallow angle and feel that discernible *give*, that change in texture, as the needle pushed through the skin and muscle and broke through into the cavernous cylinder of the femoral vein. Then push the plunger, whack it away, aloha Steve and Danno.

Veins are a kind of map, and maps are the best way to chart the way things change. What I'm really charting here is a kind of decay. The vein situation is no great exception. There really did come a point when we knew that our bodies were not in good order. That much was clear. As for our souls, well, we couldn't see the forest for the trees.

Perhaps I could have gone on with the femoral vein forever. It certainly seemed nice and big. But I think in the end, with all those holes, you kind of do something. It's like you have a container to hold your soul, and you turn it into a colander. So much of you leaks out, until there's barely anything left. And you just keep lowering your standards, to deal with the barely anything.

You just leak away. And if you're lucky, then one night in the silence, in the deep heart of the dark, you'll hear the distant trickling of the blood in your veins. A weary world of rivers, hauling their pain through the dark heat. The heart like a tom-tom, beating the message that time is running out. You'll lie there strangely alert. You'll actually feel the inside of your body, which is your soul, or where your soul is, and a great sadness will engulf you. And from the sadness an itch might begin, the itch of desire for change.

PROBLEMS WITH DETACHABLE HEADS: 2

The itch of desire for change. Even farce, in the end, seemed to be pointing toward the idea of change. Farcical situations, like the Carl's Neck Situation. By the time I was Scientist of the Year, I wasn't expecting to come across too many people with a vein problem like mine. Then I met Carl, and was reminded that there's *always* somebody worse off than you.

I grew to feel a deep sense of camaraderie with Carl in the few short weeks that he was in our lives, between stints at Pentridge Prison. I'd do a nice cook and everyone would hit up, whack whack whack whack, and get relaxed and chatty, and there'd be Carl and me fretting and prodding for half an hour, sometimes forty-five minutes.

Carl was wiry and pale, with red hair and red freckles and lots of tattoos. He was Yolanda's sometime boyfriend. Candy had met Yolanda in a brothel a couple of years earlier, where they'd often gone for the big cash kill and done doubles together, the blonde and the brunette.

Candy and O'Brien and Yolanda or whoever would be scratching their noses and smoking cigarettes in that languorous way you do when the smack comes on. They'd be sitting there going "mmmm" and complimenting me on my cook while I was the Grand Chef with the blocked esophagus, unable to taste his own food. So Carl was special, like a vein buddy in the brotherhood of suffering.

We could swap stories and hints. We could be like a support group. My name's Carl and I've got no veins. I've had no veins for four years now. Welcome Carl. You've come to the right place.

Around this time I'd been to see Doctor Feelgood for my regular backup kit visit, and in his waiting room I'd read an old *National Geographic* with a cover story about opium. It was one of those comprehensive vacuous bullshit things that *National Geographic* does, a sort of Disney version of the drug world.

There was a photo of a black woman leaning in close to a mirror and puffing her cheeks out and sticking a syringe into her neck. The caption called her a "New York City heroin addict" and explained that she was puffing her cheeks out to try and get a vein up on her neck.

I was struck by this novel idea. I thought of Carl, but of course I thought mostly of myself. I ripped out the page and put it in my wallet. That night, or maybe the next night, Carl was around.

Candy and I had been using way too much of our smack—even with the luxury of cooking, our need, as always, continued to outstrip our means—and not selling much, not keeping the turnover going.

It was becoming pretty rare for Candy to work. I almost felt like the man of the house, supplier of smack and other essential nutrients. But we still basically lived hand-to-mouth, always going for lots of hammer rather than lots of money. The odd cash injection was sometimes necessary to pay the rent or bills. One night Candy went off to work a shift so we could stock up on some expensive chemicals that were about to run out.

I was alone and chilling out in front of the TV when Carl dropped by, cashed up and hanging out, at about two A.M.

I'd had a big hit at midnight and then settled in to watch the late movie, *They Died with Their Boots On,* starring Errol Flynn as General Custer. Candy was due home about five.

Of course, I had my morning blast, and Candy's too, hidden away, and of course I felt some sympathy for Carl, begging me all snivelly and wide-eyed for a taste, but personal principles were personal principles and I would never give my morning taste to my dying grandmother, or even to Candy. Some things you had to feel secure about. Anything could go wrong.

"Haven't you got anything, mate? Just a smidge?"

"Nothing. Not a thing," I said. "I was going to cook when we woke up."

"If you could cook now," he pleaded, "I'll owe you big-time."

"Mate, it's after two already. Can't you just go home and sleep and when you wake up the dope'll be ready?"

"I won't be able to sleep. You know that."

There were fine beads of sweat all over his desperate, sad face.

More dope, I thought. Why fucking not? I already had enough packets of Panadeine capsules for the next cook.

"All right," I sighed. "I'll do a cook."

His shoulders sagged in relief and his face lit up. It looked pathetic. I'd been there many times myself.

"But it's a fucking hassle, Carl," I continued sternly. "So here's the deal. You give me eighty bucks for two nice tastes. And you come back later today with seven large packets, and after that cook I'll give you another taste to pay for the packets."

"No problems," he said. "No worries. You're a champion."

"Let's get shelling, then," I said.

I was not in a major hurry like Carl, but the way I saw it, that was essentially his problem and not mine. I was a happy cook, all cells well fed. I was feeling no real lack of anything just at that moment. I took my time and did a nice careful cook, more than two hours, everything done just right. Carl sat at the kitchen table chewing his nails and smoking lots of cigarettes and trying to act like he was enjoying chatting with me.

At four-thirty A.M., I did the demethylation and got the morphine up. Heaps of morph in the flask, a good-looking cook. I squeezed out a couple of pipettes of acetic anhydride to dissolve the morphine. I whacked on the vacuum aspirator and held the flask over the flame.

There was a luscious amount of heroin oil. Carl was almost salivating. I added the water and the drop of glacial acetic acid and dissolved it all. I poured it into my little jar and we moved back out into the lounge room.

"Got a pick, Carl?"

He fumbled in his jacket pocket and pulled out a syringe. It was a 1 mil detachable head and it looked a little the worse for wear. I looked closely at it. The calibrations had all worn off. I raised my eyebrows at Carl.

"You been camping, mate?" I asked.

He managed a weak laugh but he was pretty preoccupied, what with concentrating so fiercely on my hands and his syringe and my jar of heroin.

I dipped the needle in and pulled back the plunger and half filled his works. It was a guessing game. I wouldn't know precisely how strong the gear was until I got it on board myself. I filled my own syringe and the Carl and Me Show began.

I pulled out my tourniquet collection from under the couch.

"Help yourself," I offered with a sweep of my arm. "And Carl," I added in a serious voice.

He looked up.

"Good luck," I said.

I laughed, because I was full of heroin already, and I'd got a vein first go on my last hit. It didn't really matter if I had a little trouble. Carl, on the other hand, was really stressed.

We started fucking around, looping the ties tight around our arms, and the next thing we know the late late late movie is over and the five A.M. shit is on TV and a thin trace of gray light is leaking through the blinds.

We'd been concentrating hard for half an hour and there were dried trickles of blood all over our arms and I was saying, "Fuck this, fuck this," when I remembered the *National Geographic*.

I stopped what I was doing and pulled from my wallet the page with the photo of our New York comrade.

"Check this out," I said to Carl. I pointed at the relevant photo.

Carl studied it and then read the caption.

"Fuckin' all right," he said. He started nodding. "Fuckin' all right. Let's do it."

In a minute we had the mirror set up on the mantelpiece and the photo pinned up above us as a guide. A visual aid. The photo was grainy like it was some cinema verité shit, so it was a little hard to find the kind of clinical detail we needed. It was hard to see what she was actually doing with the needle and her neck.

We were really just stabbing in the dark.

I admit I thought about my jugular or aorta or artery or whatever the fucking thing was, but I figured there had to be veins there as well, just the normal little domestic fellows. I was tilting my head back and puffing my cheeks out and going in shallow, so the syringe was almost parallel to the line of my neck.

I was not finding anything, just adding more trickles of blood all over my neck. Carl was almost beside himself by this time.

"Maybe it's not as easy as it looks," I suggested.

I glanced at Carl's reflection beside mine. He was going in deep, at a right angle to his neck.

Just at that moment Candy's keys slipped into the door and it swung open. Carl got a shock and jumped a bit and tried to swing his head around to see where the noise was coming from. He was trying to hold the syringe in place with his left hand, but his feet were awkwardly placed and he must have pushed it in a bit farther.

I'd finally got a tiny spurt of blood back into my syringe so I was really concentrating on securing the services of that vein.

Candy walked in the room and her mouth dropped open.

"What the—" she started to say.

Then something happened that I'd never seen before.

With astonishing force, Carl's syringe shot out of his neck and out of his hand like an arrow from a bow and zoomed across the room and out through the door to the kitchen, where I heard it ping on one of my bottles of chemicals.

In that first microsecond you could see Carl's confusion as his brain tried to link the apparently poltergeistal activity of his syringe with the source of the noise at the door.

A jet of blood had spurted from Carl's neck and hit the opposite wall, spraying back out in a circle at the point of impact like a high-pressure hose. And then the jet's path continued across the room toward Candy.

Candy screamed and dropped to the floor, trying to avoid the gusher. It passed above her but her hair was sprayed with a fine mist of blood. It continued past the door and sprayed a jagged red line across the cream blinds as Carl turned a full circle.

"What's going on!" he shouted. There was raw fear in his high-pitched voice.

I had no idea what the fuck to do. Was this what happened in combat in Vietnam, everything slow motion and surreal? My wounded buddy Candy on the ground, and me trying to avoid the tracer fire coming from Carl's neck?

Carl had gone all Wes Craven, all Freddy Krueger. Carl had gone ballistic. There was blood spouting all over the room, making a high-speed pitter-patter sound on the walls.

He must have thought that the best way out of this would

be to faint. He lurched across the room, his knees wobbling. I could see him losing his balance and tottering sideways. All the while the blood kept spraying out of him. He looked like Frankenstein in a dying frenzy. One of the bolts on Frankenstein's neck had come loose and he was coming apart at the seams and roaring like a wounded animal. A stuck pig, an elephant, thrashing around the room; a demented child scribbling on a spirograph board, coloring everything wildly red.

I was in a defensive crouch by now, over beside the TV. Carl buckled at the knees and fell sideways to the floor and started to give the ceiling a spray. The blood came in ferocious spurts. Carl's eyelids were fluttering like some lame Emily Brontë shit. His head was moving purposefully toward the carpet like he was trying to get his ears down there and listen to the fleas. The wondrous music of the fleas which would deliver him from fear.

"Ahhh! Ahhh! Ahhh!"

He started wailing in terror. He was holding his hand to his slippery red neck and he looked just like Robert de Niro at the end of *Taxi Driver*. Only in *Taxi Driver*, de Niro was sitting there covered in blood and holding his neck and looking pretty calm. Almost happy. Carl didn't look calm. They were just in the same position, that's all.

All of this, the whole thing from Candy opening the door to Carl collapsing on the floor, had taken ten or fifteen seconds. I had visions of Carl's imminent death and assumed an ambulance would need to be called on this one. I imagined it would take a little explaining.

It was then it clicked. I was staring at his neck, my eyes focusing on the point where the blood erupted between his fingers like an oil strike. Jesus, I'm thinking of movies. James Dean in *Giant*.

I stared at the gusher and realized that the blood was not coming directly from his neck, but from the small piece of plastic between his fingers. The detachable head. The detachable head! Carl was in shock. *He was holding the detachable head in place with his hand!* He'd tapped into the main torrent taking blood to the brain, the most powerful vein in the body, and he'd created a berko fire hydrant in my lounge room. He was still holding the detachable head firmly in place, because he was a little panicked, and maybe also because he was a bit of a fucking idiot.

He'd tapped into an artery and blown the body of his syringe into kingdom come, into my kitchen. You would only truly be able to see something like that in super slow motion, like on a nature documentary, the way they show you a hummingbird in flight. Carl's syringe on its final journey upriver. It was a plumbing mishap of epic destructive force. And then, while unleashing the destruction, he'd had the bad manners to collapse on us.

I guess Carl's reptilian brain had taken over from the higher functions. He was keeping his fingers on that detachable head because, come hell or high water, he'd found a fucking vein, all right.

I grabbed a pillow off the couch and dived across the room and ripped his hand and the detachable head away from his neck. The blood continued to spurt out of the hole. I smothered the side of his head with the pillow, pushing down hard where his neck was.

"Get me a towel or something!" I yelled at Candy.

She ran into the kitchen and came back and threw a washcloth at me. I removed the pillow. The blood was still flowing freely, still pulsing, but it was no longer spurting to the other side of the room. Carl, however, continued to scream hysterically. It was five in the morning and I had a heroin lab in the kitchen and I was a little bit worried about the neighbors and hysterical noises and the police.

"Shut up! Shut up! Shut the fuck up!" I hissed.

"Oh God! Oh fuck! Oh Jesus!" he gurgled.

I slapped him hard with a backhander across the face. It was almost a punch. I guess it was a punch. I guess I was kind of hyped up.

His nose began to bleed. Another gusher.

"Ahh shit!" I looked over at Candy.

She was gathering her senses. Composing herself. Unsuspending her disbelief. The room looked like it had been used for a serious Satanic ritual—say, disembowelment or child sacrifice.

She was not real happy coming home to this.

"What the fuck did you two think you were doing?" It wasn't the right time to be asking questions.

I was holding Carl's head in my lap, pressing the washcloth to his neck and stroking his bloodied hair. He was blubbering gently. I think we looked like some gay fringe theater version of the *Pietà*.

"We couldn't get a vein. We just thought . . ."

There was nothing for me to say beyond the obvious. Still, I hated that. Candy standing there with her hands on her hips and giving me the steel eyeball. Okay. I made a mistake.

Carl wasn't an idiot. He was just a very distraught junkie. I felt tender toward him for a moment. I decided I would waive the forty bucks for his lost hit. Then I remembered my own blast. I'd forgotten about it in all the excitement. I scanned the floor and saw my syringe in the corner. It appeared to be undamaged by the fracas.

"Listen, Candy," I said. "I did a big cook. We've got lots of gear. Let's just all get really stoned, and calm down, and send Carl off in a cab to the hospital to get checked, and then clean up a little."

She was starting to smile, like it was so stupid being angry.

"What do you reckon?" I added.

She sighed and walked out into the kitchen. She came

back with a saucepan of warm water and another washcloth and walked across the room and crouched down to Carl. She peered at him intently.

"You okay, Carl?"

"I'm sorry, Candy, I'm so sorry," Carl moaned.

"Hey, it's nothing, little Carly," she soothed. "These things happen. Here, let me wipe you down."

She cradled him and sat him up and gently started cleaning him with the water. She looked over to me.

"How about a nice big blast for all of us, baby?"

"Yeah right," I said.

I snapped into action. Heroin jar. Terumo box.

"Hey, Carl," I said. "I'll give you a nice new syringe."

He managed a feeble laugh.

God was being extra-special nice to him now because Candy looked for a vein behind his knee, where she sometimes found one for me, and hit him up no problems and he was wasted, seriously wasted. A very happy Carl. I gave him a lot of dope, to make up for his ordeal. His lips even went a bit blue in the first five minutes and Candy had to slap him around a bit to keep him on the active list.

His neck stopped bleeding and in the end he didn't want to go to the hospital, even though you could see there was going to be a big purple bruise, like an apple lodged in his throat or a gland gone crazy. Instead he hung around with us and we made him help us clean the lounge room.

He was really grateful that we'd given him so much dope and been okay about the blood. His nose wasn't broken and he didn't seem resentful about that either. He volunteered for all the hard work, like standing on a stool and scrubbing the ceiling. We put a tape on the cassette player—*Funky Kingston* by Toots and the Maytals—and it turned out to be kind of fun, being that stoned and getting into a cleaning rhythm. In the end the walls were cleaner than they'd ever been, though it took us half a day.

No one had slept, so we all felt a bit fucked-up, but we just used dope all day and cooked again and went to bed a bit earlier that night.

Two weeks later Carl got done again. He parked his car in Carlton and walked around the corner and held up a bakery with a plastic replica pistol. The two old Vietnamese women freaked for a minute and gave him the money from the cash register. He was a wiry little nugget but he could give you a fright when his voice got going.

He had the money in one hand and the pistol in the other and he was ranting and raving about "don't follow me or I'll blow your fucking brains out" when he brought the gun down hard on the counter. The plastic splintered and the gun broke in half.

Carl ran out of the shop and down the street. The two old ladies chased him around the corner with their brooms. They watched him get into his car and they had plenty of time to memorize his license plate as he tried to disentangle his thumb from the broken plastic pistol and search his various pockets for his car keys. *His* car keys. Not a stolen car. His own car. When we are talking about Carl, we are not talking about a sophisticated criminal. But then again, I did the great GPO heist.

Maybe he spent the cash register, I don't know. The cops got him within hours. He'd worn out his welcome in the courts, and he got two years for this one.

We never saw him again. Six months later Yolanda told us he'd got into a fight in Pentridge and someone sliced him open with a knife. Carl was pretty vague, she said, about the details and the reasons. Two weeks after he got back from the prison hospital, he hanged himself in his cell.

TRUTH 4: WHERE IS THE EARTH?

When I stare at things or hear things, I think there might be some kind of beauty to them. I mean the little things, the way we make it through the day, experiencing pleasure. Trees in streets or a small bird flittering around the garden, paint flaking from the kitchen windowpane, dust motes in sunlight, the wind through poplars, the tram bell signaling departure. I'm alert, you might say, to the beauty of these things, the local nuances that bring life alive.

But all there is, is sadness.

If there's enough heroin in my blood, the world gives me comfort. If there's not enough, it makes me sad. Comfort is beauty muted by heroin. Sadness is beauty drained by lack of it.

I am so far removed, from everything, that I can't even cry. There's a chasm between me, where I am, and the world I am in. The world I move my feet through. The atmosphere I breathe is like golden syrup, twenty-seven atmospheres thick. I'm wading through the world, consumed with . . . consumed. And I'm wading through the swamp that my body has become.

Track marks. What a beautiful expression. Trail marks. I am blazing new trails all over my body in the search for virgin rivers that will carry me home to glacial happiness, to Arctic oceans of narcosis. Carry the heroin home to me. Open my blood to receive the heroin.

But I dredge the rivers with my giant harpoon until they wither and die. Gouge the rivers into rubble.

My head is throbbing. The room feels stuffy. I move the two-bar heater away from me. My arm has come up puffy and red. The red is like a rash but it's just a reaction from the needle. Or the dope maybe. Or the cut. Let's face it, I don't know what I'm talking about.

My feet are two bricks; there is no sensation of flexibility down there. Holes everywhere. I can't move my toes. I can't fully straighten my arm. It will go away but it's never pleasant. Today I found a vein on the ball of my foot. Hooray. As each vein collapses I have to look for smaller and smaller ones. A vicious circle forms: the size of the needle rips apart the tiny veins after one or two hits, setting in motion the search for other (smaller) veins, which in turn are damaged.

So I miss a lot now. So that's why everything is fucked-up. I am swollen like a balloon though I feel like a block of cement. And nothing like a vein, not even a telltale rise of the skin, in sight. This is not a weather forecast. Nonetheless I feel the outlook is bleak.

In the end I won't have veins, just some kind of trickle system, my tired blood spreading itself through tissue and skin, around bone loosened from cartilage, drip drip drip into calcified cavities.

Lord Lord I am tired.

But I have to ignore that, and hardly sleep, and scar my brain even in dreams, and wake up again tomorrow. Still, how can I think of the future when I can't even think of the past or today?

There is nothing I can do from the moment I wake up but consider the obtaining of money or smack.

Really, on heroin, even when you're sleeping you're running.

And I would fuck the whole world if I could. Fuck it up I mean. Fuck it up and take its cash. The world is cashed up, so why not me?

Most of the day I have to deal with the fact of my habit. It's a brutal kind of dealing-with, and for every hundred units of time, it takes up ninety-nine. But every now and then, even during bad times, I get a glimpse of a state where the mind is free to roam through spaces greater than what the body knows.

Waking up with leg cramps, it is possible to envision a plane of such endless proportions that every atom contains specific scenes of interest. Stone pillars crumble. This takes place over centuries. You have that much time. Follow the path of an eagle, wings spread wide, as it traces in an infinitesimal rate of curvature a swoop of beauty so painful it takes your breath away.

The eagle's eyes can hone in on a speck of dust: not forever, but for a very long time. Here is the mote growing larger and larger.

The eagle is the perfect hunter. One atom will sustain him.

It is possible to follow this thought into others (emulating, with some grace, the path of the eagle), even when stomach cramps come on. For a while, in the gray between sleeping and waking, for seconds, or even a minute, it can feel okay to be alive. And then you wake, properly.

And it all comes rushing back. You ask the question, Who am I? and the answer is always the same. I am nothing but need. I will hate today like every other day. It's so hard to experience beauty when it all stands in contrast to a greater unbeauty.

Candy is beside me, drenched in sweat. She's breathing gently, long slow breaths. I imagine her soul going in and out: wanting to leave, wanting to come back, wanting to leave, wanting to come back. The day will soon harden into what we need to do. But for now we have each other.

We run a bath. In the faint phosphorescent light of the storm, we submerge ourselves to our necks and our legs intertwine. Nothing could ever be this close. Everything is the best, or else, "I can't go on living like this. Oh God, it's all such a mess." We stroke each other softly and feel entirely dislocated from the earth, which has never existed.

CATS

There was so much wretchedness. There were so few veins. There was so little of us left. Eventually we went on methadone. Exhaustion might have been a factor. Desire for change? I guess so. Anyway, it seemed easier to drink half a cup of sweet yellow syrup every twenty-four hours than to spend seven hours a day searching for veins. So we got on a government program, for $21 a week each. We saw a doctor once every two weeks, gave a urine sample once a month. We picked up our dose every morning, and for the rest of the day we had oodles of time. What were the effects of methadone? It felt like we felt nothing. The dominant thing was the absence of the craving for heroin.

It was certainly a change. It was a tough adjustment in the beginning, after all that Yellow Jesus, but after a couple of months the methadone worked as a dull pleasantness that moved us along through our days. The relief that descended on us after heroin was like the eerie silence after a storm.

They say the Nazis invented methadone. On methadone we became obsessed with the desire to breed a race of master cats. Perhaps there is a link there somewhere.

First there was Willy, the stray we'd adopted whose cat food had made me vomit when we were living in Port Melbourne. She'd come with us to the Alexandra Avenue flat, all the time the cooking was happening. Eventually at Alexandra Avenue our landlady had brought to our attention the seven-hundred-dollar excess water bill that the council had hit her with. I assured her we used no more water than normal domestic consumption—showers, toilet, dishes—but I knew it was the vacuum aspirator, attached to the kitchen tap and turned on full blast for an hour or two a day. She was muttering about getting plumbers in to check for leaks. We let our healthy resentment build for a few weeks, then did yet another midnight flit, this time to a run-down flat we found above a shop in Albert Park.

The first day of the methadone program was the last day at Alexandra Avenue. The next day, the first day at Albert Park, was the day Willy gave birth to the kittens. We felt a certain symbolism in operation here, and settled into those first slow months to enjoy our new life with our family of cats. There was Tiger Tom, Coco, Mavis, Barney, and a couple of others we gave away. Coco stood out: jet black and long-haired in a litter of short-haired alley cats.

Half a year passed. In the back streets of Albert Park we saw an enormous and sleek black Siamese tom. Muscular, ferocious, half mad and half feral, in a rhinestone-studded necklace. We didn't really want to have him, but we decided we certainly wanted to mate him with Coco. For the aesthetics of the thing.

The cat seemed to hang around a recently vacated house we'd been checking out for break-and-enter value. A For Sale sign had SOLD slapped over it. The cat howled in the overbearing and neurotic way of Siamese, but never came close for long.

In an act of intuitive, methadone-fueled brilliance, we called the real estate agent, hoping to locate the cat's owner. We told the receptionist about our mating plan. Our story was so bizarre she believed us and gave us the new number of the previous owner.

We called him and told him we wanted to mate his cat with our cat. Not only did he not seem surprised, he told us he no longer wanted the cat, had in fact left it after he moved out, and would we like to take it?

Nothing ever seemed strange in our world, which was essentially by now a mindscape that had evolved in a Bavarian lab. We were delighted, after our initial surprise. The owner offered to come and catch the cat. He brought the psychotic thing over in the biggest cat cage I'd ever seen. The cage looked like it might have once been used for trapping small mountain lions and pumas, or maybe even feral pigs.

The cat paced relentlessly back and forward in its wire box, sniffing the air in our lounge room with the hard glint of primal stupidity in its eyes.

The owner was fully weird. No other way to describe him. His name was Darrell. He was about forty, with a graying crew cut and bottle-lens glasses. Muscular and wiry like his cat. He wore tight black jeans and a tight black Bonds T-shirt. His arms were covered with what might have been prison tattoos. Maybe not. But he had the puffed-up strut of someone who'd done time at some time or other.

I guessed he was not a junkie and never had been. Not my kind of junkie anyway. Not smack. I got the feeling his problem was speed. The creepy, off-center, hairs-on-the-neck feeling you get trying to talk with someone locked into a mean amphetamine habit. Different velocities. Especially from where we were, in the methadone crèche.

It was the old cliché. He was just like his cat. Or the cat was just like him. Darrell told us the cat's name was Sam.

Sam emerged tentatively from the cat box, all the while delivering his endless and plaintive monologue of Siamese craziness. He had the biggest balls I'd ever seen.

He sniffed around the room, checking things out in widening concentric circles. Taking his time. Next thing, he sidled arse backward to the couch leg, like a ham actor building up dramatic tension, and sprayed.

"Oh shit!"

We lunged for him. This put him into a seriously confused panic and he took off up the hallway. The flat stank with the acrid odor, which seemed in those first few seconds to be spreading through the rooms at supersonic speed.

"Don't worry about it," Darrell said. "He's just establishing himself, that's all."

Within a month we would be so numbed by this smell that only the acute embarrassment of visitors would continue to remind us we had a problem.

But Sam seemed pretty happy. Or at least, not unhappy in the primordial depths of his sharklike brain. It was not the case for all the cats.

The arrival of Sam overturned Barney's world, for instance. Barney had been desexed—on methadone we got it together to do things like that. If Barney was human he would have been just like Gilligan from *Gilligan's Island*. He was pretty laid back. Big fish in a small pond. Protector of the brood in our neck of the woods. Only months earlier, Barney and Coco, fluffily cartwheeling down the hallway, had been as inseparable as twins could be.

But after Sam, Barney was never really the same again. He lost his innocent confidence. It seemed to be replaced with various pathetic forms of insecurity, uncertainty, and trepidation.

After Sam's arrival, even tiny Mavis, the forgotten sister, desexed due to lack of potential, started having the odd shot at Barney. She would land him a hisser across the gob. He would scurry out the cat door with a wounded frown and disappear into the back alleys, to find solace in the garbage.

The mating program was fairly simple to organize.

I built a huge cat cage from chicken wire and two-by-fours and we kept Sam in it the first couple of days. This is the sort of thing you build on methadone: suddenly released from certain pressing necessities, you find there's no more need for endless plotting and scamming and rushing, and a senselessly vast amount of time seems to stretch before you. We kept the cat cage in the lounge room. I built the cat door too. These are the two things I've built in my life.

Coco was growing up. She'd been getting wet and mucousy down there, licking herself between the legs, so we knew things were beginning to happen.

On the third day we brought Coco into the room. She knew something big was going on. She was all radar ears and wide eyes and she looked a strange mixture of spooked and skittish.

She took her time. She reveled in the great luxury of checking Sam out behind the cage. She did a few languorous circles around it, then lay down and watched him. Sam was padding up and down like a lion in a circus. He was wailing over and over like some fucked-up pacer in a psych ward. It got to you after a while. But there were signals going on here that Candy and I, or any other humans for that matter, couldn't possibly pick up. The more Sam was doing this, the calmer Coco became.

Finally I got up from the couch and walked over to the cage and opened the latch. Coco was just lying there watching me do this, her ears twitching like tiny wings as she heard the noise of the clasp flick back. Sam watched my hands open the door and he went quiet.

With an effortless leap he was out of the cage. Coco jumped up like she didn't know what to do with herself. She turned in a circle, flicking her tail, then let herself fall to the carpet with a thump of abandon. Her tail whacked the floor, backward and forward in a butterfly pattern, and she began to purr.

Sam began purring too. He walked across the floor and his muscles were snapping tightly. A ripple ran down his fur like a breeze moving through a field of grass. His long face moved in to sniff her backside.

Coco jumped up and hissed and struck out at him. Sam

made a halfhearted attempt at a feint. Coco turned another circle and plonked down. This time Sam came up to her face. They sniffed noses, then she hissed again and backed off. Her tail kept flicking up like the cat that gets chased by that skunk Pepe in the cartoon.

She collapsed to the ground again, arms and legs stretched, and rolled over completely from one side to the other, meowing like she was being strangled. Sam tried to move in and sniff her backside once more. There was no pause in his loud purring.

Coco jumped up again. They moved in circles around the lounge room, and the ritual got faster and faster. Sam kept following and purring loudly. His claws were making little ripping noises in the carpet.

The next thing, he pounced. He pushed his front paws down on her shoulders and slid himself along the floor. Coco froze. Her nose pointed straight ahead. She was staring at the skirting board across the other side of the room.

Sam bit into the back of her neck. She raised her backside in the air. Her tail jerked out of the way. There was no sound at all now in the room. Then the tiny shuffling of Sam's back paws on the carpet as he moved his muscular haunches above her. He was twice her size and now he seemed even bigger.

He was having trouble keeping his balance and moving into place. His jaws stayed locked on Coco's neck, and he started to pant through his nose.

He started thrusting and he pulled back on her neck. Her head twisted upward now. She was staring at the light globe.

Sam moved in and out of Coco, faster and faster. An unearthly wail began to emanate from Coco's mouth. It started like a guttural growl and quickly became high-pitched and there was no break to it, just an increase in intensity. It went on and on and Sam held on tight to her throat and bucked into her. A rabbit, a piston, a muscle.

My heart was beating a little fast. Candy was beside me but I couldn't look at her. Complicity. I felt like I was witnessing something that shouldn't be seen.

Finally Sam pushed forward but not backward. Coco's scream reached a peak and stopped. Sam released her neck and fell back out of her. She jumped up and shook herself. Then she sat down and stuck one hind leg straight up in the air and started licking herself down there.

Sam sat like a statue. Hardly even breathing, watching Coco's every move.

"That was awesome," Candy said, the words stopping in her throat.

After about a minute Coco rolled over again and started to purr, flapping her tail toward Sam. He pounced immediately and this time they didn't do the circuit. They got straight into fucking. The same act repeated itself: the neck, the wailing, the pounding, the falling back.

And again. We watched with jaws dropped for half an hour while Sam and Coco fucked eight times. Always the same thing, short and brutal. Animals fucking. We were watching animals fucking. I had no idea what state I was in, except that it was frightening. Something primal was breaking through the methadone. That in itself was a feat. You try not to change, forever and ever, as if heroin could do that, but eventually everything changes anyway. We'd been into chemistry and here was biology.

After the eighth fuck Coco got up and sauntered away toward the back door. I followed her out. There on the veranda were Willy and Barney and Tiger Tom and Mavis. Everyone looked a little concerned, a little tense. Barney looked completely freaked. He was ready to jump off the veranda if Sam appeared.

Coco walked up to Willy, and Willy sniffed her baby's fanny. Then Coco ran away down the stairs and Barney came up to Willy and timidly sniffed her nose. It was hard sunlight out there and my legs felt very weak.

I walked back inside and Candy was still on the couch. She was wearing a faded floral print Salvation Army shop dress. She'd hitched it up above her knees and was sitting there with her legs spread wide. Her lipstick was bloodred against her pale skin, and her long blond ponytail had come undone. For the first time in months I thought about how beautiful she was.

"Come and feel my undies," she said.

"Sure."

I walked across the room to her. I leaned over and placed my left hand on the back of the couch above her right shoulder, and my right hand over her cunt. The inside of her thighs felt sticky against the edges of my hand.

Her underpants were soaked. I thought about temperature. It was probably two degrees hotter down there. I scrunched it a little with the palm of my hand, and she slid her arse out to the edge of the couch and spread her legs wider. There was no real point where flesh ended and liquid began.

"Jesus," I said. "That's wet."

"I'm so fucking horny," she said. She was trying to rip my belt open and my dick was so hard it was almost hurting.

I was never really one for damaging items of underwear, for being irresponsible with clothes, but then again narcotics kept a lid on most things. My thumb pushed through the wet fabric of Candy's undies pretty easily. Then I just took a handful and gave it an almighty heave, hard and fast. A bit like pulling a Band-Aid off. Her underpants disintegrated, all seams and frays, and I threw a handful of fabric behind me.

My jeans were down around my knees and money was spilling out and I couldn't get my boots off, but we were doing okay. We were trying to settle the frenzy down, get untwisted and organized, when suddenly we were distracted by a loud purring at close range.

Sam had lifted his front legs onto the couch. He wanted

to know what was going on. He was staring hard at Candy's pussy and his nose was twitching back and forth like Stevie Wonder singing. He didn't seem at all awkward about the possibility he might be intruding.

"Hang on a sec," I said. I picked him up, carried him over to the cat cage, and dropped him in. His whole rib cage was vibrating with purring. Before I closed the lid, I lowered my hand in there. My fingers were wet from Candy's cunt.

Sam looked almost human. He had the look I'd seen many times before, the eye-rolling bliss that comes over someone just before overdose. He strained his head up and began to smell my fingers. He wanted to lick them. I kept moving my hand away and Sam kept purring and jerking his head around after my fingers. We laughed.

I went back to the couch and we fucked, Candy sitting on top and grinding. It was good. We burst through the methadone. Her pale blue eyes turned gray and wet. She scratched my chest hard and then squeezed it. Her thighs slowed down and she shuddered a few times. Her jaw unclenched. I shuddered too and came. Her hands untensed and she fell back off me like Sam had off Coco.

She let herself drop backward to the floor, and her hair sprayed out behind her until it touched the edges of the cat cage in the middle of the room. Some blond strands fell gently through the chicken wire.

I sat there squeezing the sperm from my dick as my breath and my heart slowed down. We stared dreamily at each other, grinning.

It was a fucking nice morning and the world seemed okay. We were in love and we were on methadone and Candy wasn't working in a brothel anymore.

Candy lay sprawled on the floor and I sat sprawled on the couch. The morning sun poured through the venetian blinds and Candy's head shimmered and began to disappear in the glow. The room seemed alive with dust motes. I felt suspended in time, and almost content.

Sam lay on the floor of the cat cage and played with Candy's hair, licking it and biting it and flicking it through the octagonal holes of the chicken wire. I lit a cigarette and blew the smoke into the slants of the sunbeams. I watched the patterns of smoke swirl and fragment. After a while Sam settled back to watching them too, as he slowly fell asleep.

"I love you, Candy," I said.

"I feel so sad," she said.

There was a long silence.

"What have we done?" she said.

I knew she was talking about the long stretch, all the years.

"We'll be all right. Don't worry," I said. "We'll be all right."

She was right. It *was* so sad. It was sad that feeling sad was so rare. It was sad too that feeling happy was frightening. It only meant wanting to feel even happier. The only way to do that seemed to be heroin, and that made us so unhappy in the end. It was better to be sad, I guess.

I couldn't see a future but I wanted to. I couldn't see a future after methadone, without heroin. I couldn't see a future without guilt, for what I'd done to Candy.

Here we were. After drugs, I couldn't imagine anything but sex. I couldn't imagine growing old. But here we were. Sam slept and Candy drifted and the sunlight moved across the room.

The morning was well on its way to becoming afternoon. We hadn't gotten our methadone yet. We had to get moving.

Candy smoked a cigarette and we pulled a few bongs and got dressed and went out into the day. It was nice in autumn in Albert Park, on a methadone program. Everything sedate and easy to handle.

We crossed the tram lines and rode our bicycles down toward the bay and Albert our pharmacist. Albert the dispenser, who looked like Woody Allen.

Albert saw us come in and nodded hello. He went out the

back to his alchemist's cubbyhole and reappeared a minute later with two plastic cups. We drank the syrup and threw the cups in the bin and Candy bought a packet of jelly beans and I bought a honey and nougat log.

"Thanks, Albert. See you tomorrow!"

We picked up our bikes from the footpath outside Albert's and stood there working out our plan for the rest of the day. It was the first Friday of the month, so the first thing we had to do was give a supervised urine sample at the pathology lab. That was just a block away.

After that we could go around to Dee Dee's café and have some coffee and watch the cars go by and fuck around doing the crossword for a while. Maybe think about some food. Then we could go home and pull a few more cones and watch the afternoon soaps on TV. Later, when the kids' programs began, we could go for a long slow bike ride through the flat backstreets of Albert Park and Port Melbourne.

We didn't know there was less than eighteen months to go. We had no idea we would move to the country, and come off methadone, and try not using heroin, and go crazy, and move back to Sydney, and dribble toward good-bye. I guess there are times, in retrospect, when you can see that ignorance is bliss.

"I wonder what the kittens are going to look like," I said, gliding beside Candy with my hands off the handlebars.

"Pretty good, I reckon," Candy said. "Pretty beautiful."

PART THREE

The Momentum of Change

"I did not want to live out my life in the strenuous effort to hold a ghost world together. It was plain as the stars that time herself moved in grand tidal sweeps rather than the tick-tocks we suffocate within, and that I must reshape myself to fully inhabit the earth rather than dawdle in the sump of my foibles . . ."

Jim Harrison, *Julip*

TRUTH 5: POPLARS

I remember this, Candy. One weekend we tried to go away. This is way back. We drove three hours north, to the town with the hot springs we thought would help us detox. We picked up the old man hitchhiking. He had the sad, determined air of one who had been in the concentration camps. His wife had died and he continued to return to the holiday spot that reminded him of her, of their early years in Australia, maybe even of Europe, up there in the cold mountain air two hundred kilometers from Melbourne. When we dropped him off he said, "You are good people."

I remember—this may be the saddest memory I own—that we sat in the tiny hotel room, shivering from lack of heroin, ready for the night that lay ahead. I remember your little pill box, and how you sat on the bed and doled out so carefully our meager rations of pills. Your beautiful delicate hands. There were not enough pills to make things all right. Two little piles on the faded quilt. We gulped them down and climbed into bed and clung to each other as if only the clinging could ward off the night. We were cold and unhappy in a bed not our own.

We didn't last too many hours up there, got itchy feet, kept thinking of Melbourne and heroin, as if Melbourne was a giant finger and we were the yo-yo attached to it. It was all we could do to make it through one day. Mud baths and hot springs no longer interested us. We reached the furthest limit of the string and spun back to the city that now contained all we knew and desired.

Almost in a straight line. On the way home, in the dying glow of a cold late autumn day, you stopped the car. An avenue of poplars stretched away to the horizon. The weird ferocity of poplars. What can I say about that afternoon? The poplars, bent double, and the roaring of the wind. Such a rush of blood to my throbbing temples. Even then, such devastation already behind us, and so much still to come.

"Why are we stopping?" I asked, though the answer was already clear.

You were silent, transported, elsewhere, another. A slight grin, despite your jangled nerves, and the unswerving purpose of someone in a trance. You pushed me into the backseat, straddled me, pulled your underpants sideways, to let me in. I held my hands at the small of your back as if your hips were the fulcrum on which all pleasure turned. Everything you did was precise and to the point. At the end your eyes closed gently and you made one tiny noise. The last thing I remember is being aware of the poplars—I could see them bending and lashing beyond your right shoulder—as my fingernails made scratches in your flesh.

We didn't say a word. We never really felt complete, as if some disease already ate away inside, as if some source or spirit was always eluding us. Somehow we drove home without crying. Concentrating on what awaited us. Too many barriers already. This was all so long ago.

There are times love would seem to be the only word capable of describing the frightening physics of this momentum. There is desolation and then there is each other.

COUNTRY LIVING

Love. And then in a way it ended.

Splitting up was more a process than an event. We moved to the country, tried to slow things down, maybe stay out of trouble for a while.

After a while, on methadone, we didn't look so gaunt. Some stability must have leaked into our lives. We'd stopped hassling Candy's parents for money, and maybe they were impressed. They were hoping that this time it might be for real. All those years of false starts.

One day, out of the blue, they told Candy some old investments had come off and they were going to give her ten thousand dollars. It might have been a tax break but we weren't about to complain. It was a sign that they trusted that methadone was a step in the right direction. When we found a cheap old farmhouse on two acres in the country, a couple of hours out of Melbourne, near where Peter and Michael lived, they gave us the ten grand and grudgingly guaranteed the small bank loan. We found a country pharmacy open seven days a week and willing to take over the methadone dispensing. We planned to reduce to zero within six months.

I don't know what we thought we were going to do down

there. Maybe I would grow the world's greatest dope crop, and Candy would restore furniture or something, and we'd live happily ever after. But the silence in the country, and the not knowing each other, and the coming down off drugs, was really a brilliant recipe for disaster.

I knew nothing about mental illness. I didn't know what a nervous breakdown looked like. If any signs were obvious, I think I must have buried them. Because when you think you are in love, you don't want to know about the things that could end it.

At any rate, when you're pretty crazy yourself, you really don't want to know it. You cannot afford to know it, and you don't want to see it in anyone else. Least of all your wife. The whole thing was a lost cause. But it takes the slowing down to even see the madness in the first place. Moving to the country on low doses of methadone was a big slowing down.

I was no less crazy than her after all those years of pushing it. But I didn't end up in Royal Park Asylum. It feels like good luck, though that phrase suggests happiness. Weird luck and good luck are not the same thing. If it's luck, it's the luck of the draw.

The truth was, it was awful and frightening, having so few drugs in our systems after all those years. I could sense the methadone levels dropping lower and lower, like a pond drying up in a drought. I felt brittle and dusty, and often in the months leading up to the move to the farm, I found myself close to tears. But I couldn't cry, and at such moments I felt alarm edged with despair, and occasionally despair edged with alarm. At night I would often drink too much. Once or twice I fell over, hard, in the hallway, like I'd done so long ago on clonidine, when we'd first arrived in Melbourne and were trying to construct a new life.

Sometimes I'd be walking down the street and I'd be overcome with the dread that there wasn't enough oxygen in the thin air to sustain my lungs. I'd stop where I was and lean against a bus shelter. I might stare for a minute at my hand clasping the wood or I might look up at the strange wisps of cloud high above the bay. I would try to take a deep breath, and with a sinking heart I would be struck by the notion that only heroin would oxygenate me. My soul was a tattered rag of a thing. Heroin would, and could, if sought, do everything. And I knew it was bullshit. But I knew nothing else.

I expressed none of my doubts, my panic, to Candy. We were trying to be nice to each other, but there was a lot of damage. I figured that actions spoke louder than words, and I'd just spent a decade saying one thing and doing another. I figured it was my duty to be positive about changing our lives. I felt that talking about how I felt would be unfair to Candy. A mean, hard world without heroin loomed like something out of a postapocalyptic comic book, but I didn't see the point in getting wimpy about that. And as for guilt: fucking forget it. Bad times happen. That's what I figured. You move on.

Yet alone, with my thoughts and my growing unease, I found myself adrift on a broiling sea of guilt in a gale-force wind.

As for the future, the real tentativeness was about love. What was going to be there now, in the gap where smack had been? A crater of uncertainty. A fucking bomb site.

But we never talked, or when we talked, we bullshitted. "Things are going to be great." I tried to believe it, and I tried to not believe that there were vultures as big as pterodactyls circling overhead, waiting to descend on my soul as it expired its final weak breath. I could hear the leathery flap of their wings in the crackling air.

I'd never thought such things before and it was an effort to suppress them. I knew I was in trouble but I didn't know what it was. I had a glimmer of awareness that the spirit had been squeezed out of me. I didn't know if I could ever be inflated again, without drugs. It was a world of trepidation. Even the clanking of trams rounding bends made me jittery.

Maybe in the end we would have gotten around to taking stock of our lives. We never really got to find out. When we moved to the country, things fell apart fast. The whole thing, really, the big final thing, could in a way be measured in the gestation period of a cat. Nine weeks. It's hard to believe that all the weirdness that was about to happen could happen in sixty-three days.

In the last weeks in Melbourne and the first weeks on the farm, Candy just got speedier and speedier as the methadone went down. But that's what you'd expect, I thought. Candy was getting a little bit hyper, a little bit edgy. That's all it was. That's what I told myself. We would come off the methadone and get through the withdrawals and she'd be the queen of serene. In the meantime we started putting more and more effort into finding grass. I thought it was a slow drug. I thought it was our reward. I didn't realize it doesn't help in nervous breakdown situations. Well, I was none too slow myself. I could hear the clockwork whirring out of control, a massive background noise.

It's funny how you could come off heroin and methadone and lose your bearings like that. The whole fucking world was a blur.

The old guy we bought the farm off had been there for forty-five years. He'd bought it when he was forty, after his wife had died and his son moved out of the home. Now it was time for the retirement village.

The farmhouse was covered on every surface and in every nook and crevice with at least forty-five years of grime that we should have dealt with. We started with good intentions but the job never got done. The kitchen was particularly dark and smoky. The stove was a big old wood combustion thing which was also the heater for the house's hot water. You had to get it going at least four or five hours before having a bath or shower or cleaning the dishes. And then you had to keep feeding it and checking it. I was way out of my fucking depth, swinging that axe out at the woodpile, jarring my wrists and working on my blisters.

We never even cleaned the cupboards. We just moved everything in on top of the grime. We didn't seem to have a great deal of energy, and the move itself had been exhausting. Very quickly we were overtaken by events, and the farmhouse remained a dirty farmhouse full of unpacked boxes. Dust and grit got into our bedsheets and never got out.

I kept forgetting to feed the chickens that the old guy had left us. I didn't know if I was supposed to let them out of their little shack. I didn't know if I was supposed to clean it out, or if all the soft stuff on the ground was part of the setup. Anyway, they scared the shit out of me. I remembered I once read how Werner Herzog had said if you want to know evil you must look into the eye of a chicken. Up on the farm it made perfect sense.

The cats came with us and they seemed reasonably happy, or at least curious about their new surroundings. I was jealous of the way animals led their lives and didn't have drug problems.

I don't know what we ate but I can't remember ever cooking. There were no corner stores for miles around so it was not so simple to get a chocolate bar or a cream bun for dinner anymore. We lived on toast. But one day we tried to cook, and something happened that was one of those signs, getting harder to ignore, that things were wrong.

"We'll have my parents to Sunday lunch," Candy had said. Well, we were a proper family now, with cats and chickens and runner beans. We weren't just drug addicts anymore. It made sense to invite the folks up. And everyone had told us how lucky we were, how the old-style combustion ovens were the greatest and food cooked in them tasted out of this world. I took it that this was information you picked up in *Belle* or *Country Homes*.

I'd met Candy all those years earlier; we'd fallen in love

and our lives had begun. Everything else, other than me and Candy and drugs, was absolutely peripheral. This included parents.

I suppose her mother had tried to make an effort to like me. But you have to look at the facts. Candy's mother's grandfather was a turn-of-the-century Freemason industrialist. He hated the Irish so much that he refused to have the color green anywhere in his house. That kind of mistrust lived on in Candy's mother. I was pure CIA: Catholic, Irish descent, Addict. I'd come to sweep her daughter away, and for the better part of a decade we'd confirmed all her worst nightmares. So I guess it was an effort for her to even give me the time of day.

The best word to describe her relationship with Candy would be "strained." The best phrase: strained to breaking point. They used to just go at each other, like the meaning of life was to pull triggers and push buttons. Each thinking the other was in the wrong. I was always on Candy's side, of course.

Candy's father was pretty mellow. He'd been in Vietnam, Special Air Services or some elite shit like that, so I thought he was cool. And he was. I think he searched for the good in human nature, and I liked him because he always seemed to try and give me the benefit of the doubt: maybe next week I really *would* stop using heroin.

So they came to the farm for a Sunday roast with their Labradors, Sparky and Spanky. We were down to about 10 mils of methadone a day by now: more placebo than holding pattern, really. I suppose both our heads were coming off at the hinges, but since I couldn't see myself, I noticed it most in Candy.

We were never organized, so the first fuckup of the day was the difficulty of buying vegetables in a small country town in Gippsland on a Sunday morning.

"I can't believe you didn't get them yesterday," I said as

we drove slowly along the quiet main street, having just drunk our methadone at the pharmacy.

"Fuck you!" Candy said. "Why should *I* be the one who has to think about things like vegetables?"

Sometimes I couldn't help myself. "Well, they're *your* parents. You invited them up here."

"We were in here yesterday getting our methadone. I'm the one who's going to cook the meal, so you should have worried about getting the vegetables."

"Oh shit!" I exclaimed. "That reminds me—I haven't got the stove going yet. I haven't even chopped any wood!"

This set the tone for the day.

But we salvaged something. At the liquor store, while I was buying beer, I sweet-talked the girl at the counter into raiding the pub kitchen. She gave me some potatoes and onions. I offered her two dollars but she said not to worry about it. Then we drove half an hour to the next town and found a frozen chicken in the mixed-goods freezer of a gas station. On the way back through to the farm we dropped in on Peter and Michael, who gave us all the vegetables they had, which was half a pumpkin. Finally we picked a handful of runner beans from our own overrun garden, the old man's dying garden. The produce of the land. Good honest toil. It was the first time we'd done it. It wasn't the same as a supermarket, and all that dirt made me wary.

"They're pretty tough. They're not very green," I said to Candy, holding out my hand while she sniffed them suspiciously. "Maybe it's the wrong season. Maybe they're not ready yet."

"Don't worry," Candy said, "we'll just steam them for ages and cover them in butter."

Candy was making lots of Turkish coffee during this period of our lives, a thick muddy sludge that tasted good and really got the heart racing. So while I had a few beers to get mellow for the imminent arrival of the in-laws, Candy got snappy on the Istanbul express. We smoked a joint, thinking it would make our energy levels meet halfway, but it was strong dope and the end result was the compounding of our inability to get much of a move on.

Somehow it was midday. We had to defrost that fucking chicken. I had a manic burst with the axe out at the woodpile and got the stove going at last, but hot water was still a long way off. I filled the kitchen sink with cold water and dropped the chicken in. I put on the electric jug and added some hot water and the ice began to fall away. As I ripped the plastic off the chicken I noticed the use-by date: Friday, two days earlier.

"Ah, fuck!"

I called out to Candy. She came into the kitchen.

"Does this smell bad to you?"

She leaned over the sink and sniffed. "It doesn't smell so good."

"Shit, Candy, what are we going to do?"

"Don't worry, we'll just baste it in lots of stuff. I don't know, basil, honey, bay leaves. What's in the cupboard? We'll go through the cupboard. What do you put on a roast?"

Her parents arrived at about one o'clock. We kept them in the lounge room and made small talk for twenty minutes, but finally Candy's mother couldn't help herself. It was inspection time.

"Now, what can I do in the kitchen?" She was already out of her seat and heading toward the door.

"Nothing, Mum. Really, it's fine."

"Nonsense," her mother replied, through the door now. "There must be something I can do."

"Everything's under control," Candy said as she followed her down the hall.

"We're just waiting for the oven to heat up," I offered meekly, my voice trailing away.

Now it was just me and Candy's father alone in the lounge room. I turned to him and winced.

"We're running a bit behind."

He smiled politely and took a sip of his beer. "No worries, mate."

I went into the kitchen. You could see Candy's mother turning tight-lipped and pissed off. One minute they were niggling at each other about "you go to all this trouble to invite us up here and you can't even manage the simple decency of getting the meal together on time" and "get off my case, Mum" and "it's not the food that's even the issue here, it's your attitude." And the next minute the thing just began to spiral.

I stood in the corner of the kitchen and said, "Okay, let's just calm down. We'll be eating in less than an hour. Why don't I open one of these bottles of wine you've brought along?"

But the thing had gone too far for that. Candy's mother turned on me, a thing she'd rarely done over the years, despite her obvious dislike.

"That chicken is rock solid!" she exclaimed. "We're not going to be eating until the sun goes down!"

Candy's father was in the doorway now. "Hey, hey, hey," he said, patting the air with his hands, "let's all calm down a moment."

"Oh, she infuriates me," Candy's mother said, her back stiffening and her eyes glazing with the same cold anger that came over her during fights about money. "You really need to get ahold of yourself, young lady. It's about time you got your life together. The little details *and* the big."

She reminded me of a pit bull terrier. She was an imposing woman at the softest of times. I wanted to defend her daughter from her meanness.

I looked over to Candy. She was standing beside the stove, her shoulders hunched forward, her fists clenched, her face contorted with pain, tears flooding from her eyes. It gave me a shock. It seemed a profound change had descended. Maybe this was one of the vultures, and its shadow alone was enough to fuck your head, and it had come down on Candy, not me. Her corner of the kitchen seemed dark and different.

"Look at me!" she screamed, in a voice that was hard to recognize as hers. "Can't you see? Don't you understand? I've been clenching my fucking fists since I was thirteen years old! Look at my fists! Look at my fucking fists!" She held them up toward her mother as she sobbed and screamed. They were like two little arthritic balls of hooked bone and tight skin. They really did look like they'd been closed for years. "Look at them! Look at them, will you! I haven't been able to unclench my fists since I was thirteen years old! Don't you understand? You fucking bitch, don't you understand?"

I was scared shitless. It was a powerful thing happening, a sudden outbreak of a truth deeper than what I had known about Candy. And these were the kind of truths they locked you up for. On one level it was incoherent, and yet on another there was something about those locked fists that was clear and terrifying. I didn't know what it was, but I suddenly understood why heroin must have seemed so good to Candy.

She went on and on while the three of us stood there. It was like there were sparks coming off her. I moved toward her, to put my arm around her, to slow her down, but her body tensed like a wild animal. I retreated a step.

"Baby doll, it's okay," I said.

Her shoulders sagged and her sobbing began to increase. "I can't unclench my hands. I just can't unclench my hands. I can't relax," she blubbered.

"Candace, darling, you're overwrought," her mother said, relenting a little. "It's been a big move, it's been a big year, there's been a lot of change, adjusting to the country life. You need to take things easy."

I moved to Candy again and this time put my arms around her frail shoulders.

"Just go," she said. "Fuck off. Forget the lunch." Then she buried her head in my chest and started crying more.

"Tell them to forget the lunch. Tell them to just forget about lunch. Tell them to go."

I looked over to Candy's parents. They were pretty stunned and awkward. Obviously it was easier, clearer, more concrete, when we just hassled them for money and they could tell us we were fucked.

"I'm sorry," I said over Candy's shoulder, trying to act like not too much was wrong. "Why don't we make it another day? It's just a bad day. I'm sorry."

It *was* a bad day, a kind of marker day, from which things could deteriorate more rapidly. Her parents packed Sparky and Spanky into the station wagon and began the hungry drive back to Melbourne. Candy and I walked outside to the windbreak that ran along the ridge where the fields sloped away. We sat underneath one of the huge old pines. Candy cried for a long time. I took her hands one at a time in mine, flattening them and stroking her open palms.

"Do you know why you're crying, Candy?"

"I'm scared," she said.

"It's all right," I said, and as the words came out I realized all the times I'd said them before.

She looked up at me with her flooded blue eyes. Her lips curled and quivered in sorrow. "I think we're going to end."

I frowned. "We'll never end."

"We'll end. That's what I hate. We'll have to end."

"We'll never end."

Her palms were clammy and they trembled faintly as I stroked them. "It won't work."

"Candy, it will work."

"We think it can but it can't."

"It's all different now. We've come this far."

"Look at what we've been through. We're barely getting out alive. We should be happy with that. Happy enough with only that."

"I love you."

"Love?" she asked. "I love you too, you know. Look at where love has gotten us."

"Do you hate me?"

She sighed deeply. "Sometimes," she said. "Sometimes I hate you."

I felt what seemed like indigestion. Then I thought it might be a mild heart attack. My mind was going fast but none of my thoughts made sense as the afternoon began to cool.

After a while of silence Candy said, "I didn't mean that."

But I knew our hearts were scarred and might never get better.

Coco appeared from behind the windbreak. Her black flanks bulged with the weight of the kittens inside her. She purred and pressed herself against us. Time seemed to move in lumbering jerks, each thing separate. It was painful to be alive.

"We should feed the cats," I said at last, and we stood up and went back into the house, into the powerful smell of burned Sunday lunch.

We'd been outside for a long time and forgotten about the roast. Smoke poured from the oven. The chicken was black. The vegetables had caramelized into a gelatinous charcoal. We left them on the counter to cool down before we could throw them out. The trays sat there sizzling. It was the sound malice would make if it could talk. Candy said, "That's our Sunday lunch. Look at it, it's a sculpture. Guess what it's called?"

"What?"

"It's called, 'The Afternoon of the Closed Fists.' By Candy."

I didn't say anything.

We found some rolled oats and had porridge for dinner, with lots of sugar. We drank the wine Candy's parents had brought, and the rest of the beer, and watched TV and went to sleep.

Like I said, that was a bad day, but it was a good day compared to some that came soon after. Heroin had been hard and simple, but as Candy began to lose her mind, this metaphor stuff increased. And with it came anger. It was like the big bang theory. First there was nothing, and then the anger started, and it expanded outward in all directions, and then it was everything.

There were no more soft, sad conversations beneath the pine trees. It seemed from this point on that all we did was fight.

It was rapid and vicious. We didn't sleep much. The only good thing about this period of time was that it didn't last long, in real terms, in calendar terms.

We fought about the farm.

It had seemed so easy: money drops from the sky, you buy a farm. Yeah right. I didn't know about responsibility. I thought I deserved a medal, for getting off smack, for coming down off the methadone. I mean, I was not a danger to society anymore. Your VCR and stereo were safe, from me at least. But what did the world expect? A guy from the shire council knocked on the door one day and told me there were some weeds in one of our fields and they were the kind that had to be removed. It was the law, he said.

Fucking weeds! The field was covered with them. Leave them be, I thought. Who cares? But in the country they cared.

At the end of the first day bent double in the field, tearing the mutant kudzulike things from the soil with my bare hands, I staggered into the kitchen.

"This is bullshit!" I said, wiping the sweat from my brow, my hands bleeding from the thorns. "I hate living in the country. It's a bloody nightmare."

"Don't be a crybaby," Candy said. "It's not very becoming."

"Well, why don't you get out there and help me?"

"Listen, I just hocked my arse for five years. Pulling a few weeds is not going to hurt you."

"I just don't see the point in manual labor. It's ridiculous."

"You just don't see the point. You don't see it, do you?"

"Ah, cryptic. Very scary. Do you want me to go, then?"

"Yeah, just fuck off out of the house for a while. I can't stand you being here."

"If I fuck off, Candy, I'll fuck off out of your life."

"Yeah, you can do that too." She stared at me and her eyes seemed vacant. "Why not? It's not a bad idea."

We fought about money.

We had none.

"Then stop drinking so much," she said.

"We have to drink," I said, "we're down to eight mils of methadone. Why do you think everything's so difficult?"

"If we had some money, things wouldn't be so difficult."

"There are no jobs around here, Candy. What do you want me to do?"

"You're just a jerk," she said. "I don't want anything. I don't know what I want."

"Why do you keep attacking me, Candy?"

"I'm sorry. I'm sorry, okay?"

"Listen, how about this? I'll grow a crop, and that'll make us some money. I'll get maybe twenty plants in that gap between the windbreak and the shed. It's a wedge in there. It's nice and sunny. A thousand bucks a plant. Maybe ten thousand. I'll look after you."

"You do that," she said, smiling like she didn't believe me. "You plant those seeds."

We fought about the unknowable gap between us, in the guise of fighting about clean walls.

One day I woke up and Candy had written in lipstick, in large letters on the bedroom wall, MOTHER=SLUT. SLUT BITCH CUNT. If I felt concern for the meaning of the act, I suppressed it with anger for the act itself.

"What the fuck is that?"

Candy was sitting naked at the dressing table, putting on makeup. "It's a statement of fact, what do you think?"

"Jesus, Candy! It's all over the wall. What do you think you're doing?"

"I'm expressing myself," she said.

"Can't you express yourself on a drawing pad or something? Who's going to clean it off? Not me. What's this with your mother, anyway?"

She swiveled around. "Hey, listen. If not her, then you."

"Candy, I think you might be losing it. I think you might need to see a doctor."

"If not her, then you," she repeated, shouting this time, pointing at me. "Okay, then. You."

She stood up and walked to a fresh patch of wall.

"Let's see now."

I watched the lipstick in her hand. It swung up and touched the white surface of the wall. I could see a small red mark where contact had been made. She looked over her shoulder at me, then looked back at the wall. Her hand moved downward, an oblique stroke from left to right. There was a lovely soft texture to the unrolling of the redness, and for a moment I could see how it would be fun to write on walls with lipstick. W. The first letter was W.

WEAK.

WEAK SLIME LOSER COCK FERRET. Somehow it was the ferret that hurt the most.

"I hope you're having fun there," I said, knowing it was a pathetic thing to say. But I felt a strange surge of power. Even through the pain of coming off narcotics, I was beginning to sense that there might be a me in there somewhere. It was a scattered kind of me, but I wondered if it could gather itself together. I was all those things that Candy was writing, and yet, somehow, I didn't have to be. There was a me of the future that might be able to make choices. A me that could feel hope, and pain. With every word that Candy wrote, I felt an exhilaration. That she had been right on the afternoon of the closed fists. That we would end, and break the bonds of each other. It was as if I felt a pride about being me, and the words on the wall didn't match it. Since there wasn't a great deal to be proud of from my past, I figured it must have been a glimpse of imagined pride about a possible future.

"That's really smart, Candy. That's good. I'm glad you think that."

She dragged her arm back across the wall and underlined the words. She dressed quickly and walked outside. I heard the car start and drive away. The sense of exhilaration passed and I lay in the grit-filled bed with a hollow pain in the pit of my stomach. I stared at all the red words on the wall. After a while I went to the fridge and opened a beer for breakfast. Then I hitchhiked into Korrumburra to get my methadone.

Events like this were making me realize that I hadn't really felt anything in years. It was hard, this new business of emotions. Five minutes, like that five minutes in bed, was almost too much to bear. Something was growing inside me—an awareness of a way out of things—but it was obvious I could only take it in small doses.

Mostly, though, I still somehow figured it was just a bad patch. Maybe a break was all that was needed. A break, not a breakdown. But I couldn't sense the scale of the catastrophe that was looming in our tiny lives. My measuring devices were blunt, unsophisticated. My radar was all scrambled. Living through each day seemed such an enormous effort; it was all I could do merely to keep my own balance.

We fought about infidelity.

It was infidelity that was the final trigger, which is not as strange as it sounds. There was prostitution, of course, which didn't count, and then there was this. But this, this new thing, interest in another, was about desire or lust; was a king of turning away. It was painful, though in the scheme of things pain is a kind of strange word.

It's just a thing you sense at first, infidelity. We were moving in a new world of drugs. We met a guy called Paul

Hillman who could get good grass. We never had much money so we bought in small amounts and always seemed to be driving long distances in the quest. I suppose it kept us occupied. Paul was one of those chronic potheads who are always happy to drive two hours to pick up the dregs from a fifty-dollar deal. But he was handsome in a beaten-up way, and he was mad as a cut snake, and he was not me, so he had a lot going for him from Candy's point of view.

She started doing more and more of the dope trips with him, and after a few too many stories of car breakdowns and waiting for hours in dealers' lounge rooms, it became kind of obvious. I accused her and she denied it. I spent a lot of time repeating variations on the phrase, "Candy, it's really obvious you're fucking Paul," and she worked out many variations on, "You're wrong. You're simply wrong." Finally, one cloudless day, she said, "Firstly, you don't know what you're talking about. Secondly, I hate the sound of your voice. Thirdly, why don't you just fuck off?" It was as good as an admission. By now it seemed advice worth taking.

My knees felt weak. I walked to a pay phone a mile down the road. I wanted the privacy of that booth in the middle of nowhere. I rang my old friend Kay in Sydney, told her briefly my life had fallen apart, and asked if she'd put me up for a few days. She said sure, as if it was no surprise to hear from me out of the blue like that. Kay was a skinny, hyper-active, dark-haired girl whom I'd done some business with in the years before I'd met Candy. Back then, in the group I ran with, we'd all thought we were teenage drug barons. Kay used to do hash runs from India—strap a couple of kilos to her legs and walk through customs in a billowy dress that had quiet Christian written all over it—and get me to off-load the dope. These days she'd gone legitimate, and put all her money into a film-editing business, which was doing well. She ran the business with her husband Aaron, when he was sober enough, but since that was rare, she tended to be a little highly strung.

The bank had given Candy and me Visa cards when the loan for the farm was approved. I hated the idea of using a card with my own name on it, not the least because I had no money to make repayments. It had sat in my wallet, unused, for months, like a terrible harbinger of yuppiedom.

So I asked Kay if she'd buy my plane ticket to Sydney, and again, without missing a beat, she said sure. I asked her if she'd pick me up at the airport, and she said sure to that too. Maybe she was missing the old days a bit, all that drama and action.

Whatever. I walked back to the farm and threw some clothes and a couple of books into a bag. Candy said, "Where are you going?"

"It's none of your business," I said. Then I left the house and walked down the driveway and started hitchhiking to the train station. I wanted Candy to follow me. She didn't. I wanted to cry but I clenched my jaw instead. I thought about picking up my methadone for one last time, but I was so angry and confused that it didn't seem important anymore.

Within an hour I was on a train, heading for Melbourne and the airport. When the train picked up speed I started reading *The Unbearable Lightness of Being*, a book of which absolutely everything now escapes me other than its pervasive odor of sadness. The carriage clanked and rattled. I glanced outside. It occurred to me that the landscape was moving away from Candy.

As a drug addict, the days had always been fairly predictable: scam, get the dope, scam, get the dope. Now I felt I was balancing on the edge of a cliff in a thick fog. I had no clear notion of what lay in front; I was all spastic legs and flailing arms. I no longer knew what I thought about Candy and me. I tried to concentrate on reading the book. Our own life seemed even less concrete than the world that existed inside that ethereal fiction.

BREAKAGES

Memory is a fucker, the way it blurs things. The thing is, I can write about events. All that heroin, it was all events. When the events slowed down and emotional stuff began, well, I don't know that I know how to write about that. Perhaps it's enough to say: we fought for what seemed like a long time but wasn't, and then one day I found myself catapulted north, to Sydney and the breaking of everything that was familiar.

This was a time of life being out of whack.

When I fled the farm, I felt on top of the world. I've heard since that this is called denial. It makes sense. The brain shuts down at times of true crisis, and nothing but the locus of hilarity (or is that hysteria?) is active. Nothing could stop me, not even the depression and confusion hovering off-screen, back in Gippsland where Candy was. I went to Sydney and then farther north, to the Sunshine Coast. I plunged into sex as if it offered absences greater than overdose. For fuck's sake, I was trying to come off the drugs. There was nothing else but sex.

The first night in Sydney, I slept with Kay. I have no idea why we fucked. The situation seemed set up. Some people are attracted to sickness, to the kind of madness where sparks fly off the head, to the incoherence of despair, masked by nervous energy, which winds up looking like bewildered joy.

I think Kay was attracted to this in me.

For myself, nothing at all seemed strange during this time. Since everything was new, everything seemed correct.

Sally was Kay's trainee editor and live-in housekeeper. She was eighteen and had come down from Queensland a year earlier. She'd left school and landed what she saw as an exciting job in the big smoke through friends of friends. She was tall and confident, a rangy country girl with long black hair and sweet green eyes. I thought she was beautiful.

That first night, after Kay's husband Aaron had reached his nightly blackout, sprawled and snoring on the spare couch in the baby's room, Kay and Sally whispered conspiratorially in the kitchen.

I sat in a rocking chair on the back veranda, overlooking the freight lines at Lilyfield. It was my first night back in Sydney in four years, and that trip had just been a quick two-day heroin run. I'd done a few trips like that, but it was seven years or more since Candy and I had moved to Melbourne to get away from drugs.

And it was thirty-six hours now since I'd last had my methadone. I was beginning to feel a bit frayed around the edges. It was very uncomfortable, like I was shedding skin. I knew it would get worse before it got better.

But the smell of jasmine, at midnight, reminded me of how much I loved Sydney. I was drunk, sad, and excited, though the excitement masked the edginess, the deep unease.

Kay came out through the glass doors.

"You're going to sleep in Sally's bed," she announced.

"Sure. Fine," I said, thinking that somehow, miraculously, it had been arranged that I was to sleep with Sally. I'd been in Sydney for six hours. To sleep with Sally would have been my wish. I thought we must have all been remarkably in tune with each other's thoughts. Like I said, nothing seemed strange. I suppose it was easy that night to believe that in Sydney, magic realism was real.

I went to bed, expecting Sally to follow.

Kay came instead. I didn't really care.

"What about your husband?"

"He's too drunk. He won't wake up."

We fucked and then she went back to her room, to share the bed with Sally. Aaron remained sleeping all night on the couch.

On the second night Kay and Sally dragged me along to a party. I figured the only way to ward off the methadone devils was to get really drunk. But of course, coming off methadone, you tend to skip the drunk part and go straight to unhinged.

Everyone else was smashed so it didn't matter. It was a loud, crowded party, Sydney in summer. Coming from the darkness of Melbourne, I thought I could feel the future exploding upon me. Nothing mattered. On the stairs I said to Sally, "I didn't really want to sleep with Kay last night. I wish I'd slept with you. I'd rather sleep with you."

"Okay," she said. "Then sleep with me tonight."

This was really not good in terms of the etiquette of houseguests.

In the morning Kay's three-year-old daughter wandered into the room and looked at Sally and me and wandered back out.

"Mummy," I heard her say, "what's Sally doing in bed with that boy?"

Sally looked at me and winced and then got up and pulled on a T-shirt. She composed her face into an expression of casual indifference, and walked out of the room. It was silent for a while and I drifted back into a restless sleep.

After a few minutes I jolted awake. I could hear doors and cupboards slamming. I could hear Kay screaming at Sally. All about boundaries. "You're fired, you bitch. And you've got half an hour to get out of my house. I don't want to see your face again. This is *my* house. How dare you?"

Sally came into the room. "Well," she shrugged, "a turning point in my life."

"Don't worry," I said. "They're lots of fun."

I was feeling pretty sick by this stage. Some heroin would have done the trick and made the world nice. But I was trying to stick to my task of not using.

Sally was packing her stuff and muttering, "I can't believe it." I guess she was eighteen years old and her life had just turned upside down, but that's not what I was thinking at the time. I was thinking how much I needed to smoke a joint, to ease the creaking of the bones and make that supreme effort to get out of bed. Then Kay burst into the room.

"And as for you!" she shouted. She pointed a bony finger at me and held it there with an air of dramatic malevolence before storming out again.

I packed my bag. This took me all of fifteen seconds. In the kitchen, Aaron, always pleasant whenever conscious, was curing his hangover with a glass of wine and a grapefruit.

"Don't worry, old son," he said, tipping his glass to me. "Kay's problem is, she hasn't had a fuck in so long, she's obviously jealous of you and Sally getting it together."

I felt a bit queasy right at that moment, but knew it was not the time to show guilt or awkwardness. Not the time for public confessions.

"Have you got any of those heads left, Aaron?" I asked. "Do you think I could roll a quick joint before I go?"

In a perverse way the whole thing was a kind of bonding experience for Sally and me. We were thrown together. I was only the third guy she'd ever fucked.

All the intense weirdness of coming off the methadone over the next couple of weeks was mixed in with the strangeness of viewing an old city through new eyes. The explosion and disintegration of my relationship with Candy were briefly tempered by the alien hypnosis of sex from the unknown.

Sally didn't care too much, not after the initial shock. Kay ran a tight ship emotionally, and when I arrived, like a small typhoon, I think Sally saw it as some kind of opportunity to jump ship, to learn to swim in a bigger ocean. I was older and fucked-up, with the diamond glint of absolute abandon in my yellow eyes: everything an eighteen-year-old could dream of.

We flew north, obviously *not* courtesy of Kay's credit card this time. It was time, at last, to start using mine. Sally took me to meet her parents, in a beautiful house in the rain forest. They were nice to me, for her sake, I suppose.

I don't know what they made of me, eating their mangos for breakfast and rabbiting on in my frantic enthusiasm for a life that had been new for all of about five minutes.

I don't know what they made of the tanless pallor of years in Melbourne, or my slicked-back hair and pointy boots. I don't know what they made of the black tracks down my skinny arms, now so pathetically exposed in Sally's dad's T-shirts in the crushing Queensland heat.

They bought me a pair of shorts, so I wouldn't look so out of place on the beach. Sally gave me a Chanel T-shirt and a pair of sandals. I swear to God I looked like a fucking dipstick.

They lived in an open-plan house, cool and cedared, beautifully designed some twenty years earlier during one glorious hippie summer. There were screens and partitions and levels everywhere. Sally and I had to fuck silently, but even the stress of that was fun. Late at night the endless croaking of the frogs soothed me through the methadone pangs and into brief snatches of sleep.

Like I've said, I'd never driven much, never even had my license. In the early days, when I was a successful young drug dealer, I'd always gotten a lift to wherever I wanted to go. There was always someone willing to drive me. Later, when I was a successfully fucked-up junkie, we didn't have cars too often. In any case, Candy had always driven, since we figured if you're already breaking drug laws it's best not to compound things by breaking traffic laws as well.

Really, the sum total of my driving experience was minimal, bordering on nonexistent. Now Sally somehow convinced her trusting parents to give us—for a whole week—their brand-new four-wheel drive.

It was a Holden Jackaroo. The cabin seemed to be at least fifteen feet off the ground. It had none of the idiosyncrasies of junkies' cars in Melbourne. Nonetheless it frightened me. The concept of financial responsibility, coupled with my lack of driving experience, frightened me. Not having a license was icing on the cake.

But without the car, we couldn't get out of the rain forest, couldn't go off exploring the coast.

"Yeah, I've driven these before," I said. "No problems."

They stood on the gravel driveway, waving us good-bye. Do not crunch the gears, I willed myself, stoned on their outrageous pot, smiling through clenched teeth and sweating profusely. Do not crunch the fucking gears.

In all this madness, in all these mad few weeks, I tried to forget that back in my real life, where I'd left it in Gippsland, things were more than bad. I tried not to think about going home. I tried to maintain my anger, about Candy fucking Paul Hillman, about Candy's weeks of vitriol in the lead-up to saying *go*. But I was haunted by the feeling that I deserved everything bad that was sure to come.

After a week I called her from a phone booth in Noosa Beach, where we were staying with Sally's sister. There were years of connection. It was hard to be in new lives, other people's lives.

Candy said, "Everything's fine. Everything's turning blue here."

"Blue?" I asked, a little alarmed. "Everything's turning blue? What do you mean?"

"Blue! Everything's turning blue. Everything's fine."

I stood sweating in the hot glass booth in the tropics, feeling acids eating at my stomach.

"Listen, I'll be back sometime soon, I guess. We've got a lot to sort out. I feel okay coming off the methadone. How do you feel?"

She had stopped it too, the day I left. I don't know why. I only dropped off the methadone because I was going to Sydney, a thousand kilometers from the Korrumburra pharmacy where we were registered to pick it up.

"Fantastic," she said. "I feel fantastic. Everything's going blue."

"Candy, what do you mean? What do you mean, blue?" I gripped the phone and my knuckles were white. For the last faltering seconds I tried desperately to believe there was something here I was misunderstanding, that Candy was speaking of things that made sense, things that belonged to a world I was familiar with.

"Blue! Blue! You don't get it, do you? It's simple! I'm speaking clearly. Everything's turning blue. Everything's going to be fine."

"Okay, Candy," I sighed, overwhelmed, "I've got to go now. I'll talk to you soon."

When I came back from the phone booth, Sally knew I was no longer there. I was delving into the darker unease of burnt-out loyalties and remembrances of things past. Of an imminent horizon of collapses and breakage. Of how a mind could overload and suddenly change into something unfamiliar and unknowable. Of how something felt deeply, however misguided, could disappear forever. This must be a kind of death.

I couldn't tell Sally how I thought that perhaps Candy was going crazy, and I didn't even say it to myself.

I was hoeing into the Visa card now. It was so fucking ironic to have my own credit card at last. But I'd developed bad habits from all those earlier years of fraud. The Visa card was magic money; I had no concept of the future. At this time of my life I lived truly in the moment, in the worst possible sense.

We had dual cards on the same account. Candy was buying weird shit down in Victoria, Belgian crayons and mountain bikes and cookbooks and theatrical makeup. Up in Queensland, with not a cent to my name, the card was all I could use. In this three-week period, Candy and I took it seven thousand dollars over the two-thousand-dollar limit. Before the computers caught up with us.

Sally and I were smoking lots of dope, and suddenly all over the coast, the heads dried up. Normally this news would have passed entirely unnoticed through a consciousness preoccupied with slightly stronger drugs. But by now I was ten days or more off the methadone, all wires and pangs, and if I had to be sleep deprived, I wanted to do it on Warp 5. Up there in the lush river flats, you were about as close to the source of the warp as you could get.

Sally couldn't get any dope. When we arrived back at the rain forest, we found that even her parents had run out. I was really keen for some fucking buds, believe me. Finally we got Sally's mum revved up, appealed to her sense of the frontier spirit. I think we framed it like a challenge: if you were such a pioneer in the dope scene back then, why can't you get some now?

She rose to the occasion. She found an old hippie girlfriend still growing crops in the boondocks. As a rule this lady didn't sell dope. She was simply wire-brushing the inside of her skull, slowly, over twenty years, to let the air in.

For Sally's mum, though, in a time of need, Wirebrush would make an exception and sell Sally a pound or so. Now all we needed was the cash.

Sally sweet-talked Mac, a friend in Sydney, into supplying the dollars. He would take a cut of the dope and profits and leave me to do the business. Money had to be transferred from Sydney. We had to get out of the rain forest and straight into the nearest bank. And we had to get Sally's mum to ensure that Wirebrush was punctual and business-like. It's funny, but it felt good to be doing that shit again. What's more, it gave me something to keep my mind away from things turning blue.

All this would take two days. Maybe Wirebrush had to check the runes, work out the most opportune moment. On the first night of waiting, the call came, the call with the bad news.

I was trying to be invisible. You drop off methadone as if off the face of a cliff. In the raw pain of being flayed and crazy, you want to disappear off the very surface of the earth. Through a convoluted route, Candy's parents tracked me down. The call came at midnight. It was her dad, such a decent and bewildered man. He got straight to the point.

"Candace is in the hospital."

"What's happened?"

"She's had a bit of a nervous breakdown."

"Where is she?"

"Royal Park. You'd better come down."

"All right. I'll try to arrange for a bus or a plane. I'll call you tomorrow and tell you what's happening."

There was not much to say. I guess I had known this was coming, but now I could feel my heart going up into my throat. The holiday was over.

I climbed back under the gauze mosquito net.

"Are you okay?" Sally asked.

"I don't want to talk about it," I said, and already the cool tang of Melbourne was prickling up my arms.

But we still had to organize the dope deal. Late morning and early afternoon we fucked around, panicking when the money hadn't arrived, making urgent phone calls to Sydney. Finally we got the money five minutes before the bank closed.

I called Candy's parents, believing that the best defense for odd behavior was offense. I told them I was having trouble getting a lift to the bus depot from the rain forest.

Her mum's tone of voice was perplexed and dubious, but what could she do?

"Is Candy okay?" I asked.

"It's not good," she said. "Just get down here."

All through the next day, the time for the deal kept getting shuffled. Old Wirebrush was nervous about the "karma" involved with capitalist transactions. Kind of interesting for someone who certainly had their finger on the pulse of current market prices. Sally's mum decided to come with us, to help with the distasteful business of handing over and counting money.

We met in a picnic area beside a six-lane highway. Wirebrush's weird choice. Her hippie kids played on the swing. Sally's mum sat with Wirebrush in her car, counting the money.

Sally and I sat in the four-wheel drive and checked the dope. When I opened the shopping bag, I knew it was a winner. The pungent smell, the globules of resin on the hairy gold heads. I broke off a branch, nothing but head. Sally rolled a huge ragged joint.

The dope hurt the throat. We gave the thumbs-up to Wirebrush, or Farmer Shiva the Destroyer, as she was rapidly becoming. I began to clench my teeth. Within two minutes I was wired beyond what was pleasant, and paranoid about having so much dope in a public place. We waved our good-byes—I never actually met her directly—and pulled back out onto the highway.

Sally and I were giggling, already wasted. Her mum was driving and serenely finishing the joint.

"I'm ripped. I am fucking ripped. This is good dope," I said.

"Mmm," Sally's mum said, like a wine taster who's been there, done it all. "I suppose it's not bad. It's got a nice soft edge to it. Kind of mellow and golden."

A soft edge? Mellow and golden? Yelping noises were coming from deep inside my brain, and behind that the clang-clang-clang of giant machinery. I imagined the police were behind us. Sally's mum continued speaking.

"Let's go up and look at the view from Arundel Rock."

"Yeah!" Sally said. "You've got to see this place. It's really special."

I realized they were talking to me.

"It's an Aboriginal sacred site. A very magical place."

Oh Lord untie the stomach knots! I was not well. My wife had been committed to a mental hospital. I wanted to do a business deal and turn a profit. I wanted to curl up in a ball and I wanted the world to quiet down. I did not want to see an Aboriginal sacred site.

But I was just too stoned to try and talk them out of it. The real world, away from heroin—I was not handling it.

Sally's mum had the goods on me. I think she could see very clearly that the state I was in was one of such distorted ugliness that even high-quality marijuana could do nothing more than intensify the distortions. I think also she wanted to calm me down, put me on a plane, and get me the fuck out of her daughter's life.

And Arundel Rock did calm me down. The huge granite dome rose abruptly out of a luscious green floodplain. We drove until the driving trail stopped and then walked to the top. Directly below us, a thousand feet down, was the darker green of the rain forest canopy, skirting the river that snaked around the rock.

We stood awestruck in the sunlight on the flat bald summit of the granite giant. All around us were rock pools and carvings. I felt like an intruder, and rightly so. I had no connection with anything, least of all the earth. Only the cushioning effect of these monstrously potent heads prevented me from falling to the ground and weeping—for everything that flooded out of me as the methadone faded; for my absence from myself for so many years; for Candy, whose fragility was now exposed by the absence of drugs; for the terrible tragedy I sensed I was about to enter.

"Look at the way the light falls everywhere in gold particles," Sally's mum said.

She was holding her arms above her head and wriggling her fingers like the storyteller on *Playschool* imitating rain. If anyone else had been there I would have cringed. But I was so stoned I saw the gold particles too.

That night we triple-wrapped the pound of heads into separate, smaller packages, placed the packages in front of the Jackaroo's tires and gently rolled the four-wheel drive over them to compress them for my flight home. Even though customs wasn't involved, I was nervous about my first plane flight with drugs. Especially such smelly drugs.

In the morning I learned too late that even the tiniest amount of this stuff was enough to make you comfortably stoned. All I had wanted was to be laid back going through the airport shit. I must have been overzealous in the amount I rolled.

I could feel that I'd become nothing but a huge stretched smile. It was a smile that didn't belong to me, yet I couldn't get rid of it. The hilarity of the dope was effectively nullified by a hole in my gut as big as a harbor. This had been there, slowly expanding, since the "everything's turning blue" phone call. But the corners of my mouth were being pulled in opposite directions by invisible wires.

My eyes were half closed. I needed dark sunglasses. I felt a little ridiculous, trying to keep my balance at the ticket counter as the airline clerk told me my Visa card had been canceled.

I had dope in my shoes, up my legs, in my underpants, around my stomach. I was expecting a pack of snarling police dogs to come bounding around the corner at any moment, sliding toward me on the polished departure lounge floor.

Sally, for whom nothing *other than* the cancellation of a Visa card could have been an appropriate ending to a whirlwind fling with someone so consummately fucked-up, went and had a word with her mum, who'd driven us to the airport.

They bought me the ticket.

We said our awkward good-byes. On the plane I drank a lot of orange juice, and it leveled me out a bit. Two awful airline coffees made me feel I had a second chance at the day.

Somehow I got through the teeth-gritting paranoia of imaginary drug squad cops waiting for me at Sydney. Sally's friend Mac, the money supplier, was there to pick me up, and I went back to his place to use the phone and get business rolling. It was ten o'clock in the morning. I booked a seat on a Melbourne bus for eight that night. I had ten hours in which to off-load the gear, give the money to Mac, make a profit (or at least pay for my bus fare), keep some dope—hopefully lots—for myself, get the hell out of there and get back to my life in Melbourne and Candy in the nuthouse. Which was the reason I wanted lots of dope.

I could have gone for the bigger cash profit but I knew I would only expend my energy running around trying to exchange it for drugs. Probably the wrong kind of drugs. It seemed simpler to just take the grass.

I called Candy's parents to tell them I was now halfway home. Could they pick me up from the bus depot at eight in the morning? By now Candy's mother was openly expressing her dismay and fury—it was a full two days since I'd been informed of the hospitalization. What in God's name was going on?

Knowing it was a flimsy excuse, I told her again that I'd had trouble getting a lift out of the rain forest. I was trying to create the impression that I'd been staying in some place accessible only by helicopter.

At any rate, they said they would be there to pick me up.

Making lightning deals in Sydney all day was a good way to temporarily distract myself from myself, or rather, from the concept of my life. I wrapped up business quickly and efficiently, getting in touch with old, old friends who had never been burnt by me, who were happy enough to gather the cash for a bargain deal on an ounce or two of major mindfuck.

Night came quickly. I boarded the bus to begin the horror trip I'd done several times—which is several times too many—over the years. The Sydney-to-Melbourne route. Memories of Rohypnol and Serepax, of the Big Merino towering beside the highway, of the all-night restaurants in Goulburn or Albury. The luxurious privacy of hitting up in the disabled's toilet, where you had your own basin and the door reached fully to the ground.

All memory now, I hoped. I rolled a joint strong enough to disable an ox, and smoked it quickly and furtively in the truck-stop parking lot at Albury at four in the morning. Another mistake in an avalanche of panicked mistakes.

I think the thing that disturbed Candy's parents the most about my appearance, when they met me at the bus depot, was not so much my disheveled state or deranged, clenched smile, as the size of my pupils, expanded by the methadone withdrawal. In the years they'd known me they had rarely seen me with pupils much bigger than a match head.

Now here I was, my relationship with them altered forever by a calamity that was forcing us together when we didn't want to be forced together. They stared intently at the vast pools of blackness that were my pupils.

I think they found it disturbing, as if they were looking at a different me. Of course, they were in many ways. But they didn't know what it meant: not just the methadone comedown, which lasts a month or two or three, but the well of fear that can stretch your pupils as wide as the sky at night. I was reentering the world of the woman I thought I loved, and yet the woman I thought I loved might never really be there again.

And I didn't know anything except the world of her and me.

I figured I just had to grit my teeth, get her out of the

place she was in, help her pull her socks up, and we could get our lives back together. Candy and me.

Trying to do this while trying to stop using drugs was probably overly ambitious.

Candy's parents drove me back to their house. They fed me breakfast, which straightened me out a bit. At nine-thirty we drove to Royal Park. The long driveway meandered through a mixture of Victorian and modern buildings. It was very similar to a detox I'd been at once in Sydney, before I'd met Candy, before this story began. The modern buildings had the unoffensive and unassuming appearance of a Christian holiday camp.

We drove through the curving avenues of shrubs and pulled up in the parking lot. All morning her parents had been curiously elusive when I'd asked for specific details about Candy's breakdown. Now they told me they thought it would be better if they waited outside while I went in by myself.

A nurse took me through various locked Plexiglas doors. Everywhere were the stereotype nutcases, leering at me as I passed them, or twitching compulsively, or staring intently into space. This was the movie nuthouse. These were the *One Flew Over the Cuckoo's Nest* crew. And suddenly, there was Candy.

I saw her from behind, shuffling uncertainly in the middle of the huge recreation room. I had imagined her to be frail and vulnerable, suffering this temporary and appalling injustice like a stoic and tragic heroine. A mistake: of course, a mistake had been made. I was here to sort it out. My head was full of conflicting emotions, mostly anger and fear, but for a moment my heart went out to her.

As I came closer she turned around. The ground seemed to tilt. My heart stopped in my throat. The world I had known disappeared. For a long time I'd lived with momentum. Now it flipped over into hyperdrive. And then all that could be felt was loss, and the profound bewilderment of vertigo.

HOSPITALS

I'd seen her with hep, I'd seen her stoned, I'd seen her happy, angry, beautiful, really sick. But not this, whatever it was. Candy stood leering at me. She seemed no different from anyone else in there. At first I couldn't even tell if she recognized me. I suppose it was a grin but it looked like a leer.

"Hi, Candy," I said. I felt the hesitancy in my voice.

She'd lost twenty or thirty pounds. It was worse than the time she'd had hep. She looked like a bag lady, the way her clothes hung off her. A purple dress, a cardigan. Her collarbone jutted out. She stood suspended, as if about to begin a step. Trembling, swaying. Her own pupils were so big that I could barely see the blue I'd always loved. And the smell. Candy had always been the bath queen. Now there was the faint stench of something putrid. Not only the odor of stale sweat, but something I couldn't clearly identify.

Everything was wrong.

"Hi!" she whispered conspiratorially, holding my gaze and smiling.

"Are you okay?"

"Phew," she exhaled, shrugging her shoulders, her head bobbing, her fingers fidgeting. "I am not okay."

I took one hand in my hands, squeezed it tight. A thick film of sweat covered her skin.

"Shit, Candy. I don't know what to say. What happened?"

"I don't know, I don't know," she whispered. "What's going on? Why am I here?"

She was pretty zonked on psych drugs, trying to smile but distressed, her lips quivering.

"I'll get you out of here in no time. Things'll be okay."

"Can I come now? Can I come with you?"

"I don't know what the fuck's going on. I don't think you can, baby. I don't know what the story is. Can I smoke here?"

"Out here," she said, and led me to a crowded TV room, the air blue with smoke. She started introducing me to everyone. I couldn't see the point. A couple of the men shook hands, wouldn't let go, stared into my eyes with the earnestness of the vacant. An enormous woman lifted her head from her chest. Her head wobbled as she looked at me and spittle drooled from her mouth. She spoke in a sedated drawl, as if the air could barely make it from her lungs into the room.

"Is—this—ya—boy—friend?"

We squeezed onto a vinyl couch. Everybody turned their heads to listen. I tried to whisper.

"Baby, what happened?"

"I don't know. But guess what I found out in here?"

"What?"

"Don't tell anyone. You can't tell anyone, okay?"

"Okay. What?" She was deadly serious, so I leaned forward.

"My father is not my father."

I put my face in my hands and I furrowed my brow. Then I looked up. "I'm sorry?" I said.

"Mel Gibson's father is my father. I'm Mel Gibson's sister. I'm really Hayley Mills."

I paused. My mind was racing. I was about to say, "Candy,

you're talking shit," but too many things were happening at once.

Instead I said, "How do you know this?"

"Someone in here told me. It makes sense now."

"Candy," I said.

She grabbed my hand and pulled me up. "Here, I'll introduce you to the girl who told me."

We went back out into the rec room. A pale-skinned, dark-haired girl sat curled in a tight ball on a couch in the corner.

"Helen, this is my husband."

The girl gave no glimmer of recognition. She seemed catatonic, shaking her head and repeating over and over, "Nnnnn. Nnnnn. Nnnnn," rocking backward and forward and staring at the floor.

"She only speaks to me," Candy said. "Don't you see? She would know."

I sighed and held her hand. My whole chest felt constricted. In all the rush of thoughts, the one that stood out was that it was my fault. I should never have gone away.

"Candy, things are fucked-up. I'm sorry, baby. We're going to fix this up. You'll get better, we'll get better, everything'll get better. I'll get you out of here soon. We'll go back to the farm. We'll just calm down."

She started crying then. I hugged her tight and understood the real meaning of the phrase "bag of bones." I concentrated all the pain into my head—that way I didn't cry. I didn't want Candy to think that things were worse than they were.

"It's all right, it's all right," I said. There they were again, those words.

Candy was the coolest junkie I'd ever known and the person I'd loved most in my life. I wasn't prepared for what was happening. It seemed a quantum leap from *everything's turning blue* to this. And yet everything around me, in this mental hospital, was undeniably real.

They let me out of the locked section. I located the admitting psychiatrist and sat in his office for five minutes. He used a lot of technical terms, like "psychotic episode" and "manic-depressive." He told me she'd been sectioned for her own safety. None of it meant much, not compared to what Peter and Michael would later tell me, about what actually happened down there on the farm in the last couple of weeks. Candy demanding they close all their blinds, to keep the sun out, to keep things blue. Candy explaining that the sun was a god that was trying to kill her. Candy pleading with them to take their money out of their banks, as the world was about to collapse and electronic systems would no longer work. Candy sleeping in the shed because the cats had told her to get out. Candy running naked through the back paddock, telling Peter and Michael, when they finally coaxed her down from a tree, that clothes hurt her skin. At which point Peter, unable to find me, had called Candy's parents.

I walked out into the sunlight. Candy's parents were sitting in the car. They got out when they saw me coming. I sucked in my breath as I approached, felt it whistle between my teeth. I'd gone inside thinking, We'll fix this, and they probably knew that I'd be coming out a little different.

I heard my shoes crunch on the gravel. I couldn't feel my body. I wanted to melt into liquid, flow down the path and into the gutter, disappear into the earth. But I wanted to hold myself together too. I figured that when you gave up smack, the penance must begin. Obviously this was the first task. It was the Catholic coming out in me. I didn't know that things can get better too.

We didn't say anything. Candy's parents looked at me expectantly.

"Well . . ." I shrugged, and then two strangled sobs emerged, unexpectedly, from deep in my throat. I lowered my head and splayed my hand over my eyes.

Candy's dad put his hand on my shoulder and half

hugged me, the way men do, with absolute awkwardness. Then I cried a little more, for maybe thirty seconds. He patted me on the back and said, "There, there." He was a nice guy, and the thought that he might be in my life in the future, if it ever worked out with Candy and me, was like an oasis in this desert of dread.

The rest was a long haul, but not such a long story. I stayed on the fold-out sofa bed at Candy's parents for a couple of weeks. In the morning I'd wander over to feed the ducks on the lake in the park across the road. I'd smoke a big joint and wonder where my life was going to go and what would happen to Candy.

It occurred to me that I owed it to Candy to stick by her, no matter what happened. But then it occurred to me more strongly that Candy, should she ever get through this, would no doubt have the sense and strength to see that she was better off without me. I knew that even if I could change, as in really stop using dope once and for all, there was still a past that was fucked-up and wrong. It had never really occurred to me that for a long time love may have only been loyalty, and that work, Candy's work, was degradation, pure and simple. How effectively I'd blocked it out became apparent as the methadone withdrawals began to taper away. Maybe the only way to make an amend for all that was to let her walk off to her future, should she choose.

In the early afternoon I would visit her at the hospital. She was moved out of the locked ward after a week. After a while she was less crazy, but so heavily sedated that she was just not there. We talked about taking it easy when we got back to the farm. I saw all the antidepressants and antipsychotics as the new problem, but the doctors took me aside and assured me that these things would be necessary for a period of time. It was Candy with no spark. They were telling me I had to accept that. That the alternative was Mel Gibson's sister, messages from the CIA, and a gradual buildup of the anger and anguish I'd seen in the months before I left. They told me we'd done a big thing, coming off heroin and then methadone after all those years. Don't give yourselves a hard time, they said.

Later each afternoon I would feed the ducks again and smoke another joint. Then I'd come home, have dinner and a glass of wine with Candy's parents, make small talk, watch a bit of TV, and go to bed, hoping I would sleep, though I didn't much.

The first time I went back to the farm, it was like the cats had all gone wild. I don't know what they'd been eating. They were almost hysterical, clustering around me frantically as I fed them. The whole house was overrun with fleas.

Coco was skinny now, and when she finished eating I followed her into the spare room. She nosed her way into a pile of old clothes and I could hear the tiny squeaking of kittens only a few days old. It was a magic moment, a patch of softness in my brittle life. I reached my hand in to stroke them as they flailed toward their mother's breasts. But one seemed to be asleep. I rubbed its head with my finger, then recoiled as I realized that the head was all there was. The body was gone. The kitten's head rolled out and landed on the floor.

I stared in horror at the raw pink patch that was its neck, where the head had been bitten off at the shoulder. I didn't know then that when a cat is malnourished it will sacrifice one kitten in order to let the others live. Candy's mother explained that later. All I knew was that this was awful, and I didn't know how many more awful things I could take.

I picked up the head and carried it outside, balancing it gingerly in the palm of my hand, careful not to make contact with the wet pink insides of its neck. I took a good windup and launched it like a catapult over the windbreak and well out into the field. The wind seemed to help it along. The tiny head landed and bounced several times and disappeared behind a tuft of grass. I screamed at the top of my lungs, "Fuck you! Fuck you! Fuck you!" though I don't know who it was directed at. And then I stood there for a long while and didn't move or make a sound, other than the occasional dry sob.

Candy came out at last, fragile and scared of the world, and I picked her up and brought her back to the farm. In the final week, before Peter and Michael had called her parents, she'd written strange poems, meticulously lettered with nail polish, all over the walls and doors. They said things like, "Mother of the blueness. Angel of the storm. Remember me in my opaqueness. Of the flooding. Hit me up. Dear Mother says you were born in Vietnam. Whistle down the wind (Alan Bates). You said you would look after me. Fly away sun."

I found some old cans of paint in the shed, all different colors, and tried to paint over the poems. I didn't prepare the surfaces or use an undercoat. My heart wasn't in it. The inside of the house looked like a strange patchwork, and as the paint began to dry, the faint outlines of the poems reappeared, like the return of ghosts.

In the first months, Candy slept up to sixteen hours a day. The doctors said it was okay, a natural side effect of the drugs. When she was awake, she shuffled slowly through the house. Our lives didn't seem exciting. We had nothing to talk about. We were utterly trapped by the heavy weight of lethargy.

No matter how hard she tried, Candy just couldn't stay awake past eight o'clock each night. I thought if we could just stay up together, sharing the experience of watching TV, it would mean something.

"Please stay, Candy, the fire's going, we'll watch this show."

"I'm sorry," she'd say, "I can't hold my eyes open anymore."

I'd kiss her good night. Often she'd cry and say, "This is so awful." I'd sit on the couch and smoke cigarettes—the buds were long since gone—and watch bad television long into the night.

One night I stood up and walked outside, past the windbreak of pine trees and into the paddock beyond, where I'd thrown the kitten's head. The countryside was all around, utterly dark and silent. I lay down in the wet long grass and looked up at the night sky strewn with stars. I thought, If the universe is infinite, if there are stars in all directions, then why isn't the night sky entirely white? The answer, I knew, was that this is the local galaxy, in the local cluster. Everything was local. Everything else: too far away. The light would never reach us. Local pain was all we'd ever know. My entire life seemed weightless, and yet I felt pinned down, as if the night were a weight of pain pressing on my chest. At least with heroin we'd had a purpose. Yet I sensed, at last, clearly, the worthlessness of the world I had constructed.

The farm was too fucking depressing. Even Candy, on the psych drugs, thought so. Almost as quickly as we'd got it, we sold it, and hightailed it out of the battlefield. We gathered our straggly lives and moved back to Sydney, to start afresh. We only had one agreement: no smack.

Within six months Candy came off the psych drugs completely. It was as if the very color that came back into her cheeks was flooding into her soul as well. For the first time in all those years, she started going back to acting classes. She began to laugh a lot, like she had when I first met her. We were in Sydney, where we'd started so long before. It seemed we might have a second chance, might be able to make up for lost time, to turn bad fortune into good. I got my first real job in many years, as a kitchen hand in a busy pub restaurant.

It was good, in a way. It should have been good. But I felt I was sitting in a little wooden boat that had been cut adrift from a big ship. The boat was leaking and I had no oars. I felt a big hole in my gut, the one that heroin had always filled, and I didn't know how to live. What could I do in that boat? Dip my hand in the ocean, drink salt water? I knew it would make me sick.

And then I bumped into Casper again.

Casper was in Sydney now, working on enzyme inhibitors in the research division of a big inner-city hospital, staying late each night and brewing up the Jesus-in-a-jar. I'd lost touch with him entirely and our meeting was accidental. It was his lunch break and he was striding along a busy street in a white lab coat.

I saw him from a distance and stopped still. Chemistry tingled up my spine, and even in the mere anticipation I felt I'd been descended upon by the doves of absolute peace. He was lonely in the new city and happy to meet an old friend.

I thought to myself, Just this once. It's been so long now. Almost six months. "Hey, Casper! How's it going?" Ten minutes later I was struck by the thunderous heat once more. Dumbstruck. But just this once.

That was a Monday. By the Friday I was edgy, so I called him again. On Sunday I woke up and his phone number was in my head and my hands were lifting the telephone. You know the story. Candy said I broke the rules. She said she was going back to Melbourne if it kept happening. After two weeks I couldn't stop. Once the wiring's there, I guess it's like a switch. Bang, you flick it on.

Candy gave me a couple more warnings. Then she said, "This is a definite decision. You're using. I'm going back to Melbourne."

It was almost sad, the lack of animosity. There was not even much to divide. One day she kissed me good-bye and climbed into a rented car laden with her possessions and said, "I hope it's only temporary. I have to go." Her eyes glanced back at me in the rearview mirror as she pulled away, but I couldn't read them anymore.

So then I was left alone, in a flat where I stopped paying rent, and Casper—can you believe this?—got sloppy, and got caught. He was a good research scientist, and hospitals hate scandals, so they gave him one chance and sent him to detox and threatened him with police action if it happened again.

But Casper lasted three days in detox. He must have been thinking, How can I possibly stay here, in all this pain, when I still have the key to my lab? He must have also known that leaving detox was the end of his career.

He left anyway. He went to a doctor, and then a pharmacy, and then a liquor store. It was a Saturday; there was no one in the research division. He cooked one final batch. He downed a packet of Serepax and drank a bottle of scotch and had a big shot of Jesus and out he went.

Leaving me, as I saw it, in the absolute fucking cold.

I really didn't have much energy left. I just couldn't contemplate returning to crime, to being a petty criminal with a petty habit. I couldn't even contemplate trying to get a lab together again: it was all I could do to gather each day's scoring money. Even working as a kitchen hand had made me think there might be a better life.

Casper was gone and I was reduced to scoring shitty deals off shitty dealers. Candy was gone too, maybe forever. It was clear to me that there was no pleasure anywhere in my life. Even when I used, even if the dope was good, I didn't seem to get relief anymore. I'd have the shot, and feel the little rush, then straightaway find myself in the middle of a fidgety low-key fear, about how I was going to obtain my next one. The high point of my day, the apex of anticipation, was when I got the dope in my hand. After that I knew it was all downhill.

I trudged the streets unhappily. I avoided going home to my empty flat, where the only knock on the door was likely to be the landlord's.

This was the time of the world being gray. Even Lex wouldn't lend me money anymore. One day I got home to my flat and the locks were changed. I broke a window and climbed inside but all my stuff was gone.

I took to sleeping in doorways. For days I lived on chocolate bars: Fry's Five Fruits, Rocky Roads, Cherry Ripes. Good stuff for energy, easy to steal. I needed all my money, which wasn't much, for heroin. Then some ancient Social Security fraud I'd forgotten about caught up with me. My check wasn't in the bank when it should have been, and I learned I'd been cut off welfare.

And so at last it was *my* turn for the hospital, the thing I'd been putting off for so long. One day I just walked to a detox, somewhere along Moore Park Road, and pressed the buzzer.

Detox. I'd never even liked the sound of the word. I'd only ever preferred tox and more tox. And now here I was.

They told me the first step toward change was not to use any drugs at all. It was so simple that I'd never thought of it. Swapping one drug for another, that was as far as I'd ever gone. What I liked about their advice was that not using anything seemed just as extreme as using the amounts I'd been using. An extreme solution for an extreme situation. It was okay by me. And when I stopped using, they said, then the changes could begin to occur. Look at your life, they said. Try not to kid yourself anymore. If you stop using and stay stopped, you have a chance to open out your future in ways you can't imagine. You even have a chance to clear some of the wreckage of your past. One day you might try to contact your father, for instance. "I suppose that's possible," I said. "I suppose I could think about that."

I gave myself over to all these extraordinary new concepts. The swirling in my head was almost unbearable as it gathered force each evening and built into a cyclone by dawn. For nine long nights I didn't sleep a minute, racked by spasms and nervous electricity in a sweat-soaked bed in the men's ward of the detox. I stayed for three weeks, moving like a sleepwalker each day through dream states of delirium beyond pleasant and unpleasant. The pain, at last, was beautiful.

I thought I'd been running, and that exhaustion had pursued me relentlessly across the years. Instead I arrived at exhaustion. "I've never moved a muscle," it said. "All I ever did was wait here for you to come."

I surrendered to my tiredness. On the eleventh day of my delirium, alone in the hospital courtyard, I found myself smiling, so astonished had I suddenly become by the mere fact of eleven days. Could I turn eleven into twelve? A counselor passed by. "So why are you smiling?" she asked.

And all I could say, with a heart full of hope, was, "I have no idea in the wide world." It was a good enough starting point.

BLINDING TRUTH: FRISBEES

Everything changes so rapidly it's hard to believe. There's no Candy and there are no drugs. They tell me in the detox that I'm a bit like a "clean slate." It seems to be true. At any given moment I have no idea what's going to happen. This should mean that nothing comes as a surprise. And yet everything that happens is unexpected.

The planet spinning round and round, for instance. Suddenly, in the middle of your life, or late in your youth—it doesn't matter which, because after a decade or more of arrested development, it might as well be one and the same thing—you get a vivid physical sense of what this actually means.

I come around the curve, the ground drops away. Space surges toward me and I'm frightened, for a moment seeing blueprints behind the sky. The indelible traceries of physics. That moment of adjustment when the cortex dissolves and the stomach locks tight and you resist the urge to vomit.

In that rush of atoms I feel lightness and hysteria, a giddiness that seems boundless. My pupils are huge yet they flood with light, as all the static lines of the physical world before me surge into movement.

I begin to see objects—actually see them. Around their

well-defined edges I see their colors. The colors that they are; the things themselves. Such surgical, such molecular, clarity.

For months the world appears to me this way. After the drugs begin to leave my system, after I get out of detox, the world explodes upon me with an intensity that's almost too much to bear.

At night I lie awake trembling in bed, in a shared room in a halfway house, my eyes full of tears, unable to cry. I feel exhilarated and raw, full of fear, full of hope. Astounded by consciousness.

Somehow I make it through the bright strange winter days. Inside me, fragility and enthusiasm seem to reach a compromise that ensures my survival. As the days become longer, Ken and I play Frisbee in the glare of the setting sun and into the purple dusk.

I met him in detox. It seems to me now that friends will be important. He has the top bunk in our room. I won the coin toss, got the bottom bunk. We're thirty years old. It's not embarrassing. It's where we've arrived. How old we are means nothing after living half of a lifetime that ends in a detox.

We take turns playing into the sun. I see Ken's silhouette as he steps forward into the air and flicks his wrist to release the Frisbee. The glow of his dirty gold hair, his grace and finesse. The things you never notice, all those years. The jolt of being alive, right now, without a meter running on the smack in your blood.

The Frisbee spins toward me and disappears, directly in the path of the sun. As I look into the sun, searching, the world glows white, all outlines disappear; blinded, I can see the red of the blood vessels in my own eyes.

Suddenly, above my head, the Frisbee bursts into my vision, a hard black circle moving through the sky. I spin around and begin to run. The Frisbee hovers over my shoulder and descends.

I follow long, luxurious arcs through the cool of the evening and Ken does the same and we pass our time this way, experiencing moments of convergence. I reach up and pull the Frisbee down from the sky. My spine tingles, I gasp with joy. The emotion of awakening—is there a name for it?—floods my body.

We're like some elastic machine, running all over the park, tuned, tight, uniquely monocellular, locked into trajectories, aware of every angle. It becomes apparent that throwing a Frisbee is the most spiritual, the most poetic, of all sports.

We walk together and talk together—long rambles through Redfern and Surry Hills and Darlinghurst—made partners by the common bond of having recently emerged from a weird situation of fear and trauma, from the psychic shredding machine of detox. We catch the bus to Bondi Beach. It's as if we're going to another country. What a frightening thing, the ocean. The sheer physicality of swimming.

They've got strange rules in detox and halfway. They say no contact with Candy for ninety days. Except for the phone call to tell her no contact. Who am I to argue? And what do I know, what's good for me or not? I have no strength other than the strength to survive.

I make the call. Twelve hundred kilometers of cable and wire and yet her voice is right there, in my ear, as if I could merely close my eyes and she would lean toward me and kiss me. Since all we know is the past, we don't yet know that the future between us is doomed. We know but we don't know. We're operating on habit. "Please come to Sydney," I say. We arrange it for the ninetieth day.

At the end of the three months she arrives in Sydney. There's not much privacy in a halfway house. We go to a Lebanese restaurant on Cleveland Street.

"Things are possible without drugs," I tell her.

"I guess so," she says.

"What's going to happen with us?" I ask.

"Who the fuck knows?" she says. Her eyes are sad, the way they look away. She tells me she's seen another guy a few times, and maybe she'll keep seeing him, and maybe we should just give it a break, let it ride, see what happens. After all, she has no intention of being in Sydney and I have none of being in Melbourne. It's a very sad truth. I say a prayer, not out loud: God, make it okay for Candy.

We pay our bill and leave. We drive one street away. Candy stops the car, like she did once before, a long time ago, along the avenue of poplars, in late autumn in the country way north of Melbourne, in the time when our lives were always misery. We'd fucked then, on the side of the road back to Melbourne, in the backseat of the car. The wind had rushed across the desolate surface of the earth and poured into our brains and given us respite from the frantic pounding of our hearts and the chase for money and smack.

Is it possible the chase is over? Nothing seems real. I feel I'm wading underwater. And if the chase is over, then is it over with Candy too? It's hard to say aloud the words inside my head, that things have run their course.

She pulls the hand brake and says, "We have to fuck. It's been a while."

"It has," I say.

We climb over into the backseat. She hitches her dress and slides off her underpants.

"We can go somewhere else," I suggest.

"Fuck it," she says, "there's no time."

This is the last fuck, ever, and we know it. Even as it's happening it's already over. She straddles me. I cling to her arms, to her breasts, to her back. Across the road the neon lights of the South Sydney Leagues Club blink.

After we fuck, we sit there for a while, Candy still on top of me, hugging each other tight, both of us crying.

The next morning she goes back to Melbourne, and I know I'll never see her again, or that our life, the way it was, is over. For a very long time we've been going in one direction, and now we're going in two. Candy disappears from my life at this point, and so she disappears from the story, or the story disappears. Later I will hear she's traveled a bit, is doing okay. I will hear she had a baby. For a couple of years I will hear lots of things, some good, some bad. And then after a while I'll hear nothing.

But for now I drag through the weeks, one foot in the past and one in the future. I feel I am nothing but a dividing line. I don't know who I am. They tell me there's nothing wrong with that. They tell me today is all I have, and for the first time it begins to make sense. At times it seems like such hard work, to make it through each day. They say, of course, it's early days, everything is new, what did you expect? You can't sit on your arse and slide uphill. And I come to realize that all my small todays, the way I act, will lead into my tomorrows.

When I was using, it was like, tomorrow everything will be all right, so today doesn't matter so much. I thought if I could hold my breath for long enough, then finally tomorrow, full of light and pollen, would arrive.

And here it is. I can start breathing again.

Epilogue

CANDY

In the beginning: Sydney, summer

Everything's fucking beautiful! I'm so in love. I've just met Candy, it's been a month or two. We're discovering each other's bodies. Candy's just discovered smack and I've just discovered she's got a bit of money. Keen as all fuck to get dirty.

Candy's got the bluest eyes I've ever seen, a kind of mist you fall into. It's weird how you can be going along, and all you're thinking about is heroin, and then you meet someone, and other thoughts get in there. It makes it like meeting Candy was meant to happen. Things were getting hairy, as they tend to when you're using. As always, I was enjoying the gear. It can be all right being alone. But partnership is a good thing and helps focus your energies.

We did a credit card scam together, and Candy's still reeling from the adrenaline rush. She thinks we can be like Bonnie and Clyde, me handsome, her beautiful, both of us glamorous and full of sex and ready to take on the world. I suppose I mean Dunaway and Beatty. Anyway, falling in love is kind of exciting.

She walks around the house naked all day, her body lithe

and lank and lovely. She's the most beautiful girl I've ever seen, naked or clothed. Not a blemish. Her cunt smells nice. She laughs a lot. She runs several baths a day and splashes about. She fools around with makeup for ages. She wears her long blond hair in wild pigtails. She looks like Annie Oakley on a windy day. She reads sad Virago books with flowers and pale languid women on the covers.

She's just finding out what I found out a few years back, that thing that heroin does to you the first few times. She is over the moon. She's in the Miranda zone—O wonder! O brave new world! Things are good beyond belief. I envy her that innocence. Nowadays, when it really works—which is beginning to be not always—what I get from hammer is a kind of deep comfort. An absence of this and an absence of that. Absence of everything that prickles and rankles.

What Candy's getting is the angelic buoyancy, the profusion of colors. Good luck to her; it won't last long.

We fucked a few times then I told her I had a problem. Crying and all that. Holding my head in my hands, at least. Oh my life is so fucked-up, I've got to stop. Can you lend me some money? At the time it's happening, misery is real. She was game. She was curious. Sure. How much do you want?

Really, to be honest, I guess I was just scamming for a bit of cash. Then the falling in love part began to happen a few days later. Because she came along for the ride. Because she was so willing.

She watched me bang up a few times. I told her, make sure you don't ever do this. She nodded, watching the plunger slide down the barrel. I don't know what it was she saw when I untied that tourniquet and lolled back, but it didn't make her go away.

After a week she started asking questions—what's it like? and how come you can't stop?—and I said to the first question, that's such a hard question to answer, and to the second question, I don't know. I said, if you really want to try some you can snort a bit. She was silent for a moment and then she said, nah. Nah, I don't think so.

The next day I had to go out and do stuff and I left a little package for her and said, if you want to snort some of that, feel free. But I don't mind if you don't. I got home in the afternoon and Candy was lying on the bed reading *The Robber Bridegroom* by Eudora Welty and the package was still on the dressing table where I left it. Did you use that dope? I said. No, she said uncertainly, I didn't feel like it. That's good, I said, because I'm going to have it now.

I didn't offer her any more after that. Two days later I was mixing up for myself and she said, okay, I want to try some.

I was scraping some dope from a package into my spoon. I stopped what I was doing and laid out a thick line on a glossy magazine. She rolled up a twenty-dollar note and snorted the heroin. It seemed she started to really feel it at about twenty or thirty seconds. She was touching her nose and making short sniffing sounds and then she said whoa.

She was puffing, like her breath was trying to catch up with something bigger and faster than her, something that was catching her unprepared and slamming her into a world that was different.

To me it seems, despite the signs that are beginning to say otherwise, that heroin is the greatest thing there is. I'm not trying to give Candy a habit. I'm not trying to fuck her life. I'm trying to make mine better. I'm falling in love with her and want to share with her absolutely everything, especially the best bits. And who wouldn't?

There are no glitches in everything we do. Everything is perfect, agreed upon, unspoken. Everything moves forward as if oiled by God's own grease.

That first snort, Candy had a ball. She lay around on the bed, mostly with her eyes closed, saying this is incredible, saying kiss me, touch me. After a while she said, I feel nauseous, I think I'm going to spew. I grabbed a bucket from the laundry and I said, after you vomit you'll feel better, it happens the first few times. She vomited into the bucket and wiped her mouth and said, even that feels fantastic.

She said, I want to try sex on this. I said, you probably won't be able to come and she said, *this* is coming. Everything was electric, the horniness, the erections, the wetness, and of course we didn't come but fuck it was nice, in a trippy gymnastic kind of way.

The next day she was phased and didn't talk about it. Then a couple of days later she says, can I have some more? I say, sure, and start to lay out a line for her. She says, not that way, I want to try it your way.

At that moment my heart moves and I feel so in love I want to cry. I know what's going on. What she is saying is, I don't want second best. She's sensed already that if snorting is good then this will be infinitely better. I can feel the deep tugging of a kindred spirit, a twin.

I say okay. I look at her for a moment, at her big pupils about to become small. I nod my head. I say, sure.

I remind myself I have to be careful here. I get out my spoon and I mix up the smallest amount of hammer I can possibly imagine would do anything to anyone. Candy's wrapped a tie around her upper arm and it's way too tight. I unwrap it and there are purple lines like bands on her delicate skin. I show her how to tie a hoop that can be tightened or released quickly.

She holds out her arm and looks the other way. I tap the soft skin on the inside of her elbow and it's easy. The needle slides in and I pull the plunger backward and a strong spurt of pink erupts into the liquid in the barrel, spreading up toward the 50 calibration in a cauliflower shape. I hold it steady and carefully push the plunger forward.

There, I say.

I pull the syringe from her arm and drop it on the table and hold my thumb down over the tiny hole I've made. I release the tie with my other hand. Candy looks down at her arm like a child who's relieved that the inoculation is over. Then she says mmmm, and her facial muscles relax and she lies back on the bed and says, that is heaps better. Heaps better. Fuck oh God. Fuck fuck fuck. This is the best. Oh God, this is awesome.

It's a beautiful afternoon in Leichhardt and I want Candy to experience more of it, not just the heavenly weight that descends on vertical bodies, not just the exquisite crush of inertia. She vomits a couple of times and I wipe her face with a towel and then she wants to close her eyes and nod off but I say, come on, let's go for a walk.

First I have another blast and get pretty ripped myself. The phone rings and it's Micky Fleck wanting a hundred and I tell him to wait along the bottom of Norton Street, at the Memorial Park, and I'll be coming through the park in half an hour. I make him up a package, and Candy and I walk out into the sunlight.

We're arm in arm and I've never felt better in my life. The world is full of promise. My plan is that love will be stronger than heroin, and then we can get stuff done. The things we're meant to do in life. Candy's going to be an actress, and I'll work something out too. We're just having a bit of fun right now, and soon, I suppose, it'll be time to stop. This is the way I'm thinking, when I think about it.

I can't see Candy's eyes behind her sunglasses, but I can tell from her grin that she's loving everything, the way you do in early days, the way narcotics integrate all the parts of the world. That's not an easy task. She's loving everything: the sunlight, the heat, the greenness of the day, the trees, the cars, the children in baby carriages. There's a little council fountain in the middle of the park and Candy stops and sits beside it and runs her hand back and forth through the cool water. She's staring mesmerized at the water. I know what it is: she's intrigued by the way her wrist breaks up the scallops of silver light that bob on the surface. It's summer, in a world that is shining and good.

I see Micky's car pull up and I wave and we wander over. Hi, mate, how you going? I say. I lean into his window and drop the package in his lap and he tucks a hundred-dollar note into my top pocket. Micky, this is Candy, I say. She's beaming. Hi. She holds out her arm and they shake hands.

Micky drives away and we walk up to the Italian coffee place and have a big plate of gelato, which Candy vomits up twenty minutes later on the way home. When does the vomiting stop? she asks, like she's preparing for a journey. Not long, I say. After a while you don't vomit, except when you're really sick.

Is that bad? she asks.

Hanging out? It's the worst, I say. Just don't get a habit, Candy, and you won't have to go through that.

We get home and lie down for a while and Candy says to me, there's better things in store for us than pain. It's an odd thing to say but I feel overwhelmed and I want to say something big in return. I really love you, Candy, I say. I was, er, thinking, do you want to— Then I feel embarrassed and stop midsentence.

She rolls toward me and smiles. What? Get married?

I was going to say have a baby, actually.

She laughs. Well, let's do both!

I think we have a great future, I say. She smiles even more, her eyes water. My heart feels it's going to burst.

I kiss her, maybe the nicest long kiss I've had to that point in my life.

Then we fuck for an hour, and don't come, and finally stop when we both get a little raw and chafed.

The next day little brother Lex comes around. I'm not always on a roll, there are bad times too, but I've been getting the good brown Sri Lankan gear from T-Bar lately. It's a time of abundance, and Lex, being family, is on the inner circle. I kind of subcontract a bit to him, and his friends get it, stepped on a little more. But still everybody's happy. Relatively speaking.

It's been a good day and I'm in a good mood when Lex arrives. Candy hasn't had any smack all day and she runs a bubble bath downstairs and says she wants to try some in the bath. She's searching for new experiences and I can understand. May she milk them until they run out. Lex and I have a whack in the bedroom, then I mix one up for Candy. I want her to have a nice blast, and she's been using for almost a week, so I make it a good amount.

We're minding the house for someone I don't even know, a friend of a friend of Candy. There are two bathrooms and the best one is under the house in a spacious converted cellar that opens out onto the backyard. The walls are rough sandstone and it's cool and musty down there. A claw-foot bath stands in the middle of the room.

I come down with the syringe. Candy has tied her hair up in a loose bun. She's pink and gleaming, sitting in the bath pouring water from a saucepan over her shoulders and back, so that steam is rising off her. I dry her arm with a towel and tie the tourniquet. I hit her up and release it.

She slumps forward and I know right away that she's passed in an instant from full consciousness to full overdose. She doesn't moan or make any sounds of pleasure or say a word to me. Her head slumps forward so fast that her spine bounces twice in the reverberation. Her hair unties from the jolt and the ends of it flop down into the water.

Hey, Candy!

I try to lift her head but her neck is rubber. I take her by the shoulders and pull her up, back into a sitting position. But her butt slides forward on the slippery surface of the bath. I'm badly positioned and her momentum carries her head backward in an arc. I hold on for long enough to keep her from cracking her skull, but now her crossed legs are sticking out of the water at a right angle down at the plug end, while her head is trying to submerge itself up at my end.

I stand behind the head of the bath and take her underneath the arms. I pull her back up into a sitting position. But she's deadweight, and the floor is wet from splashing, and it's hard to get her out any farther. I'm a little breathless. You wouldn't call me fit.

I shout, Candy, Candy, and she might as well not be there.

I scream upstairs to Lex. He's on the nod and takes a while to answer.

What? he finally says, as if I'm extracting a tooth.

Quick, she's OD'd, give me a hand here.

He springs into action then. He comes down the stairs pretty fast.

What, mate? He sees me standing there, slippery and soaked and trying to keep Candy upright.

I think I gave her too much, I say. Help me get her out.

He takes her legs and we lift her out of the bath and sit her on the edge. I slap her on the face a bit but her lips are turning blue.

This is not good, I say. I slap harder. Let's walk her around.

We take an arm each and sling it over our shoulders. We start to walk her around the room. Her head is slumped forward and her feet drag toes down on the concrete floor.

The thought of an ambulance is not really appealing.

I think of a previous mishap, how T-Bar once saved the day.

Saline solution! I say. Lex, go upstairs, get a glass of warm water—and salt, put some salt in it. Stir it, dissolve it. Hurry!

How much salt?

I dunno, fuckin' heaps. A couple of teaspoons.

Other parts of Candy's face are going blue by now. It doesn't suit her at all. We lay her on the cool floor and Lex runs up the stairs. I crouch beside her saying, Candy, Candy, wake up, wake up, and slapping her gently on the face.

Lex brings the glass. I clean Candy's syringe—some habits don't die, even in an emergency—and fill it with the salt water. Lex is one step ahead of me and tying a tourniquet. I hit Candy up with salt. It seems such a weird thing to do.

Lex unties the tourniquet and I'm wiping Candy's arm of the little trickle of blood and already her eyelids start to flutter. They open and close a few times, and she's not sure where she is. I lift her head a little. The color is returning to her cheeks.

She's beginning to take it in. Her eyes focus first on me and then on Lex. Then she smiles a huge languorous smile and says, what's the matter, boys? I feel several things at once. I feel relieved that she's okay. I feel glad that the salt thing worked, though maybe it's just a junkie myth, maybe all the slapping would have woken her up anyway. I feel proud of myself and Lex for getting it done. Most of all, I feel the thing that feels like love.

Candy is sitting up now, rubbing her face in slow motion, marveling at the way her fingers feel on her skin. She's sitting naked in a puddle of water on the concrete floor, which I know would feel cold and delicious in the state she's in, coming out of such deep bliss. A cluster of bubbles from the bubble bath hangs on her collarbone like a bunch of tiny white grapes.

That was fucking beautiful, she laughs. Let's have some more!

Like I said, I'm *so* in love. I've got a real good feeling about this thing. A good feeling in my bones.

About the Author

Luke Davies was born in Sydney in 1962. He has worked variously as a truck driver, teacher, and journalist. Luke Davies's collection of poetry *Absolute Event Horizon* was short-listed for the 1995 Turnbull Fox Phillips poetry prize.